STORM FRONT

BAEN BOOKS by ROBERT CONROY

Himmler's War

Rising Sun

1920: America's Great War

Liberty 1784

1882: Custer in Chains

Germanica

Storm Front

To purchase these and all Baen Book titles in e-book format, please go to www.baen.com.

STORM FRONT

ROBERT CONROY

STORM FRONT

This is a work of fiction. All the characters and events portrayed in this book are fictional, and any resemblance to real people or incidents is purely coincidental.

Copyright © 2015 by Robert Conroy

A Baen Book

Baen Publishing Enterprises
P.O. Box 1403
Riverdale, NY 10471
www.baen.com

ISBN: 978-1-4767-8087-0

Cover art by Kurt Miller

First Baen printing, December 2015

Distributed by Simon & Schuster
1230 Avenue of the Americas
New York, NY 10020

Library of Congress Cataloging-in-Publication Data

Conroy, Robert (Joseph Robert), 1938–
   Stormfront / Robert Conroy.
       pages cm
   ISBN 978-1-4767-8087-0 (hardback)
1. Winter storms—Fiction. 2. Escaped prisoners—Fiction. 3. Suspense fiction. I. Title.
   PS3553.O51986S76 2015
   813'.54—dc23
                                                        2015030721

10 9 8 7 6 5 4 3 2 1

Pages by Joy Freeman (www.pagesbyjoy.com)
Printed in the United States of America

STORM FRONT

CHAPTER 1

WHEN THE FIRST CLOUDS BEGAN TO CLUSTER AND THEN THICKEN over the Gulf of Mexico, the satellites tasked with observing that part of the world's weather duly noted the fact and went on to more important things. They relayed the information to computers, which opened it to human analysts who assessed the data and began to make their own predictions.

First, both men and computers quickly determined that it was not an embryonic hurricane. It was March and well before hurricane season, making such a major event extremely unlikely. It was determined to be nothing more than a large but not particularly intense storm front. It would not be given a name, or even a number. It was just to be watched. It was also noted that a line of similar, but smaller, storms followed like ducks following a mommy duck.

As the main storm moved north, it continued to grow in size but not intensity. Its winds stayed in the twenty- to thirty-mile-per-hour range, while its clouds sucked up and retained copious amounts of moisture from the Gulf and the rivers below. The computers and analysts agreed that it was going to result in a

1

very big rainstorm and nothing more. All continued to track it, though with no sense of urgency. People along the Mississippi and in the Midwestern states were going to get very wet, but that was about it.

Although there were some variances in the individual predictions, there was a great deal of similarity, even harmony, as they were all dealing with the same data, the same or similar computer models, and with human forecasters who had all received similar training. There was nothing in the storm to indicate any kind of an aberration from the data on file or historical records. Yes, they agreed that the climate was getting more dramatic and violent, but this was still nothing more than a giant rainstorm and not the end of the world.

As predicted, the storm and its trailing children headed north on a line that took it up the Mississippi River. Again, the computers and their human masters noted the fact. Its course was checked against records and tendencies of hundreds of previous storms, and it was determined that the unnamed dark and thick mass of clouds would continue north until it was over Ohio. Then it would veer east through Ohio and on into Pennsylvania. When it hit the Appalachians, it would diminish and cross into the eastern seaboard where it would die and be forgotten. Analysts noted that the heavy rains would be welcome by the farmers who were constantly complaining about drought.

The analysts were confident that the worst effects would be massive rainfalls and flash flooding. They would be damaging where they fell, but intense rains often happened in late winter or early spring. With the temperature along its intended route well over freezing, rain was the worst that would befall anyone. Tornados were extremely unlikely given its configuration. The various weather services prepared their standard warnings. Floods could kill, especially flash floods, and there was genuine concern for both human casualties and the likely loss of property. The forecasters would sound the alarm and try to save as many lives as possible, and, as usual, would be fairly successful. They would not, however, be entirely successful. At some point, waters would rise more quickly than planned for and trap the unlucky or the unwise. Or some damn fool drunk would try to drive his pickup truck across a bridge already awash in swiftly flowing water and be swept away, never realizing just how little quickly flowing water it took to float a truck.

The forecasters could only do their best, as always. Television forecasters and news directors licked their chops at the thought of nice, dramatic flood scenes. But if no river turned into a raging torrent, they would have plenty of flooded-out homes to show and distraught occupants to interview. Maybe they'd be blessed with a helicopter rescue of a family, preferably with a dog, from some otherwise placid creek's raging waters. Worst case scenario: they'd be stuck interviewing people whose sewers had backed up and were now dealing with stinky muck in their basement.

North of the storm's intended route, other forecasters read their printouts, checked their models, and were silently thankful that the storm front, now almost astonishingly saturated with vast amounts of water, would pass south of them. The Great Lakes states of Michigan and Illinois, along with their Canadian counterpart—the Province of Ontario—had received more than their share of wet weather this winter, but it had been in the form of snow, not rain, and large amounts of snow still remained on the ground. Two heavy snowfalls in three weeks had left an accumulation of the white stuff that remained in dirty piles several feet tall alongside suburban driveways, and, in larger parking lots, snow mounds resembled mountains.

They were thankful that winter was almost over and that the worst of a bad year was probably past. So said the calendar, at least. Reality told them that the wind and snow of winter could hang on into the early part of April.

Regardless, the storm was full of rain and not snow, and would be headed east, which meant it was of only passing interest to anyone north of Ohio.

Thank God it would only be rain, the Michigan and Ontario forecasters thought as they concurred with the evidence provided by their computers. The storm would pass to the south. It would rain, and perhaps there would be some flurries along its northern edge as the storm lurched eastward, but it couldn't snow.

Could it?

Old, brittle snow crunched under the wheels of Mike Stuart's four-wheel-drive SUV as he pulled into Maddy Kovacs's driveway. Maddy owned a three-bedroom detached condo that she shared with two close girlfriends. Thanks to the recession it had been in foreclosure and she'd bought it for a very low price. It needed work, and she was planning on doing a lot of it during the coming summer. She did feel that the huge whirlpool bath in the bathroom and the hot tub on the patio were almost worth it. The hot tub was connected to the house by a private door and had one-way glass. Mike had often thought of the two of them in the tub. It hadn't happened yet, but hope springs eternal, he thought.

Mike got out of the car and took a deep breath of the moist air. The early March evening was dark and overcast, damp and without a hint of spring. He looked skyward and saw nothing but clouds hanging thick and low and not at all friendly. It had been several days since he'd seen either the stars or the sun, although he had it on good authority that they were still up there someplace. He shivered. It was clammy. Pneumonia weather, as his mother used to say. Old snow was piled several feet high alongside the driveway and he had to step carefully. He'd feel truly silly if he managed to slip and fall on his keister in front of his new girlfriend.

He walked to the passenger side of the car and opened it for Maddy. He'd figured out that she appreciated the little courtesies that so many guys either forgot, never learned, or didn't think were important. Their loss, he thought as Maddy got out and smiled radiantly at him.

It had been a surprisingly good Sunday afternoon with her teacher friends. "Are you coming in?" she asked.

"Sure. I'm not on duty until eight tomorrow morning," he said as he automatically checked his watch. "Just about the same time you start."

Mike Stuart was a sergeant in the traffic division of the Sheridan Police Department. At thirty, he was young for the rank, but had a bachelor's degree in Criminal Justice and was finishing his master's from Madonna University in Livonia, Michigan. He'd also spent four years futilely fighting crime in the sewers of Detroit before hiring on at Sheridan, a growing city about an hour's drive north of Detroit.

In Detroit, he'd seen more crime than he could imagine and more brutality than he thought existed. Because his was a young, fresh face, he'd been drafted—coerced—into working the Vice Squad. There he'd seen the lowest of the low: prostitution, drugs, cruelty to children and animals, and beggars stealing from beggars. Detroit, he was told, wasn't the worst city in the world, although it sometimes seemed like it. Instead, it was rather typical of a large metropolitan area in which the more affluent families had departed to the suburbs, leaving huge pockets of poverty, thousands of abandoned homes and buildings, and resentment, even anger, at authority. White cops were considered an occupying army, while black cops were thought of as traitors to their race. After four years, he'd had enough. Many young cops just used Detroit as an internship, and Mike joined the steady exodus to the suburbs, where he regained his equilibrium and the realization that not all the people he dealt with were the enemy.

In comparison, Sheridan was an oasis. Crime was present, but in numbers and percentages well below the nearby larger and older cities. Much of the crime, as the local weekly advertising newspaper liked to point out, was imported from those older cities, or was drug-related. Sheridan was just far enough north to discourage casual forays by the criminal element in Detroit. Sheridan tallied just one murder in the previous year in a liquor store robbery gone bad, and a couple of domestic violence manslaughters. Still, hiring in at Sheridan was a good career move for Mike, as his new rank indicated.

Madison—"Maddy"—Kovacs was twenty-six and a fourth-grade teacher at Patton Elementary in Sheridan. They had met a few months earlier when Mike was called to her school to investigate an accident where a school bus hit a student and broke the boy's leg. Maddy had witnessed the whole thing and been understandably shaken. It hadn't been the driver's fault, she'd insisted, and further investigation confirmed it. For some reason known only to him, the boy had crossed back from where the bus had let him off and after it had started moving. The kid was lucky to be alive. Mike had sat her down in his squad car and calmed her to the point where she'd agreed to go out with him.

Mike was just under six feet tall, had dark hair, brown eyes, and weighed one-seventy. He was athletic without being muscle-bound like so many young cops liked to be. He'd been a wrestler in high school and had tried it in college, where he found out that intensity and determination were no substitute for talent. After licking his wounds, he'd concentrated on his grades and graduated with honors.

Maddy had been a successful college athlete, as well as scholar. At five-eight and one-forty, she'd been a starter on Michigan State's volleyball team before tearing up a knee and wasting her senior year. Although not what some would consider a classic beauty, whatever that was, she had sandy brown hair that reached her shoulders, green eyes, a warm smile, and a healthy athletic figure that Mike considered striking. So what if she thought her nose was a little big, even hawkish. Her mother called it a typical Polish nose. Mike liked it, and that's what counted. Among other things, they'd been working out together at a gym and the thought of her all sweaty in a sports bra and shorts made him feel more than a little warm this cold, wet evening.

For her part, Maddy was still shocked that she'd agreed to go out with him in the first place, and even more shocked that it had worked out so well so far. *So far,* she thought. There'd been one terrible disaster in her past that she still couldn't quite put out of her mind. She'd never thought she'd fall for a cop. In fact, she thought about giving up dating for a decade or two. Instead, she now wondered if Mike Stuart was part of her long-term future. Her parents had been quietly wondering if and when she'd marry. They wouldn't mind a cop, particularly a good-looking one with a couple of college degrees. Hell, she thought, in a few years they wouldn't mind if she married a circus clown, or the guy who swept up after the elephants in the circus parade. Then she recalled that at least one boyfriend had qualified for the position. Someday, she'd forget about Dirk and what he'd done to her, but not yet.

They entered her living room and Mike took their coats. "Wine?" she asked.

"Yeah," he said with an exaggerated sigh. "A glass would be great. I need something after an afternoon with the Harrises."

And one glass is all it would be, he cautioned himself. He'd had two glasses of merlot at the Harris's and, even though he felt great, he wasn't going to chance drinking more and getting pulled over by one of his own men. Unless he killed someone, they'd let him go. Still, he had too much to lose. He'd become a joke on the force and maybe even get fired if he got pulled over for driving under the influence and God help him if the local media got wind of it.

Maddy laughed and poured them each a glass of Chardonnay. Mike preferred red, but the Chardonnay was open and she wasn't going to waste it. "There, that wasn't so bad, was it?" she chided.

Donna Harris was a fellow teacher at Patton, and her husband Tom sold insurance. Both were in their forties and Donna had taken it on herself to be Maddy's protector and close friend. It had been the first time Mike had met them. It had been a sort of test and he thought he'd passed. The Harrises were likeable people, although Donna was a little pushy. Tom was quiet, and did not seem at all like someone who peddled insurance.

"Nah, it wasn't bad at all," he admitted. "At least they didn't ask me to fix any tickets for them or to see my gun, or ask how fast you can drive in a crowded church parking lot without getting pulled over." Dumb questions were the bane of police officers everywhere, which was one of the reasons they tended to hang together.

"Well, just how fast can you drive in a church parking lot?" she asked with mock innocence.

"God only knows, yuk, yuk."

"You left the gun in the car, right?"

Maddy didn't like guns, although she understood that a cop had to carry one, even off duty. "Yep, I was a good boy." He stretched. It felt good to not be on display. "Paybacks are hell, you know. In May there's a picnic with my buddies I'd like to take you to. By the way, where are Tweedle-dee and Tweedle-dum?"

Maddy quickly agreed to go to the cops' picnic, wondering if she and Mike would still be seeing each other in a couple of months. She hoped so. She sat on the couch beside him. "Be nice, Mike. Lisa and Vicki are probably out for a bite to eat. They may be college graduates, but simple cooking, even with a microwave, confuses them." Lisa was also a teacher, but in another district, while Vicki was a systems analyst for General Motors. Of the three, Vicki made the most money by far.

"Well, I hope they stay out," he said and pulled her to him. They kissed gently and then with more fervor. His tongue found hers and she found herself responding eagerly. She hadn't felt like this in years and it felt good.

He caressed her back and shoulders, then slid his hands onto her breasts. When she didn't push him away, he pulled up her sweater and unhooked her bra. His hands found her warm, bare breasts. He pushed the sweater and bra up and lowered his head as his tongue sought out her firming nipples.

She murmured with pleasure as she caressed his back and buttocks while he shifted himself and lay partly across her. They had never gone this far before, and she was surprised that she wasn't halting him like she had done to so many others. Maybe he truly was different. Maybe she could erase the humiliation of the past.

"We can go to your room," he managed to say.

"No."

"I feel like a teenager like this," he protested.

"I know, but my roommates will be back anytime, and going to my room is out."

"Why?"

"Thin walls," she managed to say. "Lisa and her boyfriend did it once and we heard everything. She was crying out for God so much we thought she was having a religious conversion."

Despite the situation, she giggled at the memory. "I want it to be perfect the first time for us. I want it private and wonderful. No audience."

Mike just wanted it to be right here and right now, but he respected both Maddy and her wishes as they continued to caress each other. This, he thought, was dangerous, dangerous. He was afraid he would explode.

Maddy's mind whirled. Perhaps they should go to her room and hope for the best. She was acting like a bitch in heat, but didn't care. Maybe the monster in her mind was dying. Maybe it had never really existed.

A car door slammed in the driveway outside.

"Shit," Maddy said. "Shit, shit, shit."

She stood up and quickly rearranged her clothes. Mike did likewise, hoping his unrequited erection was not too obvious. A moment later, Lisa and Vicki came in and immediately took in the situation. Lisa grinned lasciviously. "Well, fun and games with Maddy and Mike."

"Screw you," Maddy said amiably.

"Glad to see you, too," said Mike with exaggerated politeness. His erection was beginning to diminish, but he felt it was plainly visible. He tried to shift his arm to cover it, but then thought, what the hell.

Both women laughed and went into the kitchen. Out of sight, Mike and Maddy kissed again, but without the intensity of a few moments past. It was time to go. Mike held her closely. "I love you," he said.

"I think I'm getting there, too, Mike, just don't push me."

He smiled and shook his head. "Push it? Not me. I'm the Good Cop, remember?"

"You're the best cop," she said and squeezed his arm fondly. They went to the door and stepped outside. "It's going to snow," Maddy said, looking at the clouds. "Just what we need is more snow. Ever listen to Wally Wellman on Channel Six? He said it might snow, but everybody else says it's only going to rain."

Mike seriously considered jumping into a snowbank to cool off. "So now we're back to talking about the weather? Besides, the forecast is for drizzle and flurries, nothing significant. How about dinner tomorrow?"

"Okay. Your place or mine?" Mike rented an apartment just outside of Sheridan. It was small, but he shared it with no one.

"Mine. Think Laurel and Hardy can get along without you for an evening?"

Maddy laughed. It felt good. She was as happy as she'd been in a long, long time. Mike deserved a lot better than she'd been giving him. Maybe it really was time to trust him and let go of the past. Maybe tomorrow in his apartment would see the final barrier broken.

"I'll make sure they try."

CHAPTER 2

WALLY WELLMAN'S ALARM WENT OFF AT SIX A.M. ON MONDAY like it did every morning except on Sundays. It gave him time to work out on his treadmill, which he did four times a week. On Sundays he spoiled himself and slept in until six-thirty. He also did not exercise. Never on Sunday, he believed.

He pushed the button and killed the annoying whine, and let silence descend before willing himself out of bed. He had a routine to follow and it helped him through the long empty days. Routine, he told himself, provided strength and a sense of security. Sure. His life's routine was shit.

First, he smiled longingly at his wife's picture and she smiled back, just as she had done for the last several years. He wished it could talk. There was so much he wanted to tell her. Just a damn shame it was too late.

It'd been three years since the misdiagnosed cancer had struck aggressively and taken Ellen from him. There were times when he still wanted to cry and times when he did cry. There were also times when he wanted to howl at the moon. He had an adult son in California, but Wally would not impose his miseries on a thirty-five-year-old man with a career and a family. He would somehow find the strength to solve his own problems. He'd stopped the heavy drinking and feeling sorry for himself, which meant some of his friends were again talking to him, but, damn it, sometimes he did feel sorry and he missed her terribly. He was fifty-eight and so alone. He had more than enough money to last him several lifetimes but no one to share it with. He and Ellen were supposed to be approaching their golden years, but now the gold had all turned to shit.

Wally shook himself out of his reverie, and turned on his computer to check the weather. The weather occupied his waking time and kept him from thinking about how things ought to have been and not how they were. He was Wally Wellman, ace meteorologist for TVDetroit6, a large and profitable independent television station located in Southfield, Michigan, a suburb adjacent to Detroit. Wally lived in a small but expensive house in Royal Oak, another suburb only a few miles away from the station.

He sniffed at what he saw on the monitor. The storm front that was supposed to stay to their south and bring misery to Ohio was much farther north than expected. It also appeared to be picking up speed. He noted that the National Weather Service now admitted to the remote possibility of some light snow in the Detroit area, but with little accumulation to worry about. They still said it would veer east and didn't represent any major threat to the local area. Everyone was urged to drive safely.

Assholes, he thought. He'd tried to tell them otherwise on Friday, that he didn't care what the computer models said, that his gut said that it could sustain its northward direction and bring significant snow on Monday morning.

But his producer and station manager had gotten furious when he'd brought up the possibility of a serious snowfall. TV6 and others had been burned a week before when yet another Storm of the Century turned out to be the Piddle of the Morning. They'd gotten a few more inches of white stuff on top of the quantities that had already accumulated, but it was nothing that hadn't happened several times already this winter. TV6 and the others had been harshly criticized for an over-dramatic ratings-inspired forecast and weren't about to do it again—at least not for a while.

So no way were they going to go against the findings of the

National Weather Service and its computers or even the Weather Channel. Of course, each weather forecasting system, such as TV6, had its own computer program, but the initial data was provided by the weather satellites that orbited the earth.

Wally brushed his teeth, showered, dressed, and combed his thinning hair. He didn't comb it across the bald spot like some other guys did, or wear a rug, which was worse. Like nobody could tell, right? Unless you spent a fortune on a toupee, it looked like a rodent had built a nest on your head. Hell, he was getting old and going bald. What was wrong with that? At least he wasn't fat like one of the weather guys on the NBC affiliate. Still, he was beginning to look over his shoulder to see who wanted to replace him. Television was for the young and photogenic. Old farts like him were a vanishing species. Who cared if you had knowledge and experience?

The station's management wanted someone young and attractive, and, of course, cheaper. It was joked that, unless you were a young blond with great boobs, you should go into radio. Actually, it was a decent thought. He had enough of a following to ensure him a job in radio that would keep him active until he actually decided to retire. But without Ellen, why would he want to retire?

Wally wasn't even a meteorologist, as the station's management kept reminding him. His college degree was in English from the University of Michigan, and he'd originally wanted to be an anchorman, not a weatherman, and deal with the world news out of New York. But he wasn't a pretty enough face even then, so he'd taken the weather job thirty-five years ago because he and Ellen needed the money, and learned the science part the hard way. He'd read every book he could find on weather, attended seminars, milked the brains of friends, audited classes, and, later, took a few more classes online. He still didn't have the right degree, but he was respected and as accurate as anyone else in the industry.

And he had a following, although it was the older and aging demographic group, and the station wanted to attract younger viewers. In order to compensate for the fact that he really didn't know what he was doing in the early days, he'd developed a line of patter and corny jokes to distract people. When he did acquire the knowledge, it no longer mattered. People still considered him as much a clown as a weatherman. He was an anachronism. The marketing director had coldly reminded Wally that his fans were either dying off, dying their hair blue, or getting hysterectomies and moving to Florida. Regardless, his numbers were shrinking. Wally nearly told him to stuff it.

He figured he'd be eased out the next time his contract expired, which would be in a year. Management was too cheap to outright fire him, because that would involve paying severance. But they would offer him a lot less money, and demote him. He'd stop being the main weather guy and be stuck with weekends and filling in when the bimbo they would hire to replace him went on vacation with her Ken doll boyfriend.

He wondered what he'd do. He didn't need the money. He and Ellen had lived prudently, saved, and invested. They were going to have long golden years together until some idiot of a doctor couldn't diagnose a tumor the size of Rhode Island. The settlement from the malpractice suit was financial frosting, but it was money he'd rather not have. No amount of money could replace Ellen. He'd thought about giving the settlement to charity, but his lawyer had talked him out of it and, right now, Wally was grateful. He was financially secure for the rest of his life, so screw the station. If they wanted to fire him, so be it. Only one problem—Wally didn't want to stop being a television weatherman just yet. Face it; he told himself, he had nothing else to do. He hadn't begun dating again and seriously wondered if he ever would.

Of course, he no longer had any idea where to begin if he wanted to. Some friends had tried to fix him up with widows or divorcees, but he'd resisted. So far. Still, a number of women close to his age had tried to pick him up at supermarkets or bookstores, which amused and intrigued him. Statistically, there were far more single women his age than men. Of course, he could always try one of those online dating sites. He'd noted a couple that catered to older men and woman. He thought about starting his own and calling it Old-Fart-Match.com. Maybe dating wouldn't be all that difficult. If the woman didn't talk about her hysterectomy, he'd keep quiet about his prostate.

He checked his watch. It was time to go to work. Outside, the ground was wet from a fine mist and the temperature was dropping. No, Wally thought sarcastically, of course it isn't going to snow. Assholes.

Three bedrooms for three women sounded great but it still meant complications and delays getting ready for work in the morning. They had their own bathrooms, which provided both efficiency and privacy, but there was only one kitchen.

After navigating past chairs and two other people, Maddy got her toast and coffee and managed a quick look at the morning paper. The world hadn't ended, although there was madness and evil still alive in it. People were still killing each other in the name of God or Allah or some other deity just like they had been for hundreds of years. She wondered if the litany of horrors would ever cease. Not likely, she decided, thinking of the attacks on the World Trade Center and the Pentagon. Even though it had been years before, pictures of people attempting to fly out of the towers in futile attempts to live had been seared on her brain. Safety and security were relative terms and nothing would ever be the same. Thank God Sheridan was away from anything any terrorist would find interesting.

Maddy flipped to the sports section and saw that the Red Wings had lost, which meant that Mike would be unhappy. However, the college basketball season and March Madness were in high gear, which meant Mike would be happy. She smiled to herself. Men were so predictable. A rare steak, a good beer, and somebody shooting hoops and Mike would be as content as a guy could be without getting in the sack.

She had dressed casually for what was going to be an active day. Once upon a time, teachers all wore dresses no matter what they were doing and how awkward and uncomfortable they would be. Thankfully, common sense and women's rights now prevailed. She'd never worn a skirt or dress to work and didn't know anybody who had. She threw a change of clothing and some toiletries into a small overnight bag. Dinner with Mike was on the agenda and she would want the opportunity to freshen up after a day with kids. Despite the unfulfilled passion of the previous night, her indecision regarding sex with him had returned. She still doubted if she was ready to take the final step with him. Too many ghosts. Too much pain.

Finally, she was ready and out the door. The damp cold surprised her. It really felt like something wet was going to happen, but she couldn't recall rain or snow being predicted. Just what the place needed, she thought, a little more rain or snow on top of what was already on the ground.

Then she recalled that this was going to be a big week for Mike and she fervently hoped that nothing happened to screw it up for him.

Mike Stuart left the drive-through window with the necessities of a policeman's life: Two dozen Krispy Kreme donuts. No, he wasn't going to eat them all himself. That would spoil his athletic figure. Instead, he would have a couple of them and let the omnivores in the station have the rest. He decided to eat his before the others swarmed him or called him greedy for taking more than one, conveniently forgetting in their donut-lust that he'd paid for them. Hell, he was a bachelor, which meant breakfasts were usually nonexistent unless he opted for a Pop Tart.

He pulled his SUV into a parking spot and munched the first one, letting the high sugar content jar his nervous system out of neutral. Surprisingly, he had slept well the night before. After the intense but unfulfilling physical encounter with Maddy, he'd thought he'd toss and turn for hours, but it hadn't happened. Instead, he felt that he was making real progress with the lovely and very complex woman he was certain he loved. Damn, he thought, the guys at the station, especially his buddy Stan Petkowski, were teasing him enough already.

He did wonder just how far they would have gone if Maddy's damned roommates hadn't showed up. Maybe not as far as he wanted, he thought. He still sensed reluctance on Maddy's part. He would be patient. Patience was a virtue. He thought of himself as being on a long stakeout that had the possibility of a very rewarding conclusion.

A light mist was forming on the windshield, and that didn't surprise him. The air was damp, and had the feel that people said smelled and tasted like rain. Rain meant slippery roads and slippery roads meant accidents. He didn't need that kind of complication this morning. Why couldn't it be sunny and seventy?

Because this was Michigan in March and anything could and usually did happen when it came to the weather.

The sound of an approaching siren distracted him. A fire engine was nearing the intersection and wanted to go against the red light. Mike wondered how many drivers would pull over and give the big red beast the right of way. Not many. They'd just keep on driving and ignore the fire engine that was twenty times their size as if it wasn't there. He'd recently found that driver's-ed in the high school didn't even teach the necessity of giving emergency vehicles the right of way. That, and so many people played their music so loud it was a wonder that drivers heard anything short of the end of the world. Even then, they'd probably miss it.

The fire engine was blocked from crossing the intersection by a Ford Focus in front of it that had stopped for the red light. The siren wailed again and again, urging the driver to move, move, move, damn it, move. Traffic was clear, so why didn't the driver go through and give the fire engine a chance to pass? Because the driver probably didn't know any better, that's why.

Finally, the driver got the message, ran the light and pulled the car into the Krispy Kreme parking lot where it stopped a few spaces away from Mike. Two young girls were in the Focus and they seemed to be crying. He sighed and got out of his car, wondering as he walked over to them if the sight of his uniform would scare them or reassure them. Today, he would try to be the Good Cop. He gestured for the driver to roll down her window.

"Ladies," he said with what he hoped was a warm and ingratiating smile. Two young, tear-streaked faces looked up at him in horror. All they saw was the uniform and the badge, not the smile. "That was a scary situation back there, wasn't it?"

They nodded mutely and Mike looked at the driver. She probably just turned sixteen and might someday be pretty, but not this morning. Her face was puffy and red, and her makeup was beginning to streak from the tears. She was scared and doubtless thought she was going to get a ticket. "I'm Sergeant Mike Stuart. So tell me, miss, what's your name?"

"Tessa," said the driver and the passenger volunteered that her name was Lori.

"And how long have you had your driver's license, Tessa?"

"Tu-two weeks," Tessa replied. Mike knew he should be asking for it as well as registration and proof of insurance, but he didn't think it was appropriate. The little girl didn't fit the profile of a terrorist, drug dealer, or car thief. Besides, he felt wet stuff hitting the back of his neck. A sudden gust of wind sent a chill down his back. It was starting to rain and it was time to get to work.

"I'll bet they never taught you what to do when a fire engine's breathing down your neck."

The girl managed a wan smile and the passenger actually giggled. "No way."

"Scared the heck out of you, didn't it?" They nodded. "Well, you did real well. You cleared the intersection safely, just like you were supposed to."

"But I ran a red light, didn't I?" Tessa said, blinking back more tears.

"There's a time and a place for everything, Tessa. It was an emergency and your job was to let that monster get through."

The girl looked reassured and brightened. "Oh. Does that mean you're not going to give me a ticket?"

Mike laughed and couldn't resist the retort. "Not unless you really want one."

"No thanks," Tessa giggled, now in control of herself. Both girls had stopped crying and begun laughing, more out of relief than humor. They had done nothing wrong, and he wanted them to know that. They wiped their faces and became horribly aware that their carefully applied makeup had been destroyed.

"Now why don't you go on and tell your friends about the fire truck that tried to eat your car." He slapped the side of their door. "And please drive carefully. It's going to get slippery real soon."

The two girls assured him they would and maybe they meant it. He hoped so. They seemed like decent kids, unlike some of the punks he sometimes had to deal with as a cop. Mike felt the rain on his face changing to small globs of wet snow. Another gust slapped him in the face. He looked up at the glowering clouds. They seemed so low he thought he could reach up and grab them. For an idiotic moment, he almost did, but checked himself. *I don't need this,* he thought. Not today.

CHAPTER 3

THE CITY OF SHERIDAN WAS LAID OUT IN WHAT LOOKED A NEAT rectangle when shown on a map or on Google Earth. It ran two miles north-south and three miles east-west. A spur of Interstate 75 ran east-west along its southern border and carried increasingly heavy traffic into the rapidly growing suburbs. Much of that traffic was dumped north into Sheridan, where people either found homes or drove farther north to still other suburbs. Eighty thousand people, many of them affluent, lived in Sheridan's new subdivisions. Despite economic downturns, the population had tripled in the last twenty years. While there were pockets of poverty and a number of just plain average people, the norm was a large new house on a large lot, or a large house on a disproportionately small lot. For many of Sheridan's residents, these were trophy homes and they were willing to put up with long and inconvenient rides to and from work for the privilege of living in a quiet and safe place like Sheridan. There were a fair number of vacant houses because of the mortgage crises and a lot of homeowners were what the banks cutely called "underwater." They owed more than their homes were worth on the market.

Some of these people were as depressed as their property values, especially those who wanted to sell their houses so they could move elsewhere.

The last census showed that ninety-seven percent of the population was white, and two percent was Asian. Blacks and other minorities constituted the remaining one percent. Comedians called Sheridan a white ghetto, and a minister in Detroit called Sheridan segregated, but neither comment upset the residents very much. This was their new home and they liked it this way and many didn't care if their homes were underwater. Sooner or later the ship would right itself.

Although considered a new suburb by those who were just discovering it, Sheridan had begun as a village in 1830. It was originally a farming community founded by Moravian Germans, whose descendants, until recently, exercised considerable influence in the community. What was now the center of the town had been little more than a disorganized trading post until after the Civil War, when the village leaders decided to name the place after General Philip Sheridan.

Sheridan's population and growth remained flat, even stagnant, until World War II when the whole area industrialized. Later, when the war ended and people began moving from the cramped core cities like Detroit, suburbs began to grow and prosper. Still, it took decades for that growth to reach Sheridan. Many of the older families resented the newcomers, but accepted the inevitable. The newcomers now vastly outnumbered the old-timers. Providing some relief was the fact that the new people brought wealth when they bought the under-producing farmlands for houses and shopping. Of course, many of the newly rich farmers left Sheridan and moved to Florida with their booty.

The only decent north-south road was MacArthur Highway. With six lanes divided by a center median, it was the main connection with the freeway for the town. The other roads in the city were your garden variety four- and five-lane roads long overdue for expansion and improvement. MacArthur Highway was also overdue for some more lanes. Mike Stuart wasn't certain he liked that idea. Traffic on MacArthur ran far too fast already, and more lanes would just make it an urban speedway. The city had several movie theaters, a number of restaurants and one good-sized shopping center at the confluence of the interstate and MacArthur. It housed a Macy's, a Sears, Saks, and about two hundred specialty stores connecting the anchors in a covered mall. A smaller strip mall held a Wal-Mart and a local chain store, Sampson's.

Sheridan's municipal complex was located along the east side of MacArthur and was a campus of several buildings including the city hall, fire station, library, courthouse, and police station. While new, the buildings had Colonial exteriors, which made the place look as warm and attractive as municipal and administrative buildings could. Taxpayer groups thought the campus was overbuilt, but the city countered by saying it would grow and they'd need the facilities.

Inside the police station, Mike Stuart was acutely aware that he was in charge of the traffic division for the next few days. Lieutenant Joey DiMona normally commanded the division, but he was vacationing in Las Vegas. DiMona was fifty-eight and seriously considering retirement. An ambitious Stuart permitted himself to wonder if he could take over from DiMona. Certainly, the older cop was more than friendly and Mike considered him a mentor who might help the younger cop inherit the position. Realistically, Mike doubted it. DiMona's boss was Chief Bench, who didn't seem to like him very much. But then, Bench didn't seem to like anyone except the mayor.

Besides, Mike was much too young. He might have to wait until next time, or move on to another city. If he wanted to move into the management hierarchy, and he did, he felt he would have to forego a degree of job security. Too bad. He liked Sheridan. He wondered if Maddy would come with him if he moved too far away to commute. Her family was a few miles south of Sheridan and she was close to them.

Mike also liked being a cop. His career choice had been a mild disappointment to his parents—his father had been a college English instructor and his mother a nurse—but they were pleasantly surprised when they found out that many cops starting out nowadays were college graduates. As in many professions, the educational requirements had increased significantly. Of course, Mike's rapid rise to sergeant had further worked to change their minds and they became proud of him. They now lived in a condo in Arizona.

Mike forced himself back to reality. He had four one-man squad cars on patrol this morning. There should have been at least one more, but absentees and unfilled openings because of budget issues kept the numbers down. For a moment he thought about asking other department heads for manpower, but decided against it. They had their own staffing problems and, besides, he was supposed to solve his own problems like a big boy. There was only an hour or so before the morning rush was over. He would hold his breath and hope for the best. At least the weather was still acceptable. Not great, but acceptable. A little wet stuff never hurt anyone.

According to the computer-generated chart and the GPS monitoring system, all four cars were in service and moving. Even, he laughed silently, his buddy, Corporal Stan Petkowski, also known as Stan the Prick by some citizens for all the traffic tickets he gave out. Some drivers he'd ticketed thought Stan would give his mother a ticket, while others doubted he was born of humans.

Mike knew better. A few beers after work with the short, squat cop had brought out the story. Petkowski's fetish for ticketing bad drivers began one evening a few years ago when he was helping remove horribly mangled dead bodies out of a particularly awful two-car wreck in which a Chevy wagon had been broadsided by a pickup truck. He'd been stunned when he found that one horribly mutilated and decapitated corpse was his niece, a likeable and lovely eighteen-year-old college freshman with the whole world before her. The accident had been caused by a drunk in the truck who had blown by a stop sign. The drunk was dead, which Stan thought was mild justice. The son of a bitch had been driving with a suspended license for an earlier drunk driving conviction. If he'd survived, Stan thought he might have killed him and enjoyed it.

After that, Petkowski suffered no one who ran red lights or stop signs or intentionally endangered others, regardless of whether they were sober or drunk. Mistakes and inexperience he could tolerate, but not intentionally dangerous or careless driving.

A symbol on the chart was blinking red. It was on northbound

MacArthur and a little ways north of the police station. "What's this," Mike wondered.

"Water main break," came the answer. "Engineers say it'll be fixed before rush hour."

"Hope so," Mike muttered.

The area was one of a number covered by surveillance cameras, so he was able to check it visually. It was already a mess. Even with all three lanes open, the northbound rush was a real bear. Closing one would have traffic backed up for miles. Now, with much lighter traffic than would occur later, the computer said the backup was still almost a mile. This Mike didn't need. He decided to send Petkowski over to see how things were working out. It was beginning to snow and that was another complication he didn't want. Like he could do anything about any of it, he thought. The city and the county would have salt trucks out and that was all that could be done.

Then he wondered what Maddy was doing.

Wally Wellman arrived at TV6's studios a little after nine that morning. The fine mist had changed to wet, soggy snow, punctuated by nasty gusts of wind.

"I was right," he announced to the staff. "It is snowing. Wally Wellman is never wrong. You may thank me profusely on bended knee or send money."

He got the expected hoots and the finger from his coworkers, grinned, and walked over to his producer, Ron Friedman. He and Friedman had worked together for more than a decade. The much younger Friedman had helped Wally through his grief by keeping him very busy.

"Now can I tell the world it's going to snow?" Wally asked. "And maybe snow a lot?"

"Anyone with a window already knows that it's snowing," Ron responded. "Besides, the National Weather Service just predicted maybe an inch and that doesn't warrant an end-of-the-world announcement. You're still the Lone Ranger when it comes to that prediction and the big boss is still pissed at you for that prediction a while back."

Who cared what the big boss thought? He was the guy who

wanted to eliminate Wally's job. "Yeah, but I think it's going to snow a lot more. Like at least six inches."

"Why?"

"Because it's a thick front that's going to be right over us if it continues on its present heading, which, may I remind you, is the opposite of what everyone thought was going to happen with that snowfall last week."

"Including you," Ron said.

"Including me. I was wrong. So sue me. Look, the storm is a thick one, it's loaded with moisture, and the winds are picking up. It's gonna slam right into the cold front and produce tons of heavy white snow."

Friedman leaned back in his chair and gazed at a spot in the ceiling where the plaster was peeling. "Can't do it, Wally. We looked like fools last week when everyone, including you, was calling for a massive storm. Hell, schools were closed in advance and businesses called it a holiday. Then nothing happened. Yes, I know, we got a couple of inches, most of which is still on the ground, but nothing like the Sky Is Falling prediction we made. Besides, you can't go out and contradict the big guys in the government without something concrete to back you up. Sorry, but six inches is too speculative. Y'know, we had a bunch of phone calls complaining about you after the last Friday's half-baked prediction where you said that the other guys might all be wrong."

Wally laughed. "At least that proves someone was watching the show. Now, will you let me go on at ten and say there's a possibility of between two and three inches?"

Friedman ran a hand through his thinning red hair. He had forty minutes until ten. TV6 and Wally also provided the weather for a Classic Rock FM radio station that was owned by TV6. A ten o'clock announcement would reach a lot of people. By that time a pattern might be developing. Freidman was torn between his duty to announce weather problems and the desire to not look like a fool any more frequently than was necessary in his profession.

What he saw did not help him make up his mind. The charts and the satellite photos showed a gigantic mass of clouds heading towards the northeast. He'd been working with Wally for long

was almost on top of the parked squad car. She hit the brakes hard. Overpowered and overbraked, the Corvette swerved out of control while Cindy shrieked.

Stan Petkowski sat in the patrol car in front of the ditch. He was warm and dry and not at all envious of the crew digging the hole, and the work they would have to do in the cold, wet, mud. It was almost ten feet deep and a full lane wide. At least they'd stopped the water from gushing out.

The guys back at the station probably thought he was sitting in his car smoking and eating donuts. If so, screw 'em. He did have a jelly donut in his hand, but he didn't smoke. At least the sloppy wet weather and the resultant tie-up held down drivers' speed.

And, on a Monday morning, it was highly unlikely that anyone was drunk. Hung over, yes, but not drunk. He'd caught seven offenders the past Saturday and considered it a good haul. State law required jail time, but a good lawyer, or a bad one, could get that reduced to a fine and community service. Petkowski didn't care if that's all the first-time offenders got. Many of them were scared and shamed into not doing it again, and that was great with him. He wanted the stupid bastards punished, and if that meant some middle-aged businessman had to spend weekends picking up trash along the roads, it served him right. If the punishment scared the fools into never doing it again, that was even better. He was still tormented by the sight of finding his niece's head twenty feet from the rest of her body.

Stan felt secure in his car. The flashers were going and he had orange cones behind him. Thus, he was stunned when he saw the Corvette careening behind him. He barely had time to brace himself when it hit, throwing him backwards into the headrest.

The Corvette's right front fender crunched into the rear of the police car, propelling it forward, and, as Cindy Thomason watched incredulously, downward. The Corvette bounced off, spun sidewise, and rammed into the car to her left. The airbag went off in Cindy's face. She screamed with pain and fright. It quickly deflated and she checked herself. Her nose hurt like the devil and blood was pouring from her nostrils. One of her front teeth was loose and she immediately wondered if all the months spent in braces were going to go to hell. Her father was a doctor and rich enough, but he would be mad.

She held a tissue against her nose to control the bleeding and stumbled out of the car. She fell on her knees, skinning them. A cop had climbed out of the squad car, which, she saw, was now halfway down the hole in the road. The cop had a bruise on his forehead and there was gooey red stuff all over his face. Worse, he was angry. When he saw her bleeding, he immediately softened.

"You okay, Miss?"

"I'm going to be killed," Cindy wailed.

Despite himself, Officer Stanley Petkowski smiled. Even though the kid had blundered terribly, it was a relief to see she wasn't seriously hurt. He gently pulled her hand away from her face. Her nose was definitely broken.

"I think we're going to get you to a hospital."

"Oh God," Cindy moaned. "Now my parents are going to find out. And you're hurt too. Oh Jesus."

This time Petkowski did smile as he checked his face. Goop from the jelly donut was all over his cheek and forehead. "It's nothing," he said, hoping she wouldn't recognize it for what it was. He wiped it away with a Kleenex. "I think they were going to find out even if you weren't hurt."

Petkowski looked at the deepening traffic snarl. His squad car was half in the excavation ditch, while her Corvette was rammed into a Chrysler. The workers had scattered and wouldn't be back until the place was cleared, which wasn't going to be for a while. MacArthur Highway was totally closed by three corks in a plug. Nor was traffic north of the site moving. Something had happened up there as well. Probably another fender-bender, he thought. There would be a lot of them in this weather. Now the snow was almost blinding and swirling in the wind, and, along with silly girls driving overpowered Corvettes, there were too many fools who thought owning a four-wheel-drive vehicle made them invincible Gods of the Road.

No, he wasn't going to get Cindy Thomason to the hospital, or anywhere else for that matter. In fact, he wasn't going anywhere either, unless he hoofed it. Damn, he hated walking. Stan's idea of fun was riding a motorcycle. He couldn't afford one of his own, so the police motorcycle he rode in the summer was his baby. He hated his squad car. Damn. The police station was half a mile away and there wasn't anything he could do here. Trying to direct traffic would be a joke. No, he'd go to the station and later send a rookie out, on foot of course, to take control of the situation.

He and Cindy and a handful of others began to trudge towards the police station. Cindy had a nose to get fixed and Stan had a bunch of tickets to write.

"What the hell is going on," muttered Police Chief William Bench. Bench was fifty-three, seriously overweight, and, if the rumors were true, drank too much because he was grossly in over his head as chief. He had risen through Sheridan's ranks when it was a much smaller town with smaller, simpler problems. Now, confronted with the more serious and complex issues that population growth brings, even in a quiet town like Sheridan, he looked and acted more and more confused. The way he did now.

Mike Stuart turned from the television monitor. Through gaps in the wind and the snow, they could see that MacArthur was totally jammed, as were most of Sheridan's other streets. Where something did move, it moved at a crawl, and that included the interstate just to their south. The exits were backing up with cars trying to enter Sheridan's already clogged streets. This was going to be miserable, Mike thought. This wasn't even heaviest traffic time. Petkowski had reported his car out of action and was on his way back. Cops in two other cars had reported themselves totally stuck in unmoving traffic. The fourth squad car's driver was trying to figure a way back to the station by using the roads through the subdivisions and not having too much luck. In effect, there was no police presence on Sheridan's streets, and not much he could do about it.

Mike's earlier confidence that he could do the job in Lieutenant DiMona's absence was evaporating rapidly. Chief Bench wanted solutions to the problem and Mike had no idea what to do until the snow let up and they could get a handle on it.

"When will the salt trucks and plows be out?" Bench asked as he wiped sweat from his brow with a dirty handkerchief.

Mike shrugged uncomfortably. He didn't like being the bearer of bad news. "The county says they're having a hard time getting their drivers in, and our drivers and contractors say the same thing. It could be a while."

Bench grunted. He seemed pleased to find someone else was a potential source of the problem—therefore, he could not be blamed. Some of Sheridan's major roads were plowed and salted by the county, while others were Sheridan's problem. Snow removal companies had contracts, but it was obvious they weren't going to do anything anytime soon. It reminded Mike of the old Volkswagen Beetle commercial that asked how the snow plow driver got to work. Why, he drove a Volkswagen, of course. Then he realized—even if they could get drivers to the trucks, they couldn't move because the roads were getting jammed.

Mike checked some of the other monitors. Cars in the streets were now little more than unmoving white lumps when they could be seen through the snow. Sometimes he could see people standing around. The interstate was still moving, but extremely slowly and not for long.

A chilled and wet Petkowski arrived and stood beside Mike. A policewoman was escorting a sobbing Cindy Thomason to the john where they could try a quick fix on her nose and clean her up.

"Hey, Mike," Petkowski said softly as he cradled a cup of hot coffee in his hands. "Congratulations. Only one day on the job and you've gone and got your ass into a real class-A cluster-fuck."

Wally Wellman glared angrily at the people gathered in the TV6 conference room. "Okay, boys and girls, what do we do with this? Personally, I am tired of giving vague and inoffensive warnings that are a joke. It is snowing hard and it is going to snow more."

"National Weather Service and the Weather Channel now say we might get six inches," said Ron Friedman sullenly. It was beginning to look like Wally had been right and they had erred in the wrong direction.

Wally laughed harshly. "Hell, what're they smoking? We've already got more than six. What're they gonna do? Take some back?"

Wally was right. All anyone had to do was look out the window and, if they could see through the swirling gusts, they could tell that the snow was over six inches. Of course the inconsistencies could be explained by the fact that the "official" weather stats were kept at Detroit Metropolitan Airport, which was about fifty miles away. That far away the sun could be shining brightly and the birds singing. Up here, Wally joked, there was no sun and the birds were all dead.

"What do you want to do?" Friedman asked, conceding the high ground to Wally.

"What I don't want is the Isaac Cline award for stupidity."

"Who and what are you talking about?"

"Quick, what's the worst disaster in U.S. history?"

"Was it one of our syndicated reality shows?" Friedman asked cheerfully. "No? Okay, how about the San Francisco earthquake or the Johnstown flood?"

"Neither, dingus. The worst disaster in American history was the Galveston hurricane of 1900. Somewhere between six and ten thousand people were killed. They never could figure out the exact number since so many families simply disappeared. Isaac Cline was the weatherman in Galveston, and, despite evidence to the contrary, he insisted that no hurricane was going to strike, and he kept on predicting that until it was too late. What happened was the worst hurricane on record."

"Okay, but a snowfall is not a major hurricane," responded Friedman.

"Right," said Wally, "but there is still the potential for real problems if it snows and we're not prepared for it."

"How much more do you think we're going to get?"

Wally shrugged, "At least another six inches in the next couple of hours. If it doesn't slow down, then another six and then another six. For it to slow down, this front's got to move in the first place and it's barely budging. This could be the mother of all storms, to coin a phrase."

"Jesus!" someone exclaimed.

"If he's a friend of yours, call him," Wally laughed harshly. "If we give a forecast of heavy snow, maybe some businesses and schools will close early, and maybe some people won't go out shopping and get stuck. It'll give people a fighting chance to get home before it gets really bad."

"Do it," Freidman said, but without conviction. He could see the snow in the parking lot and wondered how anybody was going to get home even if they were released early. The traffic copter was down and the various television cameras situated throughout the metropolitan area were showing only a world of white. All flights either into or out of Detroit Metropolitan Airport in downriver Romulus had either been cancelled or were being delayed. How much longer would cars be able to move? Still, they had to make the announcement and let people decide what was best for them. As for closing schools, he wondered if that was even feasible. Would buses be able to move? Would parents try to pick up their kids?

Wordlessly, they all began to wonder when the first people would begin to die.

Ted Baranski regularly attended the nine a.m. Mass at St. Stephen's Roman Catholic Church in Sheridan, even though he thought the young priest, Father Torelli, was a pompous twit who thought he knew it all and didn't know when to shut up. At least he wasn't diddling the altar boys like so many priests he'd read about. At first Ted thought some people had a vendetta against the Church, but had changed his mind when the number of accusations skyrocketed and included some priests he knew, and it only got worse when some of them pleaded guilty. It had disturbed him deeply, even sickened him. Priests were supposed to be above reproach. The breach of faith and trust had almost sent him away from the Church as it had so many. So far, Father Torelli had kept his hands to himself. He had a beard that the parishioners joked made him look like a portrait of Jesus, so maybe he actually took his job seriously.

Ted also thought that the organist, an overweight woman in her forties, played with her feet and sang with her ass.

Baranski was eighty and Torelli maybe thirty-five. So how did that give the young priest the right to lecture to an old man like him? Baranski had seen the world. He'd fought and been wounded in Korea; he'd earned a Bronze Star. He'd worked all

his life, and retired from General Motors with a decent pension
that so far included damn good health care. He'd married, had
children, grandchildren, and now, great-grandchildren. If only
his wife Catherine were here to help him enjoy it.

Can't have it all, he thought sadly. She'd died more than five
years ago and his memory of her was still bright. His kids teased
him that his mind wasn't as sharp as it used to be and maybe
they were right. But he remembered everything about Catherine.
So what if he sometimes misplaced his car keys, or lost a library
book, or couldn't remember if he took his heart medicine—he
remembered his past. He didn't care much for the present and the
future at his age was difficult to comprehend. The kids wanted
him to go to a senior residence or even a nursing home, but he'd
rather die before he'd let that happen. The trouble with nursing
homes was that there were too Goddamned many old people and
so many of them had Alzheimer's or dementia. He had friends
in nursing homes and some of them didn't remember him.

He liked being independent. In his own home he could grow
his plants and flowers, and so what if he forgot to flush the toilet or occasionally peed on the floor. He wasn't starving and he
wasn't hurting anybody. His home was a ranch, which meant he
didn't have to worry about stairs unless he went to the basement
for some beer. He rubbed the stubble on his chin. He hadn't
bothered to shave today and who the hell cared. At least he'd
taken a shower. Some old people stank. He didn't want to be
one of those.

So finally Father Torelli finished the Mass and the organist
hit a last discordant note. Hallelujah and amen. Baranski had
prayed and suffered quietly through an overlong sermon they now
called a homily. Didn't matter what they called it, Father Torelli
was a bore as a preacher. He remembered when the Mass was
in Latin. At least then you could get a decent nap. Of course,
Catherine always poked him awake when he began to snore. She
was embarrassed and the kids thought it was funny, which got her
upset. She tried to be angry with him, but it didn't always work.

He dutifully shook the priest's hand and opened the door where
he was slapped in the face with a blast of snow.

"When the hell did that happen?" he asked in surprise and

laughed. Like he had a choice; everyone else was laughing, too, even Father Torelli. Hey, it was funny.

Fred Foley, his good buddy, answered. "It's snowing, you big butthead. You spent so much time pretending to be praying that you forgot about the rest of the world."

Ted sniffed. "That just means I'm a better Catholic than you are. Right, Father?"

Father Torelli laughed again. He'd watched the two old men argue ever since he'd been assigned to St. Stephen's a year before. They were part of his environment. "As far as I'm concerned, you're both great guys. Now kiss and make up."

Baranski thought that maybe the young priest wasn't as bad as he'd thought. The sermons were awful, but the skinny kid was okay when he wasn't trying to preach to the choir. Maybe he'd go to Confession and try to shock the priest by telling him he'd been practicing birth control at eighty.

Foley looked out through the window in the door. "Can't see a thing. Maybe we'd better wait until this clears up. Can't last long at this rate."

That seemed like a plan, so the two older men and a handful of others sat down to wait out what was obviously a snow squall or shower, while Father Torelli made the very short walk back to the rectory. It was only a few feet away and the bulk of the building could barely be seen. Snow showers were frequent and intense, but, like a summer thunderstorm, let up after a short while and were forgotten.

An hour later, they they'd run out of things to say and the snowfall hadn't diminished a bit. Ted Baranski stood and stretched. The church pews were tough on his skinny butt. He didn't want his hemorrhoids acting up, either.

"This is ridiculous. I gotta get home."

"You don't like me anymore?" sniffed Foley.

Baranski looked outside. The snow was blowing and falling heavily. "I just want to get home," he said softly. All of a sudden, getting home was really important.

"I think you should wait a while longer," said Foley.

"Christ, I just live across the parking lot. I won't get lost."

It was a slight untruth. He lived across both the gravel parking lot and the adjacent large field that the parish was holding for future expansion. St. Stephen's was a young, new parish and the current building was only temporarily used as a church. Someday there'd be a real church and what was now the church would become a parish rec center.

Ted said goodbye to everyone and stepped outside. He oriented himself on the light pole dimly visible in the lot, and headed out towards his home. After a short while he realized that he couldn't see much of anything and decided he'd made a dumb decision. He turned around to go back to church. As he did that, his foot caught in the uneven ground. He twisted his ankle and fell to the parking lot, knocking the wind out of himself.

"Damn it to hell," he said to no one when he could breathe again. He tried to get up, but the ankle protested. He finally made it to his feet, but walking was difficult. His ankle hurt really bad. After a few tentative steps he realized that he'd been turned around by the fall and had no idea where the church was. With a feeling of dread he remembered that it was a white brick building. It blended perfectly into the driving snow.

He lurched and took some more steps. He had to go someplace. He couldn't stay out in the parking lot. To his surprise, the snow was already over his ankles and his feet were wet and freezing.

Walk, he told himself. It wasn't like he was out in the middle of a desert. This wasn't like he was back in Korea, although it brought back some very unpleasant memories. This was a city, damn it. Sooner or later he'd either be back at the church, his own house, or at a neighbor's, feeling like a fool. Better a fool than dead, he thought.

Just a few more steps, he ordered himself. The ankle hurt and it was becoming difficult to breathe. His chest was tightening. Had he taken his heart medicine? He felt a twinge of panic as he realized he wasn't sure.

His chest constricted more and breathing became painful. He dropped to his knees. He felt like he'd been shot in the chest, just like back in Korea. I'll rest for a moment, he decided, then start over again. He thought he saw a shape moving towards him. Was it his wife? No, it was a man with a beard. Jesus? Or maybe that young priest. His chest seemed to explode and a wave of red before his eyes, followed by black, were the last things his eyes saw.

The twelve classrooms at Patton Elementary were arranged in a long row with a common area every four classrooms. Maddy, her friend Donna Harris, Frieda Houle, and Maggie Tomasi were the four teachers in the group. Because of the design, they were able to step outside their classrooms and talk while still in sight of their students, many of whom were pretending to be working while watching the blinding snow.

Sheridan North High School and Bradley Middle School were similarly constructed and the three schools occupied a large compound in the middle of playgrounds and parking lots. All three were connected and shared a main entrance and admin center as an attempt to cut costs. The compound had been constructed in the eighties and there had been many complaints about the quality of the construction.

The much older Sheridan South High School was located four miles to the south.

"We are in deep poop, ladies," said Donna Harris. A couple of minutes earlier, Superintendent Mary Templeton had called and dropped a bombshell on them. The schools were closing.

Sort of.

Unlike simpler times when kids were dismissed and walked home to a waiting stay-at-home mommy, closing schools these days was a tricky proposition. No one had any idea if or when the school buses would roll and no student would be allowed to go home without the specific permission of a parent or a previously designated guardian. Because of the sprawling nature of the Sheridan community, only a handful of students lived within walking distance even in the best of weather. Attempts were being made to contact parents. However, many of these were at work and many students normally stayed late in latchkey programs.

"Student safety is our paramount concern," Templeton had said officiously. *Like we wouldn't have considered that,* Maddy'd laughed when the message was relayed. Patton's principal, Toni Felix, was at a seminar and Donna Harris was the designated stand-in.

Donna intensely disliked being the designated principal. Toni Felix, in her opinion, was absent far too often and always going to seminars or conferences. Donna received no extra pay for the inconvenience and only did it because she felt that someone with experience should be responsible. If the superintendent felt so strongly about student safety, then why didn't she insist that there always be a principal in residence? Some of the parents had noticed and were beginning to complain.

Maddy looked out a window. A bunch of lumps in the parking lot showed where the teachers' cars were parked. Nobody was going to leave until all the students were gone and maybe not even then. Already driving looked next to impossible. No cars were moving on the normally fairly busy road in front of the school.

Maddy was thankful she didn't have a family to worry about. Her date with Mike could be rescheduled. Frieda was divorced and unconcerned about her cats, while Donna's kids were grown and away at college. Since they were already expecting bad weather, most of the teachers had dressed for it, wearing jeans and similarly functional clothing. Some of the other teachers had small children of their own. Maggie Tomasi had two daughters, both under five, and she looked distraught, even though they were safe with an adult babysitter.

"Watch my class," Maddy asked the others as she reached for her coat and boots. "I'm going to get my cell phone out of the car. Somehow, I think it might come in useful."

The others nodded and passed her their keys. "Get ours too," was the request. The school district had recently instituted a policy prohibiting students from having cell phones and other devices in the school and had "strongly suggested" that teachers do likewise. Surprisingly, the teachers' union had gone along with it.

To compound matters, someone had decreed that this would be no-tech week. Thus, there were no laptops or anything else in the buildings. Students and teachers were supposed to be reduced to pencils and pads of paper. How many students and teachers were breaking what she thought was an idiotic rule was a good question. Regardless, neither Maddy nor her friends had anything electronic on them. She'd joked that they'd all become Luddites.

Now, however, the policy was beginning to look like a big

mistake. Unless the snow stopped right now, it was going to get more and more difficult to get to their cars and their technology, their connection to the outside world.

CHAPTER 5

WHEN MIKE'S CELL PHONE RANG, HE THOUGHT IT MIGHT BE Maddy or even his parents. He was a little surprised to see that it was from another officer, Clyde Detmer. Detmer was in his mid-fifties, hugely overweight and counting the days until he retired in a couple of months. Once Detmer had been a good cop, but an accident had changed him in many ways. He'd been directing traffic when a driver who'd been texting and yelling at her kids ran him over, smashing his leg. He still walked with a limp and only recently had given up his cane.

After the accident, he'd been depressed, gained a ton of weight, and been stuck in a desk job he despised. But his sense of humor had slowly returned as well as his sense of responsibility to the job. Mike tried to recall if he'd seen Clyde at all this turbulent morning and felt a twinge of guilt that he couldn't recall one way or another. Damn, Clyde was supposed to be a friend as well as a fellow cop. He put the phone on speaker.

"Let me guess, Clyde, you're not here this morning and you're calling in sick."

"I wish, Sergeant Mike. I am stuck here at Sheridan North

41

with at least a thousand kids who are all on a sugar high and no way out. I guess you don't recall, but I was sent here to give a talk to kids about the evils of drugs." He laughed. "Like they care. Hell, they probably know more about drugs than I do. I don't do drugs, never did."

"What about Viagra?" asked Petkowski.

"Up yours, Polack. Now, Mike, you want me to come in or not? If you do, you're gonna have to send someone or something. The snow's got me locked in tighter than the mayor's heart at budget time. There's a good foot or two of snow over everything and nothing's moving either in the lot or in the streets as far as I can see."

Mike thought quickly and made an easy decision. The complex that consisted of Sheridan North, Patton, and Bradley easily contained the largest concentration of children in the area. Detmer might not be the smartest or most mobile cop on the force, but he was in uniform and wore a badge. A police presence at the complex might help calm things. That he would also be able to keep an eye on Maddy's safety was another consideration. It was a selfish one, but he didn't care.

"I think it would be best if you remained there, Clyde. Keep an eye on the kids and especially for anyone who might need meds or drugs. You may have kids who need a fix and won't be able to get one because of the snow. We both know that that kind of situation could get ugly real fast. You got any people who can help you if things go south?"

Detmer laughed, "Just a bunch of coaches and maybe some senior jocks who don't like assholes who do drugs."

"Sounds like a plan," Mike said.

Petkowski couldn't help himself. "Hey, if things really get rough, we'll arrange an emergency shipment from Krispy Kreme. A couple of dozen ought to hold you over until tomorrow, don't you think?"

"Polack, that is fucking profiling. I'm going to talk to my union rep."

Petkowski was laughing and Mike could hear Detmer laughing as well. "Detmer, you jackass, I am your union rep."

✧   ✧   ✧

In the good weather months, Sheridan's municipal campus was connected by pleasant paved walkways bordered by lush shade trees. Now the trees were bare and the walkways were absolutely useless in bad weather. Fortunately, the buildings were also connected by maintenance tunnels that were used by city employees every time it rained, or by local politicians who didn't want to be cornered by voters or the press. Dodging the pipes and stepping over the dirt was often a small price to pay for not getting wet or hassled.

Thus, Mike Stuart and Chief Bench arrived warm and dry at Mayor Calvin Carter's office. Carter was a thin and cadaverous-looking man in his early sixties. Charmless and dour, he had risen to wealth and prominence as a major builder and landowner in the area. When his riches were assured, he'd turned to politics in what many felt was nothing more than an ego-trip. He was elected mayor of Sheridan the old fashioned way—he'd outspent his nearest rival by ten to one.

"Gentlemen," Carter began from behind his massive oak desk. The desk had precipitated a small scandal until Carter announced that he'd paid for it himself. It was a lie. It was unproven common knowledge that the money had come from local businessmen currying favor. "Just what are we going to do about this mess? People are swarming all over the place like Afghan refugees and we have no facilities for them. Traffic has got to move. Emergency vehicles have got to get out and they can't. Simply put, I want this problem solved. I do not want to be associated with a catastrophe."

Mike had had very little contact with the mayor. As division head, Lieutenant DiMona had always been a buffer, as had Chief Bench. Still, the comments were puzzling. Did the man expect Mike or Bench to make it stop snowing? He said nothing and let Bench, an old crony of Carter's, respond.

"Calvin, I mean Mayor Carter; you know damn well there isn't a whole helluva lot we can do. Traffic everywhere is just about dead in its tracks. The people who've come in here are those who've abandoned their cars. We're going to stash them as best we can in the library and the courthouse. At least they'll have places to sit. We can't just boot them out in the snow to die."

Bench was visibly nervous when he finished his small statement, and was sweating even more profusely than before. Mike thought he recognized the symptoms. An uncle had been a lush and sweated like a hog when he was away from a drink for more than a few minutes. Bench's inadequacies filled Mike with foreboding.

"I know that," Carter said patiently. "I'm not suggesting that we actually throw voters out in the snow. I just want them out of here and on their way home as soon as it's safe."

More than a hundred cold and confused people had escaped from the weather and into the city hall and other buildings. "But the fire department and EMS can't move either, and that's a dangerous scenario," Carter continued. "First real emergency that gets called in to 911 and people might just die because we can't respond."

Public Works Director Dom Hassell came in and sat down. He'd heard the end of the comment. "I'd love to be optimistic, fellas, but I can't. I've been on the phone with my peers at the county and we all agree that, if the snow were to stop right God damn now, it'd be a day or two before the streets were really passable thanks to all the abandoned cars."

"So what happens?" Carter asked with a touch of incredulity. "Don't tell me we just sit here on our asses and wait for summer?"

Hassell shrugged. "We won't have to wait that long, but that's exactly what we do, sir. We sit and pray for the best, but, if we don't get it, fires will burn and people will die," he said simply and grimly. "Hopefully, the heavy snow will keep fires down and, just as hopefully; maybe neighbors can pitch in and help people out in the event of accidents and heart attacks. In fact, I think we should make public service announcements to that effect. Hell, it'll be just like people did out here a hundred years ago with some modern pioneers delivering babies and setting broken bones all by their lonesomes."

"Damn it, this isn't a hundred years ago!" Carter snapped. "This is the twenty-first century, not the nineteenth, and the people want and deserve more. They've paid through the nose for the privilege of living in Sheridan and we have got to take care of their needs."

"Which they're not going to get for a while," Hassell retorted. "Even insurance policies have disclaimers saying they won't cover stuff in the event of an act of God, and insurance companies don't even believe in God."

If Carter was unhappy, that was fine with Hassell. Carter had defeated Hassell's brother-in-law for the mayor's job, and there was no love lost between the two men. Hassell's job was civil service, and Carter could do nothing about him, although he'd tried to have him fired.

Mike decided to say something positive. "Uh, Mayor Carter, Dom, we've been trying to restore some degree of mobility. With all our squad cars out of service, I've got people calling around for snowmobiles and, of course, winter clothing. We've got a couple of snowmobiles coming in and maybe more. I understand the fire department and EMS are doing the same thing."

Mike didn't add that nothing could be done too quickly and they'd be working without many of their tools. He hoped the mayor would understand that half a loaf was better than none. One of the first things to do would be to provide food for the refugees, in particular for the children. Adults could fast for a while, but the kids were not going to go hungry if he could help it. The last thing anyone needed was a few dozen kids screaming and crying because they hadn't been fed.

Carter glared at Mike and forced a smile. To Mike his smile looked like a vulture examining a cadaver. "Excellent. At least the citizens will see we're doing something and not just sitting on our tails." He turned to Bench. "And are you recalling off-duty cops?"

"Those we can reach," Bench answered. He had recovered some of his poise. "Sad fact is, many of our people live outside of Sheridan because housing in town is just too pricey. Odds are, we'll get maybe half our normal number of people in, which won't be half bad, no pun intended."

Unspoken was the fact that the police department was seriously understaffed. In a budget-balancing move, Carter had frozen hiring in all city departments. Not only did that result in serious vacancies, but it savaged the morale of those who had to work even harder while accomplishing less. So far, the average homeowner hadn't complained much since his taxes hadn't gone up and nothing really bad had happened. Yet.

Mike thought that many emergency personnel who wouldn't make it in might not be trying very hard. He rejected that thought. The cops, fire, and EMS people he knew were pros, and would do their best and then some to do their jobs. Although he had to consider that a couple of the guys who'd called in sick this Monday might be suffering from a mild case of Blue Flu. When morale went down, the slightest case of the sniffles became pneumonia in the mind of the victim.

"You know what I'm concerned about?" Hassell injected. "Roofs collapsing. Snow piling up is gonna be a problem for the best-built building. Too much snow could be a disaster waiting to happen."

To Mike's surprise, Mayor Carter seemed to pale. "Let's hope not," Carter said.

Before anyone could amplify on this new topic, Detective Sergeant Patti Hughes came in uninvited and sat down. Chief Bench glared at her. He still had problems with women cops. Worse, since Hughes was much smarter than he, Bench felt insecure with her. Hughes was short and chunky, and wore her dark brown hair mannishly short. This led to rumors that she was a lesbian, which was a source of great amusement to her husband and two sons.

Bench snapped at her. "Is this interruption necessary? We're having an important meeting."

Hughes smiled thinly. "We have other problems than the snow, gentlemen. Anybody recall that unidentified dead guy they found up near Traverse City a few days ago? The one they found naked in a field with his throat cut?"

"Sure," said Bench. "What of it? He wasn't from here."

Traverse City was a four-hour-plus drive north from Sheridan. When the report came in, they'd done a quick check of any local missing persons and confirmed what they'd thought all along—the dead guy wasn't from Sheridan. Without a local angle, the police and the local media had quickly lost interest in Traverse City's problem. It was shocking, but too bad.

Hughes was undeterred. "Then you'll recall the speculation

that the dead guy might be associated with similar killings in Idaho and Wisconsin?"

"What does that have to do with us?" Carter said. The mayor seemed to feel that Hughes was goading him, which Mike thought likely. In the world of small town politics, the police and fire unions had supported the other guy, and Hughes was not one to back down from anyone.

Undeterred, Hughes continued, "They finally managed to ID him. Turns out he lived in a small town in a Wisconsin and was visiting a friend in Traverse City. His family said he went missing a week ago."

"So?" asked Bench, his impatience growing. "Is there a point to this?"

"Well, someone used his American Express card to prepay a room at the Sheridan Motor Inn two days ago, as well as make a number of cash withdrawals from ATMs. Pretty active for a dead guy, if you ask me."

To Joe Gomez, the onset of the heavily falling snow looked like a godsend. At only thirty-two, he was the proud owner of two successful businesses: Gomez Landscaping and Gomez Snow Removal. He originally started out with only one corporation, but his lawyer had advised him to have two. Something about liability if he should run over someone with his snowplow or accidentally mulch a customer's cat with a mower. Or maybe mulch a customer. It made sense, so he did it.

Either way, business had been pretty good the past couple of years and that was great because Joe had a lot of bills to pay. First, he owed money on everything, including his lot, garage, and, of course, his vehicles. He liked to joke that only his office stapler was free and clear. Then his wife had insisted on bringing her father in from Mexico, illegally of course, which meant other expenses, and now she was very pregnant with their third child and throwing up all the time. That meant she couldn't help out in the office, which meant he had to actually pay someone for the work Maria did gratis because she loved him.

Joe Gomez laughed when he thought about it. After all was said and done, his troubles were a lot less than other people's.

Screw it. Whatever happened, he'd make it work. Hard work and Joe Gomez went together, and he had a loyal clientele who agreed with that statement.

Gomez Snow Removal had been pretty busy this past winter, but not overly so, which was both good and bad. Good was because he had time to work on his equipment, think, attend small business seminars, and play with his kids. He also played with Maria, and he thought that sort of thing had something to do with her getting pregnant. The bad part was because snow removal revenue just wasn't as profitable as lawn moving. Fortunately, there had been a lot of snow this winter and what was happening this fine morning looked like a godsend. He considered it little more than a sideline and something to keep him busy in the winter. Grass had to be cut every week in the summer, but who knew when it would snow? He'd be busier than the proverbial one-armed paper hanger in a month or so with people's lawns, but he'd really like a little better cash flow now. That was why he'd yelped with pleasure as the white stuff started to come down.

It took Joe a little longer than he thought it would to get to the lot where he had his office and shed and kept his vehicles. Unlike many of his competitors, it was in Sheridan, which was expensive, but, so far, he'd been able to handle it. After all, it kept him close to his customers.

Traffic flow coming in to his office had been really crappy, and all the idiots who didn't know how to drive in the snow seemed to be directly in front of him. When he got to the lot, he saw that one of his other drivers, Tommy Hummel, had already taken his truck with the attached plow blade and was out doing his jobs. Tommy was a good, dependable guy, and more of a friend than an employee.

Joe had a list of business and residential clients and they would be served in their turn, and, if the snow kept up, the businesses would be plowed as often as necessary to get their parking lots clear. Joe had a Wal-Mart lot to clear first, followed by a couple of large office complexes. Schools would come later since they'd be closed anyhow. Money, money, money, he thought happily as he mentally geared up for a day of hard work.

Gomez also had a contract with the city of Sheridan to clear their streets if the snow was so great that their own vehicles couldn't do it in a timely manner. In Joe's humble opinion, that was exactly the way this snow was going to play out. No way those rich suburbanites could be inconvenienced, no sir. C'mon snow, he said to no one. The city fathers would be glad to pay him whatever it cost to keep their affluent citizens in line.

Joe got behind the wheel of the big dump truck he'd bought from a bankrupt construction company and headed out. The truck was his pride and joy, and a lot of downtime work had been spent on it. Its size was more intimidating than necessary, but it was a statement that he took his job seriously. A large retractable plow hung from the hood, making it look like some kind of prehistoric dinosaur. A stegosaurus, his wife said. Joe did not disagree. He'd seen a picture of a stegosaurus on the Discovery Channel and the resemblance was clear. It really was a monster truck.

The tires were oversized and good and he had little trouble exiting the lot and getting onto his street, which was a side street that entered onto MacArthur. Christ, it was really coming down, he thought, and immediately slowed down to a crawl. The last thing he wanted was an accident.

He'd only gotten down the side street and to the main road when he stopped abruptly. Ahead and in front of him on MacArthur was nothing but wall-to-wall snow-covered cars that weren't moving. He thought about barging his way in, but then what? He backed his truck up and pulled it aside so that anyone behind him could get through. Then he laughed at that possibility. Like where would they go if they did pass him? Besides, his street was a dead end, so he didn't think anybody would exit from MacArthur, but you never knew.

He turned off the ignition and carefully climbed onto the slippery top of the truck to see what he could see through the swirling snow. Not very much at all was what he could see. Where there was highway there were cars and they weren't moving. Plumes of exhaust were all that told him anyone was in them. Otherwise, they could have been abandoned wrecks at a junkyard, or a parking lot at a football game. What now, he wondered? The top was getting icy and he climbed down before he fell and broke something. Maria was always telling him to be careful and reminding him that he *was* the business. If he got hurt, the business hurt.

Through the snow, he saw someone walking in his direction. "That you, Joe?" Tommy Hummel asked as he emerged through a gust of even heavier snow.

"Naw, it's Santa Claus," Joe answered. "Why are you walking and where the hell is my truck, you incompetent Anglo?"

Tommy laughed. "I'm trying to do you a favor, taco-man. I'm stopped and stuck maybe two hundred yards up the road and people are beginning to leave their cars and head for warm buildings. Your precious truck is locked up and safe. Even if somebody tried to steal it, they couldn't move it anywheres. Seriously, I was really hoping to catch you before you got stuck too."

That made sense to Gomez. He and Tommy got into his monster truck and Gomez carefully turned it around and headed back to the yard. He dropped the plow so he could at least make himself useful by clearing something, if only a dead end side street.

"Tommy, why didn't you phone me?"

"I did. It helps to have it on. Works a helluva lot better that way."

"Oops," Joe laughed. He noticed that the snow was nearly at the top of the plow blade. It was getting very deep real fast. So much for making a killing, he thought ruefully. All the snow in the world and no way he could get out and shovel it.

"Water, water everywhere," Joe muttered.

"And not a drop to drink," Tommy completed and both men laughed. Not much else to do but take what they'd been handed with good humor. When life deals you lemons, make lemonade. "What now, Señor Gomez? Wanna go back to the office and play cards?"

"Not unless you have a better idea," Joe said. Nor were they going anywhere at all anytime soon. Driving home had suddenly become out of the question. There was a six pack of Coors in the refrigerator and, since they obviously weren't going to be doing any driving or operating heavy machinery for a while, it seemed a fine time to demolish it. There was a couch and a couple of folding cots that he'd put in so workers could catch naps if they had to, along with a small bathroom that included a toilet and a sink. Now it looked like they'd be using the cots to bunk down tonight. Maybe they'd catch a weather forecast on the television. Damn.

The main travel guides listed the Sheridan Motor Inn as either a three- or four-star motel. Given the fact that Sheridan was a bedroom community without any significant commercial base, and that it also lacked anything to bring in tourists, the motel and restaurant were surprisingly upscale, well appointed, and popular. One hundred and twenty rooms, restaurant, lounge, indoor pool, gym, and conference rooms made it a complete facility. Weekend getaway packages sold well and augmented income from weekday business travelers. A mini-water park brought in families and filled the pool with screaming kids on weekends.

This Monday morning, the Inn was less than half full. Most of those who were departing had made it out, and those who had reservations for Monday weren't going to keep them, at least not for a while.

Billy Raines looked out the second-floor window onto an ocean of white that used to be a parking lot. *This is not good,* he thought. Their plans were to get out of this town and on the way south as quickly as possible. Staying too long in one place was a bad idea. They could not depend on the last body going undiscovered for any length of time. For all he knew, the cops around Traverse City had found the guy, identified him, and were on their way right now. Cops and computers were a bad thing. He hadn't wanted to use the guy's ATM card or his credit card, but they needed cash as well as a place to stay. He'd figured on leaving right away and then the damn snow started.

Of course, Raines chuckled with some satisfaction, the cops would need fucking snowshoes to get anywhere near him.

"What's so funny?" asked Jimmy Tower, the other half of what Raines sarcastically referred to as their dynamic duo. Tower was anything but dynamic looking. Slightly over five feet tall and chunky, Tower was four years younger than the forty-year-old Raines. At a lean six feet, Raines dominated the other man in more ways than one. To put it politely, Tower was more than a little slow and looked it. Raines thought Tower might either have a mild case of Down's syndrome or Fetal Alcohol Syndrome. Either way, Jimmy Tower was at least one egg short of a dozen.

Raines had befriended the smaller man in prison and had become his protector from the sexual predators who had stalked him. Tower owed Raines big time. Raines was a leader who always had a small group of supporters—white, of course—while Tower was an efficient and often brutal lap dog.

Jimmy Tower compensated for his slowness with his viciousness. Jimmy had cut the throat of the guy in Traverse City, and Jimmy had beaten the hell out of a woman in Green Bay. He had also raped her. Jimmy liked women, but they didn't like him because he was such an ugly little shit. Jimmy thought most people were laughing at him, and he was often right. Raines made sure he never laughed at Jimmy Tower. So far, they'd gotten along well.

But that was the least of their problems. The mounting snow was imprisoning them as effectively as metal bars once had, and ruining their plans to move south. The key to not getting caught was to keep moving. This is what they'd done since escaping from a medium-security prison in Wisconsin. From there they'd stolen cars and driven across Michigan's Upper Peninsula and south across the Mackinac Bridge to Traverse City where they'd killed that guy. From there they'd driven the dead guy's car to Sheridan where they'd planned a very short stay.

Stand still and you become a target, so they had to keep moving. Their plan, such as it was, was to head south towards warmer weather and maybe even the Mexican border, although they knew they were well east of it. They'd heard that drug dealers south of the border liked Anglos. More reliable, they thought. Also, they could cross the border more easily since they didn't look Mexican.

Raines saw a hunched figure walking through the parking lot to a trailer with two lumps on it. The man shook off some of the snow and checked a tarp that covered whatever was on the trailer. The snow was swirling, but Raines thought he saw something like metal runners poking out from the tarp.

Raines grinned. "Get in bed and cover up," he yelled at an astonished Tower. "Start moaning like a woman when I return."

Raines opened the door and ran down the hallway, confident

that Tower would do exactly as told. The hunched over man had returned to the motel and was going into his room. Snow had fallen from his coat and was puddling on the floor.

"Sir!" Raines yelled anxiously and the man paused. "Are those snowmobiles on that truck?"

The man was wary and hesitated. "Why, yes."

Raines affected great concern. "Thank God. My wife is complaining about abdominal pains. It may be her appendix. I've called 911, but they can't help me. They can't even get ambulances out because of the snow."

The man softened. "I understand. Tell you what, my wife's a nurse. I'll let her take a look before we do anything risky. If she says we need to, we'll figure out a way to get her to the hospital."

"Great," Raines said and gave him their room number. He ran back to the room to wait. In the bedroom, Tower moaned in an awful falsetto. "Not like that! Like you're in pain!"

A moment later, there was a knock on the door and the man entered, followed by a heavy-set and concerned looking woman. They both looked about fifty.

It was so easy. Raines followed the two Samaritans into the bedroom. He suddenly pushed the woman onto the bed, where Tower grabbed her. Raines turned and hit the man on the head with a table lamp. The Samaritan dropped like a rock, while Jimmy easily subdued the woman. They tied her with torn cloth and stuffed a towel in her mouth. Jimmy was very strong for his size.

The two of them dragged the man into the bathroom where Raines hit him several more times on the head. Then Jimmy dragged in the shock-stricken woman. When she saw her husband lying in a widening pool of blood, her eyes rolled back and she moaned. Then she fainted.

Raines saw the look of expectation on Jimmy's face. The woman was fat and ugly, but she was a woman and Jimmy wasn't choosy. "No time for that," Raines said. Jimmy shrugged and pushed the woman into the tub. A quick slash across her throat from a steak knife he'd taken from the kitchenette caused blood to gush out of her. She convulsed and in only a few moments, went limp. Raines dumped her husband's body face down on top of her.

Raines and Tower left their room and dashed down the hallway.

The Samaritans' room contained everything they needed in the way of cold weather equipment. Even better, they found a pistol in the man's luggage. The dead woman's gear fitted Jimmy Tower almost perfectly, although he didn't look too mannish in pink. However, those were all details and even Jimmy recognized the opportunity that had presented itself. Now they could get out of the motel and then out of town.

That is, if they could figure out how to drive a snowmobile.

CHAPTER 6

WALLY WELLMAN STARED AT THE UNBLINKING TELEVISION CAM-
era. The lens and the red light gave the impression of otherworldly
life. He recalled how it terrified him when he was first starting
out as a television personality. Back then, he spoke hesitantly and
sometimes had an almost overwhelming urge to urinate. Now it
was just a tool of the trade. His voice would be going out over
the radio as well as television.

Genuine concern showed on Wally's face. Gone was his usual
casual and corny banter. Now he was grim. "Ladies and gentlemen, it's obvious that the weather situation has gone from bad
to worse and could easily get even more dangerous. Those of
you who are listening to me on your car radios know exactly
what I am talking about. However, those of you considering
leaving work or school or wherever you are and driving home
are everyone's concern."

Wally paused for effect. "Simply put, it is far too dangerous
to be driving in this weather. Worse, it is virtually impossible
to move even if you do try. So, if you do try to drive home you
will fail miserably and become part of a growing and dangerous

55

problem. Almost every road in Southeastern Michigan is at a standstill and relief is not in sight. It is only noon and there's much more than a foot of snow on the ground, and no letup in the intensity of the storm is predicted. We can only look at our maps and satellite photos and forecast snow, snow, and more snow. We have no idea when it will slow down, much less stop. To be candid, our science and our computers have all failed. We have no idea what is going to happen next. The weather has won this round and there's nothing we can or should do except wait it out."

The comment about computers wasn't quite the truth. Computers never fail. They just didn't have enough data to make a correct analysis. The analysts who'd assumed their infallibility had failed by providing the computers with insufficient data and not acknowledging that fact. Detailed weather records went back less than a century and satellite reconnaissance less than half that. So how could data be complete?

"Even if the snow were to stop in a few minutes, it would be many hours before the roads could be cleared. As you probably know, Governor Landsman has declared a state of emergency and ordered that everyone stay where they are. This could be inconvenient, but inconvenience usually isn't fatal. At worst, you're going to be a little hungry and have to sleep on something uncomfortable tonight. You may be concerned about loved ones, but please accept the fact that you are not going to reach them even if you try. Odds are, you won't even get out of your parking lot or your driveway. Wherever you and they are, both you and they are better off not moving."

Wally again paused to let that sink in. Hopefully. Some people were such complete and stubborn asses. "Please, use your heads and not your emotions. Stay put. For those listening on your car radio to our FM affiliate, you may already be in great danger. If there are open buildings nearby, leave your vehicles and get to them as soon as you can before the snow gets even deeper and more dangerous. If you stay in your car, you run the risk of freezing to death before the roads are reopened. If you insist on staying in your vehicle, only run your engine intermittently and then with the car windows opened a crack. If you don't, you could suffocate. Bear in mind that your exhaust pipe may already be filled with snow. Like I said, your best bet is to get out of your car and into some other shelter."

An intern handed him a sheet of paper. He read the contents and nodded. "Here's something else to consider. Check the pipes that are the outside vents for your furnaces. If this snow gets much deeper, they might get covered. If that happens, carbon monoxide could back up and into your houses and that would be very dangerous."

Wally signed off and looked at his producer. The two men were shocked by the intensity of the snowfall. The normally loquacious Wally Wellman, star of TV6, really had nothing further to say.

Two adults and three kids in a car, even a large mini-van, was a recipe for disaster, especially if the car wasn't going anyplace.

"I wanna go home," complained Milly, the middle child. She was seven. John was nine and little Amy was two. She was asleep, which was a blessing. Awake, she'd be trying to destroy the car and anyone in it. The term "Terrible Twos" must have been coined with her in mind, her parents thought.

Phil and Debbie Stiles had been taking the two older kids to school. Normally Debbie did the job, but she and Phil had the day off and decided a change in routine would be fun. After getting rid of the two older kids and dropping Amy at day care, Phil and Debbie would shop, have lunch, go home, and see about making another little Stiles. It'd been a while since they'd had any real privacy, and Phil had almost forgotten what Deb looked like naked.

But the sudden, heavy snow had been a very unpleasant surprise. They were on northbound MacArthur and not much was happening. The snow was falling heavily and he had to keep using the wipers and defrosters to see anything at all. As it was, the car in front was a white blob.

"I don't think we're going anywhere for a while," he finally admitted.

"What should we do?" Deb asked. There was a note of concern in her voice. People in their social and economic circles rarely felt helpless, yet that was exactly what they felt and neither she nor Phil liked it.

Phil admitted that he had no idea and that was upsetting. He always had ideas and he always felt that he was in control. "I suppose we should sit here until traffic clears." Sometimes he thought he could see police flashers in front, but he didn't know what they meant. Maybe they meant that traffic would move when whatever was holding them up got cleared out. If that didn't happen soon, the snow would be too deep for the car to handle, four-wheel drive or not.

"I don't know if I like that idea." Deb said.

"Well, you want to get out and walk somewhere with these kids? I don't like abandoning the car, either."

She admitted he had a point and they settled down to do nothing. Walking was not an option. For one thing, they hadn't dressed for the weather. They had no boots or heavy clothing. Hey, they were just going for a short drive in their own town, weren't they?

Phil turned off the ignition, but it quickly got cold, so he turned it on again. However, that was dangerous, so he kept the window cracked open. He decided he would run the motor for a while, turn it off, and keep repeating the process. It should keep everyone warm enough, and conserve fuel. He had a little more than half a tank. He hadn't had the radio on. Instead, they'd been listening to a CD. He and Deb always found the news depressing.

Turning the engine on and off was a good idea, but he couldn't see under the car where the rapidly accumulating snow covered the exhaust and blocked it when he turned off the ignition.

Phil began to get sleepy. A blast of snow came through the window and hit him on the face, reviving him for only a moment. He closed the window, unaware that Deb had closed the one on the other side. He yawned and closed his eyes. He needed a rest.

"Hi Mike, it's me. Try and guess where I am and what I'm doing."

Inside the police station, Mike grinned into his cell phone, happy to hear a voice that was more than friendly. Hers was a calming sound in a world that was getting more and more dangerous with each moment and not just because of the weather. He was about to embark on a job that had the potential to be incredibly dangerous. He needed a light moment.

"Let me guess, Maddy. You're at school with a couple of hundred antsy kids who are going nuts 'cause they can't leave."

"Close, but not close enough," Maddy said. "I'm in the furnace room in my underwear, and I'm trying to warm up and dry out."

"Is there a reason for this, or is it something you've always wanted to do? And if the maintenance man is in there with you, our budding relationship has just taken a big turn for the worse."

Maddy laughed. It was good to hear his voice, too. She rarely called him at work and he had little opportunity to contact her, but today was a different story.

After putting on her coat and boots, she told him, she'd gotten a list of things the others wanted from their cars. The list included important stuff like food, cell phones and medications and low priority items like books.

"Like a fool, I agreed to get them," she said. Mike laughingly agreed with her assessment.

She had made it to her own car without too much trouble. Lots of effort, yes, but no real trouble. She was the youngest, fittest, and most athletic teacher there, which made her the likely choice to go scrounging.

Then she'd gone on to other cars where she'd filled some bags with phones, boots, and all sorts of cold weather gear and whatever food that was in them. The food consisted mainly of potato chips and granola bars, which wouldn't satisfy hundreds of kids.

Thus, she'd been heavily laden down with awkward parcels as she pushed her way through the snow and back to the school.

"I was doing so well until I stumbled over one of the parking bumpers. I fell flat on my face and all the crap I'd been carrying went all over the place."

"You weren't hurt, were you?"

"No, and thanks for asking. Only my pride suffered. I must've looked like an idiot. Someone with a video camera could've made a fortune showing it on *America's Dumbest Teacher Tricks*. However, I then spent the next several minutes trying to gather up what I'd lost. I was already wet from the falling snow, and now I was up to my elbows in it. It took a while, but I got just about everything and headed to school. I almost made it."

Mike was trying hard not to laugh again. "Almost?"

"I tripped over a bike rack."

Mike couldn't contain himself. He doubled over and pounded his desk. It felt so good to back off from the horrors that were developing. "Jesus, I wish I'd been there."

Despite herself, Maddy laughed along with him. "Yeah. Me, little Miss Big Ten Volleyball Jock, couldn't even stand up without falling down. I was right outside the door, so Donna and Frieda came out to help me. When I finally got in, I was soaked and freezing. Thus, I am now in bra and panties and sitting as close to the furnace as I can without burning my butt off while my clothes dry. And I'm alone, by the way."

Across town, Mike smiled into the phone. Talking to Maddy was a bright and welcome break in a grim world that was getting worse real quickly. Without any of their normal resources or backup from other communities, the Sheridan police were planning a raid on the two men suspected of murder who, according to the motel manager, were still registered in rooms at the Sheridan Motor Inn. Maddy's voice was a beacon of light in an otherwise miserable day, one that might just turn incredibly dangerous and ugly.

"Maddy, will you do me a favor?" he asked sweetly.

"What?"

He began breathing with mock heaviness. "Describe your bra and panties?"

She giggled. They were what she referred to as "industrial strength" and not something from Victoria's Secret. She whispered into the phone, "If you're so damn curious, come and see them yourself."

Yeah, he thought after hanging up. *Right after we take down two killers.*

Six officers led by Sgt. Patti Hughes made it to the Sheridan Motor Inn on snowmobiles. Mike was one of them. Sheridan didn't have a SWAT team or anything like it, although they had a lot of weapons and other equipment thanks to Federal government largesse. It had come from Homeland Security following the 9/11 attacks. Nothing big had come up in years to require a SWAT team. Had something occurred, they would have called in the county sheriff or the Michigan State Police for help. They did not have that luxury this time. Sheridan's depleted police force was on its own. If the two murderers—alleged murderers, he corrected himself even though he knew damn well they were as guilty as sin—were still at the motel, they had to be stopped.

Mike was on the team because he had volunteered, and because his four years in Detroit qualified him as a combat veteran, even though he'd never pulled his gun, much less shot at anybody. Now, covered with snow and sneaking in the back entrance to the motel, he wondered about his sanity. They had Kevlar helmets and bulletproof vests that made them look dangerous, but they were far from being a well-trained unit.

The trip to the motel had been slow and had its own dangers. The snow was blinding, forcing them to drive their snowmobiles extremely slowly. They had to wind their way around large snow mounds that were cars and smaller ones that could have hidden thick shrubs or decorative rocks. Hitting one of them could easily disable a vehicle and possibly injure a rider. Visibility was so bad that Hughes was depending on GPS to get them to the motel.

When they arrived, they found the manager pale and shaken. He managed to pull himself together and confirm that two men had registered using the credit card of a man now known to have been murdered. He added that they were in a small suite on the second floor. He also said that the second floor was virtually empty because traffic had delayed arrivals. The men had pre-paid with a Visa card, so there was no guarantee that they hadn't left, except for the fact that their car was still in the parking lot. Mike wondered just how the manager could tell that with all the vehicles covered with snow, but was then told that the guests had assigned spaces, which made it fairly easy to keep track of things. There was closed-circuit television for the hallway showing that it was empty. Hughes actually asked the manager if there were hidden cameras in the rooms and the poor guy was shocked by the question.

He vehemently denied it. "We're not that kind of place, Officer."

Too bad, Mike thought. Just once it would be nice to have somebody break the law and have it be helpful. He asked for and was promised tape of the hallway for the last couple of days.

The suites on either side of their targets were vacant, which was also a blessing. After confirming that there were no maintenance passageways that could secretly lead police to the suspects' suite, the task force broke into two groups. Hughes, Mike and two other officers moved to a suite with a door that adjoined the suspects', while the others waited at the other end of the hallway, effectively sealing it. If the bad guys tried to exit their room, Hughes hoped she had set up a decent ambush. Mike thought it looked like the cops could get caught in a crossfire, but Hughes just shrugged and said there weren't any really good choices. Her real fear was that, despite the manager's assurances that the two suspects weren't in the lounge or anywhere else, they would unexpectedly show up in the cops' rear. Again, what could they do with their limited manpower? These guys were killers and they had to be taken down.

They'd made it to the adjacent suite without difficulty. Once inside, they listened carefully for any noise from the next-door suite. They heard nothing. Hughes put a listening device that resembled a high-tech stethoscope against the door that adjoined the suspects' suite.

"Not a sound," she muttered softly. "This thing is sensitive enough that I should hear someone breathing. They may have gone, damn it."

No one wanted to think too long about that possibility. These guys were killers and the police did not want them running around the community. Of course, they weren't all that crazy about confronting them in a crowded motel room, either.

Hughes slid a threadlike fiber-optic cable under the connecting doorway. The interior of the other room showed on a monitor. The clarity of the picture was astonishing. She moved the cable like a snake and showed still more.

Mike stood behind her looking at the monitor. He caught something in the corner of the screen. "The bathroom," he snapped. "Go there."

The cable wasn't long enough to actually go into the bathroom, but it did show part of the shower-tub combination. A shoeless human foot was visible. The toes pointed downward, an impossible situation for someone taking a bath. The foot wore a sock.

Now they were confident no living thing was in the suite. They unlocked the connecting door and rushed in, guns ready in case they were wrong. The suite was empty. But there were two dead bodies in the tub, lying in a pond of congealing blood.

Detective Hughes got the manager. His memory was good. From the description, he gave them names, Mr. and Mrs. Kellogg from Cleveland, and a room number. He then ran down the hallway and threw up. They repeated the careful process of clearing the Kelloggs' room, where they found plundered luggage and the identification belonging to Mrs. Kellogg, but no murderers.

"Why did they kill them?" Hughes asked. She was pale and shaken by the discovery of the butchered bodies and Mike suspected he looked the same way. "And why were the Kelloggs in the bad guys' room in the first place?" Mike wished he was smart enough to know. The Kelloggs had been butchered like hogs. No, he thought, even hogs were treated better. The two guys who'd butchered them were monsters.

Mike had a thought. He dashed downstairs and grabbed the manager. "Where are the Kelloggs parked?"

The manager pointed out the window to a snow-covered truck one floor down and on the other side of the narrow lot. The bed of the truck looked empty. Mike had a sick and empty feeling. He turned to Hughes and saw the same thing mirrored on her face.

"The Kelloggs had snowmobiles, didn't they?" she asked. The manager nodded dumbly. Now it made sense. They had been murdered for transportation. Along with everything else, a pair of serial killers might now be roaming Sheridan.

"Surprise, surprise," proclaimed Donna Harris. "We've gotten rid of more than half the students."

"Now ditch the other half," Maddy laughed, even though she accepted the reality that only a few more would be going anytime soon. Her clothes had dried quickly and she had left the furnace room. "What I would really like is a comfortable place to sit." There was one couch in the entire building and it was in the teachers' lounge. It looked as if those left in the school would be sleeping on the floor. Already some students had curled up on gym mats.

That so many kids had departed truly was a real surprise. Donna wasn't going to release students unless they were in the company of a parent or other adult who was registered at the school as a guardian. Even those kids who lived close enough to walk on normal days were kept in. It was too easy to get lost in the blinding snow. Some complained, but she ignored them, while other kids thought it was a lark. Wait a while, Maddy thought. Wait until they realize that Mommy and Daddy aren't coming for them. They might be dealing with scores of sobbing little ones and maybe some that weren't so little as night fell and they realized they were going to be sleeping at a school.

There'd been a steady trickle of adults using snowmobiles, cross-country skis, or even snowshoes arriving and taking their children. Donna wasn't comfortable with all the arrangements, but parents were parents and she couldn't veto them directly, especially when they showed up in person. She insisted they call her when they got home and most had understood her concerns and complied. Those who didn't got a terse call from her after an appropriate length of time. At this point, Donna didn't care if she pissed them off or not.

Donna Harris had other pressing concerns. Food and toilet paper were the two major ones. As long as the electricity stayed on, the furnace would run, so heat would not be a problem. Water would not be a problem, either. But food and toilet paper would be major issues if they had to stay overlong. There was also the possibility the ladies room would run out of sanitary napkins, which would really be a problem.

Donna had sent Mr. Craft, the maintenance man, to inventory and secure all the toilet paper they could find. With still more than a hundred students and a dozen adults remaining in Patton Elementary, rationing was likely. A multitude of bad jokes were made, generally about recycling toilet paper, but no one wanted to run out of the stuff, and some people, small kids in particular, used tons of it each time they went to the bathroom.

Ironically, food was less of a problem. A full lunch for the entire school had been prepared, and almost half of it remained. Usually, the sizeable excess would have been thrown out, but Donna put a stop to that. Health laws be damned, she would hoard what she could for an evening meal. They would also give out smaller portions. Again, people would complain but they would be ignored.

After locking up the vending machines and checking the contents of the freezers in the cafeteria, it was decided they could feed everyone for the day and maybe a second if they stretched it. It wouldn't be gourmet cuisine, or even particularly nourishing, but it would fill bellies. By morning they would surely be out of this mess, wouldn't they?

"Tits on a boar," Wally Wellman snapped, and then threw a wad of paper against the wall. "We're as useless as tits on a boar!"

"Haven't heard that one in a while," laughed news director Ron Friedman. "But I understand your frustration. Here we have the biggest news story of the year—hell, maybe the decade—and we can't get out of this building and cover it. For all we know, people are dying all over the place and we don't know enough to report it. Golly-damn, we ought to be out there running around on snowmobiles asking people how they feel about freezing to death."

"Balls," muttered Wellman. "I don't care a rat's ass about your fire-of-the-day journalism or the idea that if it bleeds it leads. I just want to know why this damn thing sneaked up on us and why we can't figure out when it's going to end."

"When you do, you'll actually be God," Friedman said with a yawn. "Instead of merely thinking you were." It had been a long day and no end was in sight. "You heard that the governor has declared a state of emergency, haven't you?"

"Yeah, and a fat lot of good that'll do. I guess she has to do something, though, even if it isn't an election year."

"Didn't you used to know her?" Freidman asked.

Wellman paused thoughtfully and nodded. "It was a long time ago in a galaxy far away."

Lauren Landsman was a second-term governor, a Democrat, and a woman Wally had known before he'd met his late wife. There had been few contacts in the last couple of decades. "Iron" Lauren Landsman was a primly attractive woman who'd patterned her behavior after England's legendary Iron Lady, Margaret Thatcher.

It had made her respected, but unloved, unlike the woman he'd known in college so long ago. Wally wondered just what the hell she was up to and just how declaring a state of emergency would change things. *State of emergency my ass,* he thought, *how about a state of chaos.*

"Can we keep this thing quiet?" Mayor Calvin Carter asked hopefully. He had just received the report of the two dead bodies in the Sheridan Motor Inn and was digesting the possibility—likelihood?—that a pair of killers was on the loose in his beloved city.

This meeting was in Chief Bench's office, with Bench and Mike Stuart the only attendees. Detective Hughes remained at the crime scene and the public works director was simply absent. Mike was mildly annoyed at being included because he had so much else to do, but understood. He'd actually seen what the killers had done. Still, there was not much he could add, even though he had been on the scene at the motel. He wanted to get back to his office. He had rescue operations to plan with his snowmobile force.

"Keep it quiet? Not a chance," answered Bench. "I've already gotten calls from television stations, and there's a reporter on the way on a snowmobile."

"Damn it," muttered Carter.

"Well, what the hell did you expect?" snarled Bench. "We sent six people in there armed to the teeth and looking like a bunch of Darth Vaders. The motel might have been almost empty but that's a long way from *actually* empty. Our people have been keeping the few remaining motel guests away from that wing and the motel has moved a couple of people to other rooms to help us secure the scene. Add to that that half the staff called their families to tell them the exciting news, and I'm surprised that more people don't know."

"And the bodies?" Carter asked.

"Packed in ice and still in the bathtub," Mike answered. The scene was almost nauseating, but it was necessary. "Right now we don't have a safe way of transporting them. They'll last."

"Christ," muttered the mayor.

"We don't lack for snow and ice," Mike added. Detective Hughes was there trying to lift fingerprints and identify the two killers.

"But do people actually know there's a pair of killers loose?" Carter asked.

"Probably."

Carter looked whipped. "Will someone please tell me they've fled the area on those snowmobiles they stole and are now somebody else's responsibility?"

Mike and Chief Bench looked at each other and the chief nodded at him to answer. For the moment at least, Bench was functioning competently. He and Bench had talked it over and Mike responded.

"Sorry sir, but we think they're still in the area. First, we don't think they know that much about running snowmobiles, although you don't have to be a rocket scientist to learn; and, second, the weather is still too rotten to travel far. The snow front extends fifty miles to our south if the weather people can be believed. We think they'll hole up and wait for the weather to break, steal a car when the roads are clear, and drive off."

Bench nodded his agreement. "They'll likely break into an empty house and live there as long as they can. I think they'll try to avoid houses with people, even though they are murderers. It's safer that way for them. With so many people unable to get home, they'll have a lot of choices."

Carter shuddered. "What'll happen when the owners finally come home?"

Bench shook his head sadly. "We don't even want to think about that."

CHAPTER 7

OFFICER STAN PETKOWSKI WAS COLD AND WET, BUT GLAD TO BE out of the station and doing something useful. He shared a snowmobile with a civilian, a young man in his twenties named Stu or Steve or something. It didn't matter. A dozen or so teams like this were scouring the streets and trying to maintain order. Cars and trucks were now dinosaurs, confined to fossil-like stillness while snow blanketed them. Steve or Stu commented that archeologists might not uncover them for centuries the way the snow was falling. Then, he added, they'd probably think they had religious significance. Petkowski thought the kid was a bore, but he was a volunteer and trying to help. It was also the kid's snowmobile.

EMS technicians rode other snowmobiles as did the fire department. Some came from private individuals, and a couple from dealerships that "donated" them. They didn't have much in the way of equipment that the vehicles could carry, but the techs did have knowledge, and the ability to communicate via hand-held radios and cell phones. A couple of bright guys had rigged sleds that carried some additional equipment.

It was a jury-rigged emergency response system, but it sort of worked.

Petkowski's crew was checking cars on MacArthur Boulevard, not very far from the police station. Word had come from on high that people in cars could die if they remained there. Freezing to death was a strong possibility. The temperature was only slightly below freezing, but that was cold enough to kill if you weren't dressed or otherwise prepared for it. If someone ran out of gas, or just decided to turn off the engine, they would get cold real fast. It was a virtual certainty that few drivers or their passengers were wearing proper cold-weather gear like the snowmobile suit Petkowski had on.

At least if someone was freezing, they stood a chance of knowing it. Carbon monoxide, on the other hand, crept up on you. If you kept the engine running to provide heat, you might just go to sleep and never wake up. It wasn't called a silent killer for nothing.

Petkowski swore under his breath. People didn't want to give up their cars; he wouldn't want to give his up either. A car was so much more than transportation. It was freedom. It was safety and security and an extension of home. And for many people it was part of their identities. Too many would remain in their cars and hope the tooth fairy would blow the snow away.

You could only go so fast on a snowmobile in a storm without endangering yourself, and the short trip to MacArthur had been slow. Except for a few people the cops thought of as flaming assholes, snowmobilers were driving slowly and tentatively. There were no groomed trails, only hints as to where a road might have been. Fences, shrubs, rocks, and fire hydrants lay underneath the deceptively gentle snow, waiting to attack the unwary.

Steve or Stu stopped the snowmobile and both men got off. Volunteers on other snowmobiles did likewise and fanned out. They began to wipe snow off the windows and windshields of the endless lines of stalled vehicles. The shined their flashlights inward and scanned for people. If they found anyone, they were to exhort them to leave their cars and they would be taken to the safety of nearby buildings. If they didn't want to go, Petkowski had decided he would break a window to ensure that carbon monoxide would not build up. If, after that, they still wanted to stay in their car and freeze their asses off, then fuck 'em. He'd brought a pipe wrench for that purpose. Chief Bench or Mike Stuart might not like it, but he wasn't going to leave someone to die in their car even though they volunteered for the honor.

Car after car was checked and found empty. Surprise, he thought. Maybe people were smarter than he gave them credit for. He sure as hell hoped so. Shops and stores alongside the road were filled with astonished and sometimes frightened people wondering when the snow would end and they could go home to hearth, family, and a good martini.

The snow was deep and drifting. At the low points, it was well over his knees and walking was reduced to lurching around the unmoving cars. He was beginning to think it was an exhausting fool's errand.

Petkowski wiped the snow off the driver's side windshield of a Ford mini-van. He leaped backward and nearly fell. A man's face stared out at him. The eyes were open, but unfocused, and the man's head was back. He'd adjusted the seat back so he could almost recline. There was no movement.

"God damn it!" Petkowski screamed and others came running as quickly as they could.

He swung the pipe wrench and shattered the side window. He reached in and opened the door. Hands pulled the driver out, inert, pale, and uncomplaining.

"There's a passenger," Petkowski yelled as someone started CPR on the driver. He unlocked the minivan's doors and pulled a woman out. She was in her thirties, limp and gray. An EMS snowmobile had been nearby and their people began to work frantically.

Then Petkowski saw the back seat. "No," he moaned. "Oh, Jesus, no!" He sat back in the snow, covered his face with his hands and began to weep. This was worse than pulling the dead teenagers from the car and finding his niece was one of the beheaded corpses. That was hell and this was worse than hell. He groaned and shook as others pulled the three small children from the back of the van and began the work of trying to revive them. One EMS tech looked at another and sadly shook his head.

✦ ✦ ✦

Wally Wellman and anchorman Mort Cristman sat behind the familiar TV6 news desk.

Cristman was the new kid in town. Not yet thirty, he'd been imported from a much smaller out-of-state channel a few months earlier. He usually did the noon anchor only, but today he was going to do the five o'clock news for the simple reason that the station's A-team hadn't made it in. Wally thought Cristman was a good enough kid, but inexperienced and with a tendency to be pompous. Wally also wondered if Cristman knew where half the now snowbound suburbs even were. He still sometimes mangled the names of streets, which resulted in angry phone calls from people who wondered why the station hired such a dummy.

"The weather is still the number one story," Cristman said with a bow to the obvious. He expected to be a major presence in either New York or LA before very much longer and spent a lot of time working on his delivery.

"However, it is now getting lethal," Cristman said, nodding his head solemnly. "TV6 has just learned that five people were pulled dead from a car stalled on MacArthur Boulevard in Sheridan. Carbon monoxide poisoning had killed them all even though they were within walking distance of safety. As a result, Governor Landsman has urged all police agencies to begin checking cars in the streets if they haven't already done so. Along with the numerous heart attacks and other injuries that have occurred, this sudden snowstorm has turned into a killer."

Wally shook his head imperceptibly. Most cities covered by the snow emergency had been doing exactly this for hours, as had Sheridan. Cristman was beginning to take credit for the discovery of sunrise.

Cristman turned to Wally. "Can you tell us when this scourge is going to end?"

Wally gagged. Scourge? Please, he thought, war was a scourge. So too was the Black Death. This was a fucking blizzard. "No, Mort, I can't, and neither can anyone else."

"Well—" Cristman started to say, but Wally cut him off. He had something to add.

"Before I deliver some thoughts on the weather, please let me amplify on what we should all be doing. Police and fire personnel are too widely spread out to be everywhere; therefore, it's up to all of us to get involved and not wait for help. The people who can help out are those of you watching and listening to this broadcast. Here's what you should do. Check on your neighbors. Call them. Walk over to their houses if you can. Form groups to check on others. Carbon monoxide is a huge danger as people get sealed into their homes and cars. New vents for super-efficient furnaces are sometimes only a few feet above the ground and may be buried. The five dead people in Sheridan aren't going to be the last. Hell, they're merely the first we've found and, count on it, there will be more."

Cristman got the hint that Wally had taken over and nodded solemnly as Wally continued.

"Inventory what medical supplies you have on hand and what medical skills people have. You don't have to be a doctor to help save lives. CPR and first aid training will help, and, if you haven't had that, just use common sense. Some of you have snowmobiles and other winter gear that can help. Figure out who has generators and knows how to use them. So far, power outages have been few and far between, but they can and will occur more frequently as this goes on. The weight of the snow is going to do some strange things.

"Finally, get those idiots off the roofs. A number of people have been injured trying to clear off sloped roofs. Most sloped roofs probably won't have any problems, but flat ones might," Wally said. Actually, he had no good figures on that, but it did sound plausible.

"It's just early evening," Wally added, "and we've officially got more than three feet accumulation, much more in some places, and not a clue as to when it's going to slow down, much less stop. All I can tell you is that it isn't going to stop anytime soon, so everyone get mentally, physically, and emotionally ready for a nasty long haul. I am very afraid that what we see now is just the beginning.

"Weather forecasters like me are going to get crucified for failing to predict this, and I accept that. Criticism goes with the job. However, please remember that weather forecasting has been a science for a very short time, actually little more than a century. We don't know if this type of storm has occurred before or not. We can tell from tree rings whether the winter of 1815 was a cold one or not, but nobody can tell whether it snowed like this anytime that year, or any other. We also know that freak storms are just that and can occur. In 1888, New York City was inundated by about fifty inches of unexpected snow causing drifts up to fifty feet high and a number of people were killed. And don't get me started on whether or not this is a manifestation of global warming, because the New York storm of 1888 clearly wasn't. Personally and professionally, I think this is just a freakish, nasty snowstorm and not the end of the world.

"Folks, I'm not terribly religious, but I sort of do recall a quote by somebody. It went, 'Man proposes, but God disposes,' and that is precisely what is happening today. Every one of us is as helpless to change or influence what is happening." He turned to the now astonished looking young anchor. "Back to you, Mort."

The young girl, a second-grade student, ran up to Maddy with a look of panic on her small tear-streaked face. "Miss Kovacs, Tom Harper went outside. He was crying and said he wanted to go home. I told him not to, but he went anyhow."

Maddy had been sitting on the floor, using her coat as an inadequate cushion. Whatever way she sat or laid down, her butt hurt. She jumped up and ran stiffly towards the open door at the end of the long hallway. Snow was swirling in, almost immediately covering the tile floor. She stepped outside and was slapped in the face with wet snow.

"Tommy Harper, where are you? You get back in here!" *So we can kill you,* she thought. Why was she surprised? Almost a hundred students still remained and, as night began to fall, the unpleasant reality of spending the foreseeable future in Patton Elementary was upsetting a number of them. Tommy Harper was a third grader and a pretty good kid. Now, though, he was just a scared little boy who wanted his mother.

Maddy bulled her way through a snowdrift that was almost waist high. She could see where Tommy's small body had tried to push its way through. She plowed her way in his quickly fading tracks.

And then they stopped. Why? Had he collapsed? Oh, Christ. She dropped to her knees and groped around through the snow, trying to feel flesh. She dived under the snow and felt like a swimmer, a diver, holding her breath and trying to find a treasure. Once she'd had to do much the same thing looking for a boy who'd drowned in a shallow pond. Fortunately, she hadn't been the one who'd found the boy's body.

"Tommy," she screamed after raising her head. Snow was in her hair and piled on her shoulders. It was futile. He wasn't in sight and, if he was buried under the snow, he doubtless couldn't hear her or respond to her even if he could. Tommy might be six inches out of her reach and she'd never know. She would have to go back to the school and get more help. She cursed herself. That's what she should have done in the first place. Now a little boy was freezing to death, perhaps even drowning, while precious seconds she'd wasted ticked away.

Damn, Maddy groaned. What would she say to his mother? It was scant consolation that Tommy wasn't one of her students and that he'd snuck out by himself. He was a little kid and she was supposed to protect him. Damn it!

She groped around some more, getting tired, wetter, and colder. Unlike when she'd gone out to the cars, this time every inch of her was getting soaked. She hadn't bothered to put on a coat and this time even her underwear was cold and wet. Maddy knew she couldn't keep this up much longer. Maybe some of the others were coming to help her. She started to shiver. She had to get out of this before she was overwhelmed and collapsed.

"Maddy, where the hell are you?"

It was Donna Harris. Maddy stood and could barely see Donna standing in the doorway only fifty feet away. "I'm looking for Tommy."

"Get back in here. He's inside."

In disbelief, Maddy stumbled through the snow back to the doorway. "What?"

"Yeah. He went out but then saw how difficult it was and returned. The girl who got you didn't know that. She only saw him leave and ran to get someone."

"Shit."

Donna laughed. Maddy looked like a drowned rat and felt worse. Her wet hair lay limp and her face was red with cold.

"Don't cuss in front of the fucking students." There were no students around the doorway.

"Shit, fuck, bitch," Maddy said, half crying and half laughing in relief. She started to shake again from the stress, the relief, and the soaking cold she'd endured. "I'm going to quit teaching and join the circus. Obviously I have a future as a clown."

Donna took her by the arm and pulled her inside. "You look like hell. Go back to the furnace room and dry off. Again."

The voice on the phone had a heavy, hammy, and throaty Italian accent. "Am I speaking to the distinguished sergeant of trafficology, the honorable Michael Stuart? The same man who has the hots for my job?"

Mike laughed into the phone. "That is the worst *Godfather* imitation I have ever heard, most honorable Lieutenant DiMona."

"Hey, how can it be phony when I'm so genuine an Italian gentleman?"

It was good to hear the voice of DiMona, the thirty-year veteran of the force, and a man who was both Mike's boss and friend.

"So, Mikey, I'm sitting here playing with myself and watching CNN and seeing how you've managed to fuck up the place in such a short while without my steadying hand to guide you. In fact, most people say you need to read the directions tattooed on your cock every time you masturbate."

Mike laughed. "I love you too. So come home and put me out of my misery and fire me. Where are you anyway?"

"I'm still in Lost Wages, Nevada, and pumping money into the local economy. My arm's sore from jacking off one of those old-fashioned slot machines that I prefer to the newer models, so I thought I'd call you and find out what the fuck is going on."

Mike updated him on the situation, beginning with the totally unexpected snow and continuing with the motel murders and the dead people in the car on MacArthur.

"How's Petkowski taking it?" DiMona asked.

"Badly. He's reliving that accident that killed his niece and he feels guilty that he didn't check that car sooner. What makes it worse is that it was almost within sight of the station."

"Keep him busy so he doesn't have time to think about it."

"Easier said than done, Joey. But he is out checking on other cars. Maybe he's double and triple checking them, but you're right, at least he's busy."

"Good. Now, what the hell were you doing at the motel with Hughes when you should have been organizing help for people in cars?"

Mike winced. He'd been asking himself that same question. What were his priorities? "Hughes asked for me to help and I know that's a cop-out answer, no pun intended. I didn't think it would be right to say no. After all, I did have a little training in SWAT tactics in Detroit, which put me ahead of a lot of other people."

"Me included," DiMona admitted grudgingly. "Life is full of bad choices and you did what you had to. What about the little pricks who killed the Kelloggs?"

"Hughes has some prints and they've been sent in. Maybe one will hit."

"You know, what you're telling me about all the snow-covered shit hitting the fan makes retirement sound real good. You really want my job, Mikey?"

Mike laughed. A few days ago he would have jumped at the chance. "I don't think I'm ready," he admitted, and then wondered if he would ever be.

"Right. You're not ready. That's why I want you to take my phone number and call me anytime, anyplace. Okay?"

"Okay."

"For starters, though, remember two things. Chief Bench is a drunken incompetent, and Mayor Carter is a crook. Other than that, they're cool. Hughes is good people and so are a lot of others. I presume, however, that a lot of the other brass isn't going to make it in."

"We're working on it, but some live so far away."

The department had two other lieutenants. One had called in sick earlier, while the second lived more than twenty miles away. He was trying to get there, but his appearance was growing more unlikely with each minute. Chief Bench ran a sloppy ship, which meant that the "sick" lieutenant had probably been at his lake cottage, working and preparing for the arrival of spring.

"Well, as the old saying goes, you play the cards you were dealt, not the ones you wish you had. Y'all go now and have fun and don't fuck the place up much more than you already have."

Raines and Tower found it ridiculously easy to break into people's homes. Just find a place without a home alarm sticker or a barking dog, drive the snowmobile behind the house and out of sight, and park it. Then break a window, reach in and unlock the door, and the place was theirs. After that, their great ideas just fell apart.

There were a lot of cars in garages, and a number of liftable items in the houses, but there wasn't much they could do about it. They could only take what they could stuff in their pockets or carry on one snowmobile. Jimmy Tower had run his snowmobile onto a fire hydrant and ruined it. So they concentrated on finding and taking cash and small jewelry. While there was sufficient jewelry, there was little cash. They concluded that the people in Sheridan lived off their credit cards, which, of course, they carried with them. After breaking into three houses, they'd concluded that Sheridan was an affluent but surprisingly cashless society.

They'd been listening to the radio and the television in their latest house and had heard Wally Wellman's urgings for all neighbors to be good neighbors and help each other out. This was the last thing they wanted at this time. The idea of some do-gooder coming to the door and checking things out horrified them. Raines made it a point to keep lights off and the noise down when they were in a house. Neither man liked this, but what were their choices? Even if they knew where to go and how to get there, they couldn't drive their one surviving snowmobile far enough to safety.

Raines checked their findings from this nice colonial house and added it to the others. All together, they had less than two thousand dollars in cash and a few bits of really decent jewelry for their efforts. The cash wouldn't get them far, and the jewelry was useless without someone to sell it to. Nor could they continue to skulk indefinitely. They had to do something to get away from this snowbound burg. The snow would stop and they had to be prepared.

But how?

Tower was getting restless. Dark empty houses spooked him, reminding him of nights in the prison. Maybe they should take a chance on one that was occupied? That might give Tower some fun if the occupants were female. Not a chance, Raines thought. They would stick with empty places.

Only a few years earlier, Sheridan and the surrounding area had consisted of farmland and small patches of woodland. It had looked tame enough, but the area had supported a number of animals that the average person would consider wild. These included fox, woodchuck, raccoon, and skunks, along with omnipresent squirrels, field mice, possum, and shrews. Also, there was the occasional coyote whose howling livened up an otherwise dull evening and who occasionally ate cats and small dogs. Wild birds also abounded, with hawks that fed on the smaller animals and birds. Non-predatory birds included pheasants, herons, ducks, and geese in great numbers.

When the farms began to evolve into subdivisions and strip malls, the creatures of the wild had a limited menu of choices: adapt, move, or die. Some, like raccoons, found attics, garages, and garbage cans to their liking, while many birds ate seed at the feeders put out by people who enjoyed watching them. Others, like ducks and geese, were protected by law. Ducks, at least, were migratory, while many geese wintered over, feeding where they could and defecating copious amounts of green matter wherever they wished to the disgust and dismay of the residents. The geese especially liked golf courses; golfers hated them.

The coyotes were ungodly smart and almost impossible to catch. Nor could they be shot since firing a weapon in a subdivision was both dangerous and illegal.

The strangest adaptation belonged to the deer. They existed in uncountable numbers in parks and golf courses, as well as in less developed areas. Statistically, each year there were several thousand car-deer collisions in the metropolitan Detroit area causing a number of human deaths and injuries. Other than cars, the deer in Sheridan had no known predators.

Sheridan, being newer and with a city plan that called for a lot of green space, saw "wild" deer frequently. They ate flowers, vegetables, and shrubs, and where homeowners were kind, waited patiently in backyards for handouts. The deer existed smugly in a kill-free zone.

Ben Goldman had retired from a stock brokerage in New York. Just a few years before retirement he'd been transferred to what many New Yorkers perceived of as the barrens of the Midwest in an effort to get him to resign. It didn't work. As Ben Goldman said to Harriet, his wife, he wasn't stupid enough to toss away a good pension when he could tread water in a Midwestern Siberia for a couple of years. Harriet would remind him that he was mixing metaphors, but he didn't care.

Then the Goldmans found that they liked it in Sheridan. The people spoke English, didn't eat their young, and best of all, the cost of living was so much lower than in New York. They wound up with three times the house at half the price. Ben and Harriet thought they'd gotten the last laugh on Ben's so-called friends at the brokerage. Other essentials, like food, wine, and clothing, were also far less expensive than New York. They loved it.

Also, they were nowhere near New York when terrorists attacked the World Trade Center and murdered a number of their friends and associates.

Like many city people, they loved the deer. In the Goldmans' extensive and unfenced back yard, Bambi lived. In fact, lots of Bambis hung around.

On this night, the company included a young deer, a buck with four small points defining what might become a quality rack of antlers if the deer kept out of traffic long enough. He was hungry and confused. Winter is the killing time for deer as much as the hunting season, and many deer died of natural causes, mainly starvation. Cold killed the grasses, and snow covered what remained. Only the hardy survived even a mild winter, and this had been a harsh one. The storm was simply one more blow to the deer population.

This buck was gaunt and ached from near-starvation, and he was exhausted from plowing through the snow. He dimly recalled getting food from a feeder near a home and went snuffling towards it. It was empty and he banged it around in frustration and then rooted through the deep snow in the area to see if anything had spilled. There was nothing.

Somehow, he understood that the food came from the houses, and the buck took a handful of tentative steps towards the intimidating dwelling. Even though deer had been around people for decades, they were still wild animals and there was but a minimal level of trust between deer and human. The house was a large, alien thing, and only his overpowering hunger gave him the strength to approach it.

As the deer ventured onto the patio, two things happened. First, the dog next door, a German shepherd named Adolf, saw the deer through the snow from a second-floor window. The dog barked ferociously and the sound carried. Second, Harriet Goldman chose that moment to turn on the patio light, even though there was plenty of outside light. Confused and frightened, the deer whirled and launched himself into some snow-covered patio furniture. Now frightened beyond reason, the deer lurched towards what he perceived as greenery. It wasn't. He'd seen the ficus plant and Norfolk pine in the Goldmans' family room.

The deer smashed headfirst through the doorwall, sending snow and glass flying. It had a fractured skull and a broken leg and was dying, but it didn't know that. It only knew that it was in agony and terrified.

Instinctively, from where she had just sat down, Harriet Goldman jumped up and screamed. The deer focused in on the sound and lashed out with its head as it crumpled to the ground. Two small antlers rammed themselves into her thigh and stuck for a moment. The dying deer shook its head to free itself, tearing the flesh on Harriet's thigh. She screamed and fainted at about the same moment the buck died.

Ben Goldman ran to his wife's side just in time to catch a flailing hoof to his mouth. He spat out teeth and fell beside his wife. Blood gushed from her leg and he nearly fainted from his own pain and the sight of such mutilation. The flesh was shredded and her leg bone was visible. He whipped off his belt and tried to fashion a tourniquet. Then he grabbed the phone and frantically called 911. They said they'd respond as quickly as they could.

Ben looked at his wife's frail and unconscious body. The color of her skin was ashen and her breath was shallow and irregular. Blood still seeped from her leg. He tied the tourniquet tighter and it pretty much stopped. Then he began to wait for the sound of sirens.

Donna Harris slipped into the furnace room where Maddy sat naked, wrapped in a couple of blankets that more or less covered her.

"Shut the door," Maddy snapped.

"What? Afraid Mr. Craft will see you?" Wilson Craft was the maintenance man and the furnace room was his office. He had been booted out so that Maddy could dry off, and he thought her predicament was hilarious.

"No, he's sixty and harmless. I'm afraid some of my students will look in and see something they shouldn't."

"Then keep your legs crossed and that blanket around your shoulders. Besides, Mr. Craft at sixty is far from harmless. I have it on good authority that men that old and older can and do get it up every now and then."

Maddy giggled. "What good authority?"

"Mrs. Severson. She and Mr. Craft have been having an affair for some time now."

"Oh my God, and nobody told me," Maddy wailed in mock dismay. Mary Severson was the food services supervisor and unhappily married. Craft was a widower who'd taken early retirement from Chrysler before latching on as a maintenance man in the Sheridan Schools. She thought the two were always friendly, but never realized it went farther. She must have been blind, she thought.

"At any rate, Wilson is busy shoveling snow from the doorways. It occurred to him that any need to evacuate this building would be hindered if snow blocked the exits."

"Never thought of that," Maddy said. "A fire and a panic would be a tragedy. I underestimated him."

"So did I, although Mary Severson says she never did. Here, take some of this."

Donna handed Maddy a plastic coffee cup. She sniffed and looked up, surprised. "Liquor?"

"Brandy, to be specific, although not very expensive. However, it'll have to do. We beggars cannot be choosers."

Maddy took a sip and then a swallow. She felt its warmth flowing through her. "Good. Where did you get it?"

Donna grinned. "From the back of a drawer in a large desk in the principal's office."

Maddy whooped. "Mrs. Felix drinks on the job? Is there anything else I should know?"

"Don't be silly," Donna laughed. "And don't be so damned naive. She's not the only one who thinks drinking very mediocre liquor isn't a violation of church and state. She waits until the kids have gone before she has a nip." Donna stood and took the empty cup. "Don't go away, now. I'll be back later with some more booze and we can have a girls' party."

Joe Mertz was convinced that his homeowner's insurance rates had gone through the roof, no pun intended, because of the claim he'd made two years prior. Snow and ice had built up on his roof creating what people called "ice dams" and what he called "damn ice." As a result, water had seeped through his roof, into his ceilings and walls, caused dry wall to buckle and paint to peel, ruined his carpets, and generally fucked up his day.

And that was only the beginning. Then he had to deal with the schmucks and crooks from the insurance companies and the bandits who did the actual repair work. In his opinion, he had been robbed blind. He just wasn't certain precisely how.

If he could prevent it, he sure as hell wasn't going to let damage from an ice dam happen again. This was his dream home, his trophy home, and he'd worked more than twenty years to get it, and so what if it was too big for just the two of them now that the kids were grown and gone? No snowstorm was going to take it from him. And so what if he was overweight and didn't spend much time on roofs? Hell, he was an appliance salesman at a local retailer, not a roofing contractor. However, the pitch wasn't all that steep and he could stand up there fairly easily. He'd done it before while cleaning out gutters and nailing down wind-blown shingles. Heights didn't scare him. He would solve his problem. It was all part of the joy of being a homeowner, he thought sarcastically.

Mertz climbed the ladder to the roof and began to shovel the snow off. He was astonished at the volume of snow and how heavy it was. He congratulated himself on being smart enough to shovel it off before it caused a collapse, much less a leak, although it seemed like it was coming down as quick as he shoveled it. He also was smart enough to pace himself. It was exhausting work and he wasn't a kid anymore.

He shoveled and pushed the stuff downward, letting gravity do as much of the work as possible. Each shovelful landed on the snow below with a satisfying whump. He was working up a sweat and working hard. It felt good. He wasn't at all fatigued. Joe Mertz was not a man to sit back and let things happen. He was an action kind of guy, and he felt he was in charge. He almost thought he was on top of things, but that was just too lousy a joke.

Then he felt something in the roof shift beneath him. He froze, wondering just what had happened. He'd laughed at a contractor who'd told him, while repairing the earlier damage, that some of his roof might be rotten. He'd thought the prick was just trying to con him for some more money and he hadn't gotten the suggested additional repairs done. After all, it wasn't covered by insurance. Now he suddenly didn't know if he'd done the right thing. The roof below him felt mushy.

"Gwen!" he yelled for his wife. "Come out here. Now, please."

A moment later, his wife stood on the ground by the ladder. "What's up besides you?" she joked.

"Feels squishy up here. Steady the ladder. I'm coming down."

She nodded and grabbed the ladder. Her Joe was aggressive, but not stupid. Getting up was easy; getting down was the hard part. He always said it was like flying a plane—any fool could take off and fly, but landing was another story. Joe took a tentative step towards the ladder. It felt like he was on weakening ice and realized he'd made a big mistake by coming up and stomping around. Careful. One more step and he'd be by the ladder and safety.

With a crack, the roof opened and Joe's leg disappeared into the void. Something hit him in the groin and he screamed.

Something else jabbed into his leg and, as he fought off dizziness and nausea, he felt a warm trickle running down his leg.

"Oh Christ. Gwen! I'm bleeding to death."

Mike Stuart signaled Petkowski to come into DiMona's office. With the lieutenant gone, Mike had simply taken it over. It gave him a little privacy in an increasingly congested environment. Even though fewer people were abandoning their cars and crowding into the station and other city facilities, the buildings were filled with refugees.

"How're you doing?" Mike asked.

The other officer looked like hell. Why not, Mike thought, after what he'd seen and gone through. The story of the car filled with dead people had become major news. It had even been picked up by CNN and Fox. If nothing else, it had scared some people into being conscious of the fact that they could die from suffocation.

"Some things you never get over, Mike, and maybe it's better you don't. Christ, I'm being philosophic. I must be getting old. Bottom line, I think I'm okay. I'll have nightmares, but I'm kind of used to that after what happened to my niece. But it does kind of make me wonder why I wanted to become a cop in the first place."

Keep him talking, Mike thought. "So why did you?"

"The cool uniforms, of course. And you get to carry a gun, get to ride a motorcycle, and it really impressed the chicks. At least I thought it would. Then I realized it was the Marine Corps uniform they really liked." He laughed harshly. "Nah, I became cop because I ruled out just about everything else. Didn't want to work in a factory, didn't want to work in an office, couldn't sell stuff worth shit, so that left either the military, delivering mail, or becoming a cop. Being a cop won out. Sometimes I still wonder if I should have done the factory thing. I needed a job. I'm not the altruistic type."

Mike nodded sagely. "You chose wisely, my friend. You are a damn good cop. The fact that things still get to you means that you are human, even if you don't always look or act it."

Petkowski chuckled, this time genuinely. "Don't make me laugh. Now, why the hell did a bright guy like you enlist? And please don't tell me you wanted to make like Batman and save the world from evildoers. I've seen too many people motivated by altruism and watched them go down the toilet when they realized their efforts weren't going to add up to squat."

Mike smiled inwardly. Actually, that's exactly what he'd felt in the beginning of his police career, except that he wanted to help the victims and punish the criminals. It stemmed from a carjacking in which his mother had been mugged and another incident when a great-aunt had been beaten and raped. The old lady never quite recovered and had died a few years later. She used to brag about living in a town like Detroit, but she'd died in a nursing home completely unable to remember her own name. If he ever did become a lawyer, he would be a prosecutor, not a defense attorney.

For a while, he'd been a good hater, but the years on the Detroit force taught him the futility of that, and the move to Sheridan's Police Department had further softened his attitude. Now he liked to think of himself as almost human, too.

"I didn't know you knew the meaning of altruism," Mike teased. "Nope, I wanted to impress chicks, too. Actually, I made the same kind of process of elimination you did. Funny, but a lot of people choose careers on the basis of what they don't want, rather than what they do want. All I knew was that I wanted to be involved in the law, and now I am. Is this the end? Hell, I don't know. Ask me five or ten years from now."

"Any cops in the family?"

"An uncle," Mike said, "And a good guy. Kind of a role model, I guess, along with my dad. My dad is a retired accountant and my mom was a teacher. One of my brothers is in commercial real estate, and the other is a veterinarian."

"But being a cop in Sheridan isn't your life's ambition, is it? I get the feeling you aspire to greater things."

Mike nodded. "Maybe I do. I came here because they were hiring and it looked like a nice place to learn after spending some interesting combat time in Detroit. I'll have my master's in a few months—if it stops snowing, of course—and then I'm thinking of going to law school. After that, who knows? Maybe I'll get a better job in a bigger town, or a job in corporate security."

"Or how about a run at politics?" Stan teased. "Or maybe you won't be a prosecutor. Instead, you'll become a high-priced defense attorney and get all the bad guys off while hard-working cops like me bust their balls arresting them and trying to get them convicted."

Mike laughed. "Well, hell, I didn't take a vow of poverty. Or celibacy, for that matter." He thought quickly of Maddy and wondered what she was doing. He'd called her a couple of times and knew that she'd gotten herself stuffed in the snow for the second time. He told her he wanted to rub her body to help it warm up and she hadn't said no. Of course, he was miles away.

It was getting on in the evening and Mike wondered where he was going to sleep, or if he'd even be able to sleep. The floor was covered by a layer of commercial carpeting, which was only slightly softer than a rock, but it might have to do. He didn't feel sorry for himself. There were literally hundreds of refugees in the buildings, and they would be sacking out on cold and unforgiving tile, which was marginally better than sleeping on an office chair.

"Can I sleep with you tonight, Mike?" Petkowski said in falsetto and blinked with mock coyness.

Mike laughed. "Sure can, sailor, pick a spot of floor and don't fart. God, I hope it's a quiet night. We're the only ones left in here, right now."

A quiet night following a miserable day. Five people dead in a car, one woman had bled to death from a deer accident because EMS couldn't get there in time, and an old man had suffered a fatal heart attack in the snow at St. Stephen's Church. The pastor had gone out looking for him and dragged him in from the cold. CPR hadn't worked and, again, the EMS techs had difficulty getting there, only arriving when it was far too late.

Stuart had several teams of police and volunteers continuing to patrol the city on snowmobiles. On the positive side, the number of calls to the 911 center across the hall had dropped to almost nothing. It was a small blessing, but they'd joked that the storm had kept all the drunk drivers out of their cars, and most people had given up trying to shovel the snow, which cut down on heart attack runs. The same with thefts, although everyone in the department wondered where the two killers had gone. Not far, was the worried consensus.

There was a tap on the doorway and Thea Hamilton, the 911 supervisor, stuck her head in. "If you guys are the reserves, you'd better saddle up. Some guy just went through his roof and thinks he's bleeding to death. He's only a couple of blocks away and you're the closest."

Both men jumped up and, in moves now practiced, got into their cold weather outfits. *So much for a quiet evening,* Mike thought. At least he didn't have to sleep with Stan.

CHAPTER 8

MIKE AND STAN LAID THE LADDER AGAINST THE MERTZ HOUSE and climbed up it as quickly as they could. It had fallen to the ground when Joe Mertz went through the roof. The victim's wife was being held and comforted by a neighbor woman. Mrs. Mertz was sobbing and looked at the two cops with gratitude.

On the roof, Joe Mertz's head and shoulders were covered with a thin layer of snow and he was groaning. With only half his body protruding, it looked like someone had planted him in the roof as an obscene decoration. His eyes were open, but it didn't appear that he was comprehending very much. Mike and Stan crawled to him on their bellies, as if they were on thin ice, and hoped the roof would hold their distributed weight. They reached Mertz and quickly checked him for vital signs. They figured he was going into shock as well as maybe bleeding to death. Mike jerked on some soggy plywood to widen the hole in the roof so he could see what had happened while Stan tried to hold Mertz steady. Both were nervous. They had zero confidence in the roof holding three people if it had collapsed under the weight of one.

Mike took a deep breath and stuck his head into the enlarged hole. A piece of plywood had split and was driven into Mertz's thigh. Bad news was that the piece of wood was attached to a larger piece that was still connected to the roof. *Damn it,* Mike thought. How to get him out of there without killing him was the question.

Mike managed to slip his arms down into the hole and tie a crude tourniquet around Mertz's leg. It didn't stop all the bleeding, but it did slow it down. But how to get the victim out and down with that piece of wood in his leg? And how much blood had the victim already lost?

"Officers, you need help?"

The mustached head of a middle-aged man wearing a ridiculous ski cap appeared at the top of the ladder. "Not unless you're a doctor," Mike snapped. "Otherwise please get down and let us do our jobs."

The man beamed happily. "Good, because I am a doctor. My name is Scarborough and I'm a gynecologist. Guys like him aren't exactly my specialty, but I think I can be useful."

That said, he slid over and onto the roof and plunked down a gym bag. He crawled on his belly like they had and checked on Mertz. He seemed blithely unconcerned about the structural integrity of the roof. "Not bad," he said of the tourniquet. "Good of you not to try and remove the wood. That might have started him bleeding more. I don't think he's cut an artery, but we do want to be careful."

Mike said nothing about the gratuitous but well intended advice. Both he and Stan had experience and training and knew how to handle stabbing victims. The doctor took some things from the gym bag, leaned down into the roof cavity, sliced Mertz's pants, and gave him an injection. Mertz groaned and swore at the indignity, and then went silent.

Dr. Scarborough continued to check Mertz's vital signs. "I just gave him a sedative to keep him calm and not get in our way while we get his worthless butt out of here. Last thing we need is him thrashing like a whale while we try to get him out of this stupid situation. He's a good neighbor, although somewhat of a doofus. Thinks everybody's conspiring against him. Personally, I think his wife's a saint for putting up with all his crap."

Scarborough crawled back to the roof edge and yelled something down. A few moments later, another man handed him a tool and Mike grinned—it was a battery powered saw.

"Everybody hold him steady and don't let him fall father through," Scarborough said. "And let's try not fall through ourselves. I'm going to cut the wood in his leg away from the roofing." The saw buzzed and whined, and then Joe Mertz was free. They pulled him onto the roof and laid him flat.

The doctor checked the wound and again decided against pulling out the piece of wood from his thigh. It looked like he'd been struck by some kind of spear or arrow. Better, it looked like the bleeding had entirely stopped.

"I still don't think an artery was severed, but I'm not going to take a chance," Scarborough said calmly. "I'll pull the wood out when he's on the ground. I'm also afraid that too much jostling could cause the wood to shift in his leg and do some real damage, maybe even find that artery, so we'll have to be extra careful moving his worthless carcass."

Mike nodded. "You're in charge, Doctor. Let's just get him and us down from here before the roof collapses some more." Now there were four people on the roof and it appeared to be holding. Maybe Joe Mertz had found the only bad spot on it.

They tied a rope around Mertz's chest and gently lowered him over the edge and down the ladder. Petkowski went before him to cover and steady the victim as they went. Petkowski and another neighbor laid Mertz on a blanket on the snow while Mike and the doctor clambered down as quickly as they could. They made no effort to cover the hole in the roof. That would be somebody else's problem.

Dr. Scarborough looked at the snowmobile Mike and Stan had ridden and shook his head. "No way you're going to get him to a hospital in that, are you?"

"Not likely," Mike said. Several neighbors had gathered. An EMS team was pulling up on their own snowmobile. It was dragging a sled with supplies that, Mike guessed, could be used to transport a victim if necessary.

Scarborough shrugged and looked at Mertz, who was unconscious and snoring softly. He nodded and grinned at the two cops. "He should be okay for now. Despite his fears, he wasn't bleeding to death. Still, he could have died if you two hadn't gone up there. You saved his life."

Mike grinned. "Same holds for you, Doctor. Not bad for a gynecologist."

"I did some time in an emergency room, although it was a couple of decades ago." Scarborough sniffed, "Some things you never forget. Now I have to get him indoors so I can perform some kitchen table surgery. Then EMS can take him to the hospital on that sled."

"You need help?" Mike asked.

"Just getting him in. After that, your EMS people can assist me. This should be interesting," Scarborough chuckled. "As a gynecologist, I never see men patients. I wonder if I'll cut out the wrong thing. If I do, I'll just reduce his bill."

Mike and Petkowski were soon on their way back to the station. Joe Mertz was shot full of Tdap and morphine and was having happy dreams. Doctor Scarborough and the EMS crew had removed the splinter, cleaned the wound, and sewed it up. Mertz would live. They decided they would not transport him by sled, but they would get him to a hospital for a better checkup when the weather got better. A couple of other neighbors had covered the hole in the roof with fresh plywood and a tarp. Everything was under control.

"Hey, Mike," Stan called from the rear seat.

"What?"

"We just won one, or hadn't you noticed?"

Mike smiled. He was cold and tired, but Stan was right. They had done good work and it felt even better. "You're right. The bad guys don't win all the time, do they?"

Thea Hamilton was one of the few black people working in Sheridan's city offices, and nobody was quite sure how she'd first gotten the position since she'd been around for almost forty years. Maybe it had been part of an affirmative action program, or maybe she was simply more qualified than the other applicants. Anybody who might recall was long since dead, quit, or retired. The city of Sheridan certainly had nothing to regret about her hiring. She had served them well.

For at least twenty of those years, she had worked as an EMS technician and prided herself on the number of lives she'd saved. She'd been saddened by the ones who died, but she rarely let it get to her. She'd always been satisfied that she'd done her absolute best and if God said that wasn't good enough, then so be it. She was deeply religious and would not argue with a higher power. But she would argue with everyone else.

Arthritis, encroaching age, and a bad back had forced her to give up making ambulance runs. This frailty came as a shock to both Thea and her coworkers. She was six feet tall and weighed over two hundred pounds. Most thought she was indestructible, but she wasn't. Instead of feeling sorry for herself, she applied for and became the supervisor of Sheridan's 911 call center. When she got the job, another surprise emerged. Somehow, along with being a single mom raising three children and working full time, she'd gotten a liberal arts degree from Saginaw Valley University by taking off-campus courses, which put her light years ahead of her competition for the job.

Recently, Thea had been giving retirement some serious thought. But when she did, she wondered what she'd do with her time, especially since the kids were fully grown and her new husband wasn't. She liked her work and needed it to get away from Bert. She loved him dearly, but he'd retired a couple of years earlier and no way was she ready to spend all day with him and the stupid television shows he insisted on watching. She hated reality TV and he loved it.

Conscious that she was doing what she thought was right, she never took crap from her coworkers, most of whom were white. She especially disliked white hypocrites who pretended to be pro-black, whatever that was, and who emphasized their point by trying to talk jive or ghetto. Thea did not live in the ghetto, physically, psychologically, or emotionally. Thea considered herself an equal opportunity person—she didn't take shit from anybody regardless of race, gender, age, or religion.

Thea strode forcefully into Mike's office and slammed the door behind her. "This is bullshit, Sergeant Michael Stuart. You are nothing but incompetent white, honky trash!"

Mike leaned back in his chair and grinned. "I love you too, Thea. And saying white and honky in the same sentence is redundant."

Thea sat down heavily. "I'll redundant your ass if the snow causes me any more problems."

"Oh, yeah, like I can make it stop."

"I wish somebody would, Mike. I just lost another one."

The outburst was over. Anger and frustration were subsumed. "What happened?" Mike asked softly.

"A lady died. Can you believe it? She was gored in the leg by a deer and she bled to death on the floor of her very own house. Two firemen got there and managed to stop the bleeding, which wasn't too difficult since most of her blood was all over the place, but she died about five minutes later."

Mike shook his head sadly. He'd already heard the story from Stan, but didn't think it was time to mention it. "They didn't have any blood with them, did they?"

"Of course not. How do you carry blood on a snowmobile unless it's already inside you? Naw, they were okay to set a leg or do some rough stitching or perform CPR, but they had no blood to give her. They even considered a direct transfusion, but none of them was her blood type. Damn, how do you get killed by a deer in your own home in the middle of a city? It's the dumb things like this that really get to me. Damn it all!"

She stood and smiled a little. The tirade was over. "As always, Mike, I am truly sorry for having dumped on you."

Mike smiled. "As always, Thea, you are very welcome and feel free to do it anytime. My turn's next."

Thea took a deep breath. It was time to change the subject. "At least I am thankful I have enough staff to work things."

Sheridan's 911 call center was small, but there were always at least two people on duty at all times. That way, it would not be left unattended when somebody had to go to the john, or more than one call came in. There'd been two plus her when the snow started and that was proving more than sufficient.

"At any rate," Thea added, "it's otherwise been a slow day. A lot of accidents, but all fender-benders and no injuries. A couple of heart attacks and one pregnant woman worrying about going into labor, but I've got them covered. A couple of people got hurt on their roofs, but you know all about that. Also, no crimes, excepting your two murders, which I suggest you solve fairly soon."

"They aren't my murders, madam; I had nothing to do with them. My hands are clean. I am not a crook," Mike said, doing his best Richard Nixon imitation.

Thea sat back down and sighed. "You know what I mean, Mike. At any rate, how's your love life? How'd it go with dinner yesterday with those other teachers?"

For reasons hard to define, Mike had been confiding in Thea as well as Petkowski. A lot of people confided in Thea, who never breached a confidence. "It went really well. Nobody asked me to fix a ticket, or how to avoid a ticket, or how many miles over the limit you can go before getting a ticket. We just talked about stuff. It made me realize that cops and teachers have a lot in common."

"Come again?"

"Really. Cops rally around the badge and are suspicious of anyone who isn't a cop. If you're not a cop you really can't understand what's going on, and what it's really like to be a cop. Same with teaching. A teacher's enemies are the students, the parents, and the administration. In short, anyone who isn't a teacher or married to a teacher is the enemy. All of those other people are trying to second guess the teacher, just like civilians are always second guessing cops. At any rate, Maddy's friends are nice people. I think I scored some points."

"That's very profound," Thea said. "But then, bullshit often sounds like it is."

"You're right as usual, but there is a kernel of truth in it."

"Maybe, just maybe. Are you any closer to figuring out what Maddy's hang-up is?"

Mike shook his head. "All I know is that it happened while she was in college and involved a guy, and he was probably a boyfriend. She was betrayed and hurt and she hasn't worked her way through it, even though it's been several years. It must have been more than the standard now ex-boyfriend dumping her crap for it to have hit her so hard. I think she's in love with me, but just not ready to admit it or to make a commitment."

"What's your guess? Date rape?"

"Possible. Maybe a combination of things. I just wish she'd open up with me. I just don't know and it frustrates me. I want to help her, damn it."

"Does it bother you, the fact that she might have lived with a guy?"

Mike thought about the number of women he'd had sex with. Although it wasn't a large number by some people's standards, he had long ago given up any thoughts of taking a vow of celibacy.

"I can't throw stones. Hey, this is the twenty-first century, isn't it?"

Thea laughed. "Some people don't think so. Bet you had your first sex in high school, didn't you? A good-looking stud athlete like yourself didn't have to beg for it, did you?"

Mike thought quickly back to his junior year in high school. The girl's name was Mitzi, which was a nickname for something else he never cared to find out. All he really knew was that she was pretty and eager. She'd had sex with him and he'd later realized that she'd done the same for every other member of the wrestling team. He'd felt cheap and ashamed that he'd taken advantage of a pathetic little high school groupie who likely had all kinds of emotional problems and maybe just wanted to be "popular." It wasn't until much later that he realized he'd been lucky not to have gotten AIDS or some other sexually transmitted disease. Guys that age thought with their peckers.

Mike's first real relationship hadn't come until college. Her name was Aggie and they'd been desperately in love for a couple of torrid months. She'd dumped him claiming a need to not get tied down and to find herself. Mike had been relieved. It was going too far and too fast.

"High school wasn't all that much fun," Mike said. "For that matter, neither was college. Besides, Maddy is the one with the problem, not me." *At least I hope I'm not the one with the problem,* he thought. "Her past life is no concern of mine and mine is really no concern of hers. What I'm really interested in is her future, our future."

"Good speech," Thea said. "Have you tried it out on her?"

"Yeah, but it hasn't worked yet. I just hope we have a future."

Maddy's clothes were still a little damp when she put them on, but she didn't feel like spending any more time in the furnace room, and Donna hadn't returned with the promised brandy. The hell with it, the clothes would dry on her body soon enough.

She checked on the kids in the gym and saw their emotions covered all ranges. Some seemed to be enjoying the adventure, while others looked shocked and confused. One boy was crying and a teacher was trying to comfort him. A TV in the corner was playing an old video of Disney's *Lion King* in an attempt to keep them distracted. They'd all seen it a hundred times, so it really wasn't going over. Remnants of a poor substitute for a dinner from the cafeteria filled the waste baskets. For a moment, Maddy felt sorry, and then she realized that they were so much safer where they were than trying to get home. It was still snowing with an intensity that was sometimes blinding, but it seemed to be tapering off a little. Or maybe it wasn't tapering off, she thought. Maybe it was her imagination.

Donna Harris emerged from the principal's office with an angry look on her face. "Parents are all assholes," she said in a harsh whisper. "Do you know the Hardingens?"

Maddy nodded, amused at her friend's outburst. The Hardingens had a girl in first grade and a boy in third.

Donna continued. "Would you believe that Mrs. Hardingen somehow made it home and she just phoned me and wants me to send her little dumplings over to her?"

"What's wrong with that?" Maddy asked.

"She wants me to let them walk. They live several blocks away, it's still snowing heavily, it's dark, and the kids don't have winter clothing. Mrs. Hardingen is one of those parents who doesn't seem to care how they dress themselves in the morning. They came to school today in light jackets, tee shirts, and gym shoes. They would be soaked and frostbitten in a hundred yards, not to mention lost. The woman is totally clueless. I can't figure out whether she's lazy or stupid. Or both."

"So you refused?"

"I politely told her to stuff it. She then called the superintendent and our beloved Dr. Templeton told me I should do what the parents want. After all, they are taxpayers who vote on millages and elect the board members who chose the superintendent. So I told Dr. Templeton to stuff it, only this time I wasn't so tactful. Damn it, I am not going to have kids getting lost and freezing to death while I am in charge here, even though I'm not the principal."

"Good for you," Maddy said, "but what kind of trouble are you in now?" Templeton was known to have a short fuse.

Donna grinned maliciously. "None that I can think of. She backed down and admitted I was right. Besides, I have tenure and a union to back me if it comes to that. I don't think it will. Our beloved superintendent is just as frustrated as I am. Let's face it; she's got a whole bunch of schools with children in them to worry about. I got word from a friend that the kids at the high school end of the building are going crazy, while the ones at the middle school are a little worse. Something about raging hormones and an utter lack of discipline. A couple of high school seniors got caught having sex in a locker room. I think they're having their version of end of the world parties. I think I like the little kids better."

In the gym behind them, a child began to cry. Dinner had been less than wonderful, with dry cereal and leftover salad and fruit from lunch as the main and only courses. What they'd earlier thought might last through morning had turned out to be a laughable miscalculation. Some of the kids had refused to eat, and Maddy could hardly blame them. While what they'd been served would fill the belly, it was a long ways from Mom's home cooking. Or even Burger King. Maddy wondered how well anyone was going to sleep this night.

"Enough feeling sorry for ourselves," Donna said. "Let's have a two-teacher staff meeting in the office and see what we can do about the rest of that brandy."

"Is that a good idea?"

"Well, I don't plan on getting sloshed, if that's what you're wondering," Donna laughed. "I also don't plan on driving, performing surgery, or operating heavy machinery, so screw it."

Wally Wellman slammed down the phone. His producer, Ron Friedman, looked at him curiously. "Another satisfied customer?" he asked. Incredibly, the station had gotten calls demanding they do something about the weather. Wellman told the old joke about a television weatherman being in sales and not production, but it hadn't gone over. People were angry and frustrated. Well, so was Wally.

Wellman shook his head. "Worse. This guy says it's God's punishment for our sins that this is all happening. He wants to go on television and lead a prayer for deliverance, and then call for the elimination of all sex and violence on television and in the movies. I think he used to be one of the Taliban."

Friedman yawned. "I knew there had to be a reason. Are they going to sacrifice a virgin to make the snow go away, or have they given up trying to find a virgin?"

Wally laughed and looked at the monitors that should be showing traffic in various spots around the metropolitan area. Streetlights were on, which provided a faint jewellike glow to the still heavily falling snow. The snow already on the ground covered everything, making the area look surreal, even, in a strange sort of way, lovely. Outside, nothing moved, except an occasional snowmobile.

TV6 finally had a couple of reporters out on the snow-covered streets, but reporting on the snowfall had become an exercise in journalistic redundancy. Otherwise, there was no traffic, vehicular or pedestrian. The stillness was haunting. Every now and then, a gust of wind would make the snow swirl and the camera would go totally blank.

Wally checked his watch. In another hour, he was going on camera again to give another update. What could he say besides the obvious—Hey gang, it's still snowing! Wow! He was tired from his all-day vigil and wanted to go home.

The phone on the desk buzzed and Ron picked it up. "If it's God," Wally said, "I don't want to talk until He makes it stop snowing."

"Don't knock it," said Ron, covering the receiver with his hand. "Remember, many are cold but few are frozen."

"Yeah." Wally laughed through his fatigue.

"Actually," Ron said with a wicked grin, "it almost is God."

"What?"

"It's the governor, and she's asking for you by name. I told you you should have paid your taxes."

Jamal Wheeler knew he'd made a big mistake. He'd only been working for United Parcel Service for a little more than a year and wanted to make a good impression. A lot of people said that working for UPS sucked because of all the picky regulations and the strange, uncool, brown uniform, but Jamal had seen it as an opportunity, not a curse.

At twenty-four and with only two years of college, Jamal had been going nowhere fast. Still, he'd managed to get out of the inner city where so many young blacks like him were gang-bangers, did drugs, committed crime, or all of the above. The UPS job was the best money he'd ever earned and he got to drive the truck all by himself without some supervisor looking over his shoulder. There was no way he was going to screw this up. He had already paid off a lot of debts and was seriously considering going back to school and finishing his degree.

His aunt was the only relative with a degree, although Jamal's cousin Byron had gone to college for four years on a basketball scholarship. Only he'd returned as illiterate as when he'd left for school and now was wandering around the city doing nothing but odd jobs.

Thus, even though he wasn't a mailman per se, Jamal remembered the stuff about delivering through sleet and storm and felt that today's weather certainly qualified. It might be difficult, but he was going to deliver the stash of packages in the back of his truck. He'd been told that a lot of drug dealers used UPS, but he didn't think much of that happened in Sheridan.

At first, his truck, a big ugly brown diesel, had managed to bull its way through the deepening snow with not too much difficulty, but then problems began to add up.

Jamal's real problem in the short run was that he had to leave the truck to make his deliveries in the residential area of Sheridan. By the time he got back to the truck each time, it seemed like another foot had fallen. That was an exaggeration, of course, but walking was even more difficult than driving, particularly when he didn't have boots. Hey, it wasn't even supposed to snow today. Whatever. His feet were cold and wet and his shoes were ruined. Of course, most of the houses didn't have anybody home, which meant that items that needed to be signed for had to be brought back to the truck.

Finally, it happened. He'd learned to hate stops since it took so much of the truck's energy to get started again. Now, he was confronted by a stalled car directly in front of him and another one off to the right. Under optimal circumstances, he might have finessed his way around them, but his situation sucked. He didn't know where the road began and ended, and he didn't think the United Parcel Service would want him driving over the nice lawns hidden under the snow.

He called his office on his cell phone and got the surprising comment that they'd thought he'd already returned to the barn. Since he hadn't, he was urged to do so immediately and in no uncertain language. The implication was clear—he'd been stupid to stay out.

"How the hell do I get out of this?" he asked himself after hanging up. Jamal considered backing up, but he couldn't see very much at all. Then he became aware that another car was stalled behind him. It was empty. The driver must have bailed right away. He was trapped.

He called his supervisor again and informed him that he was going to have to sit out the storm. Jamal's supervisor was more sympathetic this time and agreed, then wished him good luck. This time he seemed concerned, not angry, and Jamal realized that the man was frustrated. Well, who wasn't?

Jamal understood all about carbon monoxide poisoning and turned off the ignition. He grew rapidly colder and his wet feet felt like they were freezing. The fact that it was night only made him feel colder and lonelier. A check of the remaining boxes suggested nothing that would keep him warm. Certainly, there was nothing from Land's End, or anyplace like that. He had a couple of boxes from Amazon, but they were heavy, like they contained computers. He doubted he could warm himself much by hugging a monitor.

That left going to a house. He left his vehicle and locked it. He had on a jacket, which had already proved to be useless. He could barely see the shapes of the houses, much less a light on, and he nearly exhausted himself before convincing himself that he'd have to break into one or freeze to death.

A red-brick colonial looked inviting. He rang the doorbell several times and waited. Then he knocked hard. Nothing. Nobody was home to get upset if he broke in and, just as good, he hadn't heard a dog barking.

Jamal was a church-going young man and had never done anything even remotely illegal before in his life, but he'd seen enough movies to know what he had to do. He went to the side of the house and found a door leading to the kitchen. He took off his sodden shoe and used it to smash in the glass above the knob. As he did it, he wondered if UPS would reimburse for the damage or if he would have to pay for it himself. He decided it didn't much matter.

Jamal cleared the window of glass shards that would have sliced him and stuck his arm through it. He found the inside knob and opened the door. He stepped in to the welcome warmth and took a deep breath.

He'd scarcely taken a step into the kitchen when the blast hit him square in the chest, lifted him into the air, and slammed him against the wall.

Through fading vision and waves of pain that swept through his shattered body, he became aware of a shape standing over him. It was an older white man and he had a double-barreled shotgun in his arms. Both barrels were smoking and the man looked wide-eyed and terrified. An equally frightened woman peeked over his shoulder.

"Damn it, Shelly," he said to someone Jamal couldn't see through his fading vision. "I told you the son of a bitch was trying to break in."

CHAPTER 9

THE FRIGHTENING AND UNEXPECTED SOUND OF THE DOORBELL chiming froze Raines in his tracks. He stared at Tower in shock and dismay as the chimes rang melodically. Who the hell could it be? They'd only been in the house for an hour and Raines had hopes of staying there all night. It was large, empty, warm, and had a refrigerator full of food and a dozen cans of beer. It was dark out and the snow was continuing to pile up. How the hell could anyone even make it to the house? He knew it wasn't the Avon lady, so it had to be a do-gooder neighbor.

The ringing was followed by a loud pounding on the door and the muted sound of voices. Raines broke from his trance and picked up a gun. One of the few ways they'd managed to help themselves while looting houses was in firepower. If they couldn't find much money, they did find some excellent weapons. The people of Sheridan seemed to be well armed, although cashless. One of the places they'd plundered contained several highly illegal fully automatic weapons and a lot of ammunition, and they'd helped themselves. It amused him that the owner was unlikely to report the theft to the police. He would be in deep trouble himself.

Raines had a full clip in his stolen M16, and the safety was off. He was ready. Tower was similarly armed. His face twitched in either nervousness or excitement. Raines could never tell.

A muffled voice sounded through the door. "Hey, Phil, we know you're in there. We saw the lights. What gives? Talk to us, buddy."

God damn it, Raines muttered. He had yelled at Tower to keep the place dark, but that was after the idiot had already turned on a couple of lights. The fucking troll was afraid of the dark. Raines had switched them off as quickly as he could, but they'd obviously been noticed. It was too late for regrets. Now what? Blast your way out or bluff your way out? Or maybe stay silent and hope the neighbor would go away. Not a chance. They'd obviously seen the lights go on and off.

Tower went to a window and peered through the drapes. He signaled that there were at least two men outside that he could see. Finally, the little jerk was doing something right.

First try to bluff, Raines thought. "Sorry guys, but I can't come to the door right now," he said in a deep voice that he hoped would pass for the homeowner's. "I'm all wet and I'm changing. You know how it is."

There was a pause and then laughter from outside. "Yeah, we know all about that. We're freezing our asses off. Are Lisa and the kids home yet? Marie and our kids are worried."

Who the hell is Lisa? A wife? A child? His wife, he decided. "Nope, and it doesn't look like anybody's gonna be home for a long while."

"Ain't that the truth? Well, when you get yourself settled, come over and let's talk. We're setting up ways to protect the neighborhood from whatever comes along. No way we can't drink some beer while we're doing it."

"Sounds great," Raines answered with what he hoped was the proper enthusiasm.

Raines crept to a window and looked out. He could make out two men on snowshoes walking away with an awkward shuffle. To his dismay, they had shotguns over their shoulders. The logical assumption was that this "Phil" had snowshoes as well; otherwise the neighbors wouldn't think he'd be able to move around at all.

"Fooled them, didn't we?" said Tower happily, unconcerned that his mistake had caused the dilemma.

"We wouldn't have had to fool anyone if you'd kept your hands off the lights."

Tower looked hurt. "How'm I supposed to see without lights? If I can't see, this is as bad as prison. At least we can stay here with the lights on now that they know we're here."

He had a point about prison, Raines thought. Freedom, though, was more than turning on a switch when you wanted to. A thought suddenly jarred Raines. He ran upstairs to the room the owner used as an office. A desk in the corner was covered with papers. He turned on the light and searched through the papers. There it was, the homeowner's bank statement. The name on the account read Philip and Amy Jakobowski. He checked for photos and found an adult man and a woman. No child. He checked the other rooms and only the master bedroom was lived in. That meant there was no Lisa and no kids! Oh, Christ! The fucking neighbors had tricked them. Damn it.

"Grab our shit and get moving. We've gotta leave," he yelled.

"Why?"

"Because there ain't nobody named Lisa and there ain't no kids, and they'll be back soon with cops and guns."

Already, Raines could visualize cops on snowmobiles surrounding the house, while citizens on snowshoes helped them. In moments, the two criminals were ready and on their remaining snowmobile. They'd stashed it in the family room to keep it out of sight and free of snow. It made a mess when they'd opened the double doors, but they hadn't cared. They weren't going to clean it up. They quickly topped off the tank with gas from a container in the attached garage.

Raines had already plotted an escape route. Exiting the back, there were fences to his right and rear, but not to his left. The rear fence would prevent him from cutting to the street behind. He thought the snowmobile might clear the fence if he gunned it, but he couldn't take a chance. Raines was an amateur driver and knew it. Jumping a fence was something you saw on commercials or in movies, not in real life. Lose their one remaining snowmobile and they would be hoofing it as wanted men in a strange town in the middle of a blizzard. Assuming, of course, that they weren't hurt in the crash.

He drove the snowmobile out and swerved to his left, nearly overturning it. He drove down several back yards and gunned it left again towards the street. To his astonishment, several men stood directly in front of him. They were as surprised as he and scattered, allowing him to drive through them and turn away. One of them had a rifle or a shotgun. Tower fired a wild burst from his M16 that ripped through the night, and the men threw themselves into the snow. Someone howled in pain as Raines turned to the right and down another street.

Not good, Raines thought as they roared away from near disaster. Not good at all. But at least they were away from immediate danger.

Mike Stuart looked around the conference room. Where was Chief Bench, he mouthed as a question to Detective Hughes. She shrugged. The mayor was there, and he looked tired and frustrated. Well, that fit a lot of people, Mike thought.

"Chief Bench isn't with us tonight," Mayor Carter said. "He's not feeling well."

Mike suddenly understood. The chief was drunk, just like DiMona had said. Wonderful. Now he and Hughes were the senior officers present in the building, if you didn't count a couple of elderly sergeants in supplies and records. Obviously, the mayor didn't either, or they'd have been invited to the meeting.

"Detective Hughes," Carter began, "do you believe the two men on snowmobiles who shot up Almond Street are the same people who killed those people in the motel?"

The calls had come in a few minutes earlier. No one had been hit in the shootout, although one citizen had fallen over an ornamental boulder and broken his ankle. The real shocker was that the criminals had used automatic weapons and scared the hell out of the citizens. How they'd gotten them and from where was a moot point. They had them and that made the two shooters even more of a threat, especially if they actually were the motel murderers.

"Probably one and the same, or two and the same," Hughes said. "They left the motel with two snowmobiles, but they may have damaged or dumped one of them. Either way, they fit the profile and the rough description we now have. It ain't perfect confirmation, but logic says it's them."

She'd just come from the site of the abortive shootout on Almond Street and had spent fruitless minutes looking for shell casings, before deciding that they wouldn't be found until the snow melted, sometime around July. Another cop remained at the site and was lifting fingerprints from inside the house where the suspects had been hiding.

Earlier, Hughes had sent fingerprint information from the motel to the FBI and gotten a quick response because of the savagery of the murders. They identified two criminals named James Tower and William Raines. They were from Oklahoma and were suspects in a series of violent crimes, and had each been in jail for several years. Until recently, they had assaulted, robbed, and beaten, and there was a suspected rape, but they had not killed. Nor did they have any known drug problems. At least the Sheridan Police were not dealing with half-crazed addicts looking for their next fix. But that was scant comfort, because Tower and Raines had now killed. They'd crossed a new threshold of violence and that made them infinitely more dangerous.

Of course, knowing who they were and finding Tower and Raines were two different things. The two suspects had made a mistake in turning on the lights in a house that was presumed to be vacant. It was highly unlikely they would make the same mistake twice. Mike had little respect for the so-called mind of the criminal. Most people stole and killed because they were too stupid or uneducated to do otherwise, and, so far, he'd seen nothing to indicate a higher level of intelligence in either Tower or Raines.

Of course, that did not mean taking them for granted. Tower and Raines were now desperate and remorseless killers. The chatter of full auto guns made them extremely dangerous, stupid or not.

"Does anybody have any good news?" Carter asked.

There was silence; then Mike spoke up. "I can give a little highly qualified good news. We do have a couple of snow removal teams in action with more to follow."

Carter raised his hands high in mock joy. "Hallelujah. Finally. Now, what do you mean by teams and why is it qualified good news?"

Mike explained that he, Public Works Director Dom Hassell, and their counterparts in the county government had decided on a way to begin to clear the roads. This, of course, was the main reason that Hassell wasn't at Carter's meeting. That Hassell couldn't stand Carter was another.

First, they used the snowmobiles to get snowplow drivers to their vehicles. However, the plows could not operate alone. With the roads clogged with abandoned cars, it was necessary to first find a place to put the empty cars. Thus, tow trucks had to drag abandoned cars someplace where they wouldn't be in the way. Usually this would be a temporary site, like a nearby lawn, or median. Once a path was cleared, plows would then go off-road and clear some of the parking lots that were empty as a result of businesses sending people home early. The tows would again drag cars into the lots and leave them.

"We're making progress," Mike said, "but it's progress measured in feet per hour rather than miles per hour, and the snow is continuing to come down. At least, though, it gets the roads cleared so we can plow again." And again and again, he thought.

Patti Hughes laughed. "How are the good citizens taking to our towing their cars? I'll bet we're killing a lot of transmissions and causing tons of other damage."

Mike grinned wryly. "How can I argue? Of course we are. What's funny is that some of the people who've abandoned their cars see us doing the work, and they believe they can hop in and drive home, and we've got to tell them otherwise, which pisses them off. At least we can get those people to put their cars in neutral and save on repair jobs."

Carter shook his head in anger. "That way'll take forever, damn it. Can't somebody think of something else? I'm going to get crucified if this can't be cleaned up promptly. What the hell went wrong? Why weren't we prepared?"

Mike was tired and didn't feel like playing nice. "Mr. Mayor, we were as prepared as we could be, especially since nobody predicted any snow in the first place. Look, this isn't Buffalo or some town way up north or out west in the ski country, like Denver, where they deal with huge amounts of snow as a matter of course. A foot of snow in this town can close almost anything, and we've got more than three feet on the ground, and that's on top of what had fallen last week. And it really hasn't even begun to slow down. Add to that the fact that it started during a workday and caused everybody to get stuck in traffic and you have a better feel for the mess we're in. Sir, if you have a better idea, we'd all love to hear it."

Carter pulled back as if slapped. "If I had, you're right, you'd hear it. I'm frustrated, pissed, and angry, Sergeant Stuart." He softened slightly, although his expression showed residual anger. He didn't like being talked back to. "I guess we all are. Do you know how many people we're warehousing here in this civic center compound? No? Well, I'll tell you. Four hundred plus. And would you believe that some of them are complaining about the facilities? We've got some food in here from some of the closer restaurants and stores, although the vending machines are now empty, but there's no satisfying some people. Would you also believe that a couple of assholes have complained that I didn't have bottled water brought in instead of food? When I told them to drink from the drinking fountains, you would've thought I'd asked them to commit incest or turn cannibal. Jesus!"

Mike laughed ruefully. "I guess you do have problems, sir."

"We all do, Sergeant Stuart," Carter said grimly. Mike winced. The honorable mayor had not forgiven Mike for his outburst. Someday he might regret being blunt with Carter. Tonight, however, he just couldn't care.

"Governor," Wally purred. "What a pleasure to hear your sweet sexy voice."

Governor Lauren Landsman chuckled. "You are so full of bullshit, Wally. You should have been a lawyer or a politician, or both, like me. No, you had to be a weatherman type and lie to the world on a daily basis. I only have to do it when it's time to get re-elected or otherwise politically expedient."

"Thanks for putting things in perspective, Lauren."

"Seriously, Wally, how are you doing?"

Wally took a deep breath. Usually, he gave a generic answer to a question like that and said he was doing fine, thank you. He couldn't do that to someone like Lauren.

"It still hurts. God, Lauren, it hurts. Some days I think I'll make it, and other days I just don't know how. They say it gets better, but I don't know. Don't get me wrong, I'm over my feeling sorry for myself and I really am doing better."

"I'm so sorry, Wally. You know Ellen was one of my best friends, too. I just wish I could have made it to the funeral."

She had been in Japan on a trade mission drumming up business for the state when Ellen died.

Lauren Landsman and Wally's late wife had been roommates in college. Wally had actually dated Lauren and the relationship had been quite serious, even intimate, until Lauren dumped him for someone else. He had dated Ellen on the rebound and it had blossomed into a long and successful marriage. As to Lauren Landsman, the guy she left Wally for was long forgotten. She had never married. Instead, she'd gone to law school and become a career politician, rising from state representative to state senator and then governor. Governorship of the State of Michigan was the obvious high point of her life to date, although there were rumors that she'd consider running for the U.S. Senate the next time around. Term limit legislation said she would be through as governor. Throughout the years, she, Ellen, and Wally had remained in contact and continued to be friends.

Lauren Landsman was still slender and extremely attractive for a woman her age, and Wally found himself thinking about the great physical fun they'd had when they were young and lithe and limber. Then he wondered if either of them was anywhere near as limber as then.

"Wally, what's happening to us with all this snow? And don't tell me the world's ending."

Wally smiled. "Not hardly. What we have here, Lauren, is a meteorological stalemate. We have two weather fronts in collision with each other and neither one will budge. It happens all the time, but it usually doesn't last very long and, sooner or later, and generally sooner, one of the fronts gives up and is pushed away. This stalemate is lasting an ungodly long time and I don't know when it will end. Maybe it's our turn, though."

"What do you mean by that happy thought, Wally-man?"

Wally smiled. She used to call him that when they were an

item a century or so before. "Well, let's see. California has earth-
quakes, brush fires, and storms off the Pacific, all of which makes
one wonder why anybody would want to live there. Florida has
hurricanes, gators, snakes, and a swamp that burns, while Kansas
has tornados that take little girls to Oz. New England has Perfect Storms, and the Mississippi and Missouri flood all over the
plains. What do we have in Michigan? Nothing. Oh, we get an
occasional tornado that generally finds a trailer park, but nowhere
near as many as other areas. Compared with other places, our
weather picture is really very sedate. So, maybe it's our turn for
Mother Nature to zap us and remind us who's really in charge."

Lauren Landsman sighed expansively. "Wally, I cannot go before
the people of Michigan and tell them what's happening is our
turn and we should learn to love it. They'd tell me to shove it,
and with a snow shovel no less."

"Lauren, I'd love to tell you it's going to end soon, but I can't.
Sure it will end—I just don't know when. The stalemate could
break in five minutes, although not bloody likely, or it could
break in five hours. Or maybe not for five days."

"During which time it keeps on snowing."

"You got it."

"And other meteorologists agree with you?"

"Yep," he said with a degree of pride. It was small comfort,
but Wally was now the acknowledged prophet who'd been proven
correct. He would not get the Isaac Cline award, although his
warnings had come too late and against an astonishingly strong
storm to be much help.

"Well, I guess I'll have to tell everyone that this whole thing is
your fault, and that they should send all their cards and letters
to your home address, which, of course, I'll provide along with
your home phone number."

Wally laughed and remembered how close they'd been in college before he'd met Ellen. "You do that, my dear governor, and
I'll tell the whole world that I've seen you naked."

The Sampson's Super Store in Sheridan was an outlet of a small
Midwestern chain that emulated the more numerous Wal-Mart
and Target chains. Like its larger brethren, the Sampson's stores

were one-floor, huge, sprawling, and had an almost all-inclusive
inventory. They sold food, clothing, alcohol, prescription drugs,
camping gear, car and home improvement supplies, and God
only knew what else. Some of the more cynical said that God
really didn't know.

A store the size of Sampson's could easily hold several hundred customers at a time, and handled far larger crowds during
peak shopping periods. When the snow started falling, the store
was almost empty. Then, as manager Tyler Holcomb watched, a
trickle of people seeking shelter became a relative torrent. As
people coming in laughingly told him and his staff, Sampson's
was the best possible place to wait out a storm, and Holcomb
had to agree with them. It pleased him that they felt comfortable in his store. He just wondered how long they'd be there. It
quickly became obvious that closing the place and booting them
out was not an option.

Tyler Holcomb was in his mid-thirties, well-educated and
considered a real possibility to be Sampson, Inc.'s first African-
American vice president. That is, if another major competitor didn't
snag him with an offer the smaller Sampson's couldn't match. It
was also rumored that Sampson's was having financial problems.

Tyler liked working at Sampson's. His pay and benefits were
more than adequate. But he would go with an offer of more money.
He had a wife and a couple of young kids who would want their
own turn at college, even though they could barely walk right
now. All other things being equal, or at least equivalent, money
talked and bullshit walked as his father liked to say.

Holcomb was a very humane man. As people streamed in, he
tried his best to make them comfortable and urged his staff to
do the same thing. As a parent, he was amused at the way the
mothers in the crowd took charge. They were the first to buy up
items that their children could eat without cooking or trouble.
This included cereal, milk (which necessitated buying plastic cups
or bowls), fruit, veggies, and anything else that came to mind.
Despite the snow, it was going to be a very profitable day. And
night, he thought ruefully. He'd much rather be home.

Some of the more pessimistic bought Holcomb's stock of
camping gear and even the pillows from the home section. Since

just about everyone had cash or plastic, they paid for what they took, and everyone was as happy as they could be under the circumstances.

However, Tyler could see problems arising. Sadly, he knew he could not predict all of them. First, he called his home office and told them of the situation and his conclusion that he, his staff, and his customers were going to be in the store for the foreseeable future. People, he said, were going to need help, and his staff should be paid for their overtime efforts. His corporate bosses agreed, and also gave him the go-ahead to distribute whatever was needed and let people use what was required without charge if necessary. They did not have to tell him that any inventory losses would be covered by insurance and that the subsequent "good neighbor" publicity would do the chain well. He was certain that Wal-Mart and other stores were doing the same thing.

Requests for food and other supplies from City Hall and elsewhere put an additional strain on his resources. While it looked as if he had an abundance of food on his shelves, that was an illusion. What was on the shelves was practically it. There was no huge quantity in a back room. In fact, there really wasn't a back room at all, just loading docks and handling spaces. They depended on a constant stream of trucks bringing inventory, and the snow had put an end to all that.

Still, there were lighter moments. The request for toilet paper from City Hall made Holcomb's irreverent assistant manager laugh. "Always thought there were a lot of assholes in that building, and now this proves it," he said to general agreement.

There were laws forbidding the eating of food in the store proper—the small snack bar was an obvious exception, but Holcomb judged that circumstances required that the rule be ignored. He was not going to ask people to take their food and their little kids outside in the snowdrifts to eat, or jam themselves into the snack bar.

Nor was he concerned about the purchases of beer and liquor. For quite some time, he wasn't even aware that such purchases were being made. It simply never occurred to him. Nor did it occur to him that some people would steal the alcohol. Thus, when one of his security guards told him there were some rowdy teenagers in the rear of the building and that they were upsetting other people, he thought it was just kids making noise, and went to ask them to put a stop to it.

Five of them were squatting in the aisle around women's cosmetics, three boys and two girls. Cosmetics was a good choice for some privacy. Not too many people had a need for nail polish at the moment, so they pretty much had the place to themselves. The kids looked about sixteen and there were empty beer cans half hidden in a bag. Holcomb quickly had the security guard take what was left. The kids didn't protest, other than to swear. One, however, called him a motherfucking nigger in a drink-slurred voice. Holcomb was shocked and barely controlled his rage. He'd played football in college, defensive end, and could have wiped out the little shit, which he dearly wanted to. It'd been years since anyone had called him a nigger and that had been one of his own family after Tyler had fouled him hard during a pickup basketball game.

He had no choice regarding handling the punks. At least a couple of them had the decency to look shocked at the outburst, while one of the girls simply giggled drunkenly and belched. He would have to endure the idiots. His only alternative was to throw them out. He couldn't bring himself to do that.

Holcomb walked to his office and gathered his department managers. "I want all alcohol taken off the shelves and moved to the back and locked up," he said angrily. "Start with the hard stuff and then do the beer and wine. If anybody asks, I'm going to announce that the mayor has ordered all sales of alcoholic beverages stopped."

"Has he actually done that?" the supervisor of the cashiers asked.

"No," Holcomb said, "but I think he should have."

"What about those who already have stuff? Should we remind them it's illegal to drink it in here?" asked the same assistant manager who thought City Hall was filled with assholes.

Holcomb thought that would be impossible to enforce. The aisles were filled with people and packages, and who knew what was in them. Besides, why punish adults who wanted a drink because some punks acted up?

"No, do not take anything from adults who've already paid for it."

"What about smoking?"

Holcomb shook his head. The store was an old building. Sampson's had bought it from K-Mart after their bankruptcy, and, at best, the circulation in the store was barely adequate. Already the air was getting stale because of the numbers of people. This law he would obey. "No smoking. If anybody complains, tell them there are kids in the building with asthma. Hell, there probably are."

As he went back into his office, he wondered: What the hell am I, a cruise ship director? For the first time, he began to feel both weary and to understand that he had maybe a thousand people to manage. Maybe he really was a cruise director. He laughed harshly. Just so long as this wasn't the *Titanic*.

"I'll make a PA announcement about booze and smoking, however useless it might prove to be. I'll also threaten to throw out anybody who is disruptive."

"Would you actually do that?" he was asked.

"I honestly don't know," Holcomb said and thought: *Just don't let anyone call me "nigger" again.*

CHAPTER 10

"MIKE, I'M GLAD I GOT HOLD OF YOU," MADDY SAID INTO THE phone. "Donna's told us to cut down on our cell phone calls and preserve our batteries."

Mike had been dozing with his head on his lieutenant's desk. His brain was not fully engaged and his tongue was fuzzy. "Don't you have a charger?" he finally managed.

"Two, in fact. One's still in the car, wherever that is, and the other's at home. Donna's afraid we're going to lose the phone or electricity or both at any time."

Mike yawned. "She's probably right. There've been some power outages already, and the repair crews aren't going to fix them for a long time." Another yawn. "So why'd you call, other than to tell me how much you miss me?"

"Yes, I miss you. I wanted to have dinner with you tonight. Instead I'm stuck in this dull school with scores of hyper kids and some strange people who call themselves teachers. I think I'd rather have a root canal or be a lawyer than be stuck like this."

Mike laughed. "I miss you, too, and I'm sorry you chose the wrong major in college. And don't knock lawyers. I may be one, someday."

117

"How's your night going?"

"Other than nagging phone calls from women who can't do without me, it's okay."

"Not much crime, I'll bet."

"Dull. Without getaway cars, criminals are staying home. A high-speed chase is out of the question."

He decided against telling her about the two murderers, Raines and Tower. Their pictures had just been faxed in, so now the names had taken on substance. The two killers looked so innocuous, even dull. Nor did he tell her that there had been a number of instances of domestic violence, resulting from situations where people who couldn't stand each other now couldn't escape each other's presence. That was leading to potentially violent flareups that the police could not respond to.

There'd been a couple of fires that neighbors had banded together to put out. Firemen on snowmobiles had arrived with small lengths of hose only to confront a new problem—Where the hell were all the hydrants? Invisible under gentle mounds of snow, that's where. So far, catastrophe had been averted. It was as if people realized that nature was in charge and that was making them relatively meek. Mike didn't think it would last too much longer. Sooner or later, someone would get cabin fever real bad, find a shotgun or an ax, and there would be hell to pay.

"So far, the city's existing," Mike said. "Personally, I rather be snowed in with you, and not Petkowski or Bench." Petkowski was asleep on the floor, or at least pretending to be, while Bench was down the hall, passed out in his chair and with his head on the desk. The scent of peppermint schnapps was heavy above the chief.

Maddy laughed. "There are lots of places I'd rather be, and with you is very high on the list. Have you talked to your parents?"

Mike's parents were retired and lived in a condo in Arizona. They spent a lot of time golfing. He'd spoken to them, and they'd told him to be careful. Thanks, Mom and Dad. He hadn't spoken to his younger brother in Chicago. The sky was clear in Chicago and he didn't feel like taking the ribbing his brother would inflict on him.

"Yeah, they're fine. How about yours?"

Maddy's parents lived in a house in a nearby suburb that was a lot less expensive than Sheridan. Maddy's father was a fore-man at a Ford plant, and her mother was an office manager at an automotive supplier.

"They're safe at home."

"When we get out of here, how about a hot tub for two and a bottle of champagne?" he said.

"Sounds good," she said, "But just one bottle? That sounds very inadequate. Speaking of inadequacies, are swimsuits optional?"

"Very optional," he said.

"Michael, I will hold you to that. Now I've got to make sure my battery doesn't run down."

"Mine's already recharging, Maddy."

Raines and Tower drove their snowmobile slowly and carefully through the almost invisible streets of residential Sheridan. It was night, but the reflections off the snow made it easy to see and to drive, providing, of course, that they didn't hit anything that was buried. Had they not been cold and confused, they might have noticed a strange beauty the storm had created. Street lights were on, and they glowed like Japanese lanterns through the swirling snow. The snow itself glittered like so many small jewels.

However, the effect was totally lost on them. They needed a place to stay, but one that was far enough away from prying neighbors. That, Raines conceded, was going to be hard to find. He really hadn't noticed it before, but, like so many affluent suburbs in the area, the houses were large, but the lots were small; thus enabling neighbors to easily see what was going on next door. They had been lucky with the last bunch of cowboys they'd almost run over in their escape, but they might not be so lucky the next time. Now the police knew they were armed to the teeth.

"I'm cold," Tower complained. "Hungry, too."

"So am I," Raines answered. He didn't add that they wouldn't be in this mess if Tower hadn't insisted on turning on the lights in their last place. "I'm looking for just the right house and I know what I'm looking for."

It wasn't far from the truth. Raines understood that many subdivisions had farming roots and that the original farmhouse, and sometimes the complete farm complex, often still stood. When the farmer sold out to the developer, he either took a ton of cash and moved elsewhere, or he remained in the farm house and hung onto a decent chunk of land.

He'd seen several farmhouses, but they had the bad fortune to be on main roads. That, too, made sense. Years ago, when there were only farms in the area, the only roads were those that later became main roads.

Then he saw a shape through the snow and smiled. Perched on a low hill, the house was two stories and had a gabled roof that hid a third. In a way it reminded him of the house from the old movie *Psycho*. Raines didn't believe in ghosts, and, since they were the ones who were the killers, there was no threat from that quarter, either. There was a three-car garage and other outbuildings. Better, it was on a very large lot and surrounded by extremely tall pine trees. A couple of outside lights provided some illumination and were probably on timers since there were no inside lights visible. He steered the snowmobile up where trees indicated there might be a driveway.

"Jimmy, I think we found us a home."

"Still up to your ass in the white stuff, I see," said DiMona over the phone. "And not the stuff you can suck up your nose."

He had just called from Las Vegas. He said he'd forgotten what time it was, but he didn't sound sincere.

"Yeah," Mike replied. "I just never thought hell would be this cold." There was a small town in Michigan named Hell. It often got very cold in Hell and everything froze over.

"If it's any consolation, little buddy, the whole nation is watching this thing go down. This is the disaster of the week, my friend. You may be having it bad where you are, but it's looking a lot worse elsewhere."

"You're joking."

"Naw. You're too close to the forest to see the trees. Of course, it's snowing so hard you can't see shit, much less the forest. The mayor of Detroit is screaming for help. Detroit doesn't have all the snow you're getting but they're still getting a lot. Roofs on old buildings are collapsing all over the place and fires can't be controlled. With houses so close to each other in the older sections of Detroit, Highland Park, and Hamtramck, real blazes are eating up city blocks, and there ain't a Goddamned thing anybody can do except maybe throw snowballs at them. Fortunately, there's been so many abandoned homes torn down that it's created fire breaks. In the big city, you've got thousands of people wandering about in the snow and looking for a place to stay. It's not quite as bad as that in the other 'burbs, but it's still no picnic."

"I had no idea," Mike said honestly. He'd been too focused on his job to pay attention to anything but the unchanging weather report. The rest of the news might as well have involved China.

"Our beloved governor has called out the National Guard and they are trying to clear paths down the major highways. From what they've shown on the tube, it's an almost hopeless task."

Mike then took the opportunity to tell DiMona how crews were attempting to clear Sheridan's roads. "It'll work when the snow stops," Mike said, "but until then it's not accomplishing much."

"But it shows you're actually doing something instead of sitting around pulling your pud," DiMona said. "Later, when everybody's looking for someone to blame, you can piously say you stuck your dick in the dike to stop the ocean from leaking in."

"You shouldn't make me laugh. I'm too tired."

"Where's your little Polack buddy, Petkowski?"

"Out on a domestic problem run. I was doing something else and couldn't go with him."

"He's alone?"

"Couldn't be helped, boss. We're really spread thin."

"I guess it couldn't," DiMona said with a sigh. Domestic runs were among the worst. Husband, wives, sons, and daughters who'd long ago decided they hated each other could suddenly explode and take all around with them in a final and irrational act of violent desperation. Petkowski was a good cop, but sending him alone on a domestic violence run was an act of desperation.

"Bench is drunk," Mike said. "Carter's been okay, although he'd like someone to pull off a miracle and end this." He didn't say that the mayor was pissed at him for not toadying to him. That was water over the dam, although DiMona would hear about it when he got back, if he ever got back.

"Carter's got problems," DiMona said. "Maybe more than you know."

"Like what?"

"Like the FBI's been investigating him."

"You're joking."

"Do I look like I'm joking? Of course, since we're on the phone, you don't know what I look like, which is just as good 'cause I'm sitting here in my underwear. But I'm not joking, Mikey. Remember what downtown Sheridan looked like about ten years ago?"

Ten years ago, Sheridan was little more than a dot on a map to Mike. One of many towns he had never really seen, although he'd driven through it a forgettable number of times. That the city had a past was something he'd never really thought much about.

"Mike, ten years ago, the city got a federal grant to renovate MacArthur Boulevard and the old, sleazy properties along it. They even closed down a porno video store that me and the missus really liked. It really turned her on but then we got divorced. Ah well. About that time, a little company called Carter Siding and Home Improvement became Carter-Sheridan Construction with a lot of money to bid on contracts. They got more than their share and now Calvin Carter's both rich and mayor of the town he helped rebuild. The Feds are looking into where and how he got the initial money to go big all of a sudden, and where all the grant money went. There are rumors of queer accounting practices and offshore banking accounts. The Feds love that kind of shit."

"Son of a bitch," Mike said. "Does Carter know this?"

"Possibly not for certain, although I'm sure he suspects. I only hear rumors and leaks from friends of mine, but I'm reasonably certain it's true."

"But what has that have to do with us and the price of snow?"

"Y'know, Mikey, that's the damndest thing. I don't really know, but I'll bet there's something going to come up that we don't suspect."

Mike laughed. "Yeah, like a blizzard."

Traci Lawford was napping in her upstairs bedroom when she heard the noise. She was exhausted, but she'd accomplished what she'd feared all day was impossible: She'd actually made it home from work. Of course, she'd only had a couple of miles to come and her car was abandoned in the street about a half mile away, but she was home after bulling her way through the drifts. Wet, cold, and exhausted, but home. And safe.

Traci was quietly thankful that she was in excellent physical shape. Many her age, she was thirty-four, were in crummy shape. Her husband was one and, although she loved him dearly, she despaired of getting him to eat right and exercise.

Small and slender to the point of being thin, she exercised daily and was working her way up to running her first marathon. She wondered just how people who weren't in shape, like her husband, managed to get around in days like this. Maybe she wouldn't live forever, but it wouldn't be for lack of doing the right thing. Well, at least most of the time.

Alternatively dazzled by the beauty of the snow and fearful of its implications, she'd watched both it and the weather reports. It was obvious that her husband would not be home this evening from his business trip to Indianapolis, where it was also snowing, but not nearly as bad, and that she would be alone for the night. She changed into sweats and decided to make the best of a bad situation. A shower, a microwaved dinner and a couple of glasses of inexpensive wine and she was ready for bed. She stripped off the sweats and was half asleep when she heard something.

At first, she was confused as to the sound's meaning. She and her husband Tony had only been living on Beckett Street in Sheridan for a year even though it had been in Tony's family for generations. It came to them as an inheritance when his grandmother passed away. The house was far too large for their needs and tastes, and it didn't look like it would be filled with a ton of kids. If they had any, it would be one or two. Sometimes she wondered if they had sacrificed their chances for a family on the altar of career. Traci was an accountant and Tony was a lawyer.

The sound grew closer and she recognized it as a snowmobile. She'd been on them a couple of times and couldn't see the thrill it gave some people. Freezing and getting snow in the face was not her idea of fun. She felt the same about riding motorcycles in the summer and spitting out bugs.

Perhaps it was Tony, she thought hopefully. Maybe he'd figured a way to get home. She hopped out of bed and looked out the second-floor window just in time to see the snowmobile pausing under the utility wires. Through the falling snow, she watched as a man in the back reached up and sliced a wire. Stunned, Traci ran to the phone. It was dead and she realized that the people on the snowmobile were a danger to her.

She had been napping in her bra and panties. She quickly threw on her sweat suit and slippers. Where was her cell phone? Downstairs in her purse. Where was Tony's shotgun? All locked up in the basement for safety's sake. Besides, she thought ruefully, she didn't know how to shoot the damn thing anyhow.

A noise downstairs told her the strangers had forced their way into her house. This is my home, she wanted to scream, but reason held her tongue. Would her screams scare them off or excite them? She would be prudent and try not to draw attention to herself. They had talked about getting an alarm system, but hadn't convinced themselves of the need. Sheridan was a safe community, wasn't it? Or maybe there was no place safe anymore.

Where to hide? The attic crawlspace was a good choice, but then she remembered that a wall of old clothes was backed up against the closet ceiling hatch that led to it. Along with taking forever to clear, the noise would attract too much attention.

She heard more noises downstairs. She willed herself to be silent. Where would they search, and what were they looking for? Valuables, of course, and the most likely spot was the master bedroom, and she was in the master bedroom. After mentally racing through a number of bad alternatives, she took the best one available and crawled under the bed. It was so silly, she thought. Only in bad movies did anyone hide under a bed.

She heard footsteps on the stairs. Traci willed herself not to breathe, not to make a noise. They were in the hallway, and then the other rooms. She heard their voices, male voices. She was too terrified to make words out of the sounds—she only knew that they were as menacing as a tiger's growl. She felt utterly helpless.

They were in her room. Strange, but they hadn't turned on any lights. No one looked under a bed, she told herself. No one was even looking for her. They didn't even know she was home. She'd cleaned up the kitchen, hadn't she?

She screamed when a hand closed around her ankle and began pulling her out from under the bed.

As he pulled up on his snowmobile, Petkowski realized he had been to this place before. It was one of a number of nice, expensive detached condos on small lots. Affluent couples lived there, and, if he recalled correctly, association bylaws prohibited children. He thought the only way to really prevent children was to prevent screwing, but that was none of his business. He liked kids and hoped someday to have a handful.

These particular people were real winners, or whiners, he thought as he pushed his way through the almost waist-deep snow to the door. The woman seemed nice enough, petite and cute, although who knew what she was like when she was alone with her husband. Maybe she was a real viper who dared him to belt her and then she'd call the cops when he did. Regardless, that didn't give her gonzo of a husband the right to slap her around. Mr. Happy Homeowner was a big guy, which suddenly gave Petkowski pause. He was all alone and he'd better not forget that. Backup was nonexistent.

He pounded on the door. Someone had cleared a space on the small porch so he could stand. Their names were Fred and Cindy Baumann and they were about thirty. The condo was expensive and maybe they had money problems. Probably cost more than they could afford. Thanks to the housing collapse, they probably owed more on it than it was worth and were trapped in a place they could neither sell nor afford to keep.

Or maybe their problems were more traditional. Maybe one was doing some extracurricular screwing. Hey, maybe both. Cindy Baumann was pretty good looking. Too bad she was married to such an asshole.

Petkowski pounded on the door a second time. It opened and Mrs. Baumann stood there. Her face was red and there was a welt forming under right eye. She looked physically and emotionally defeated and very much like a candidate for a personal protection order. Petkowski wondered if he should suggest it to her.

"Police," he said and showed a badge. Otherwise he looked like anybody in a snowmobile suit. If the situation wasn't so serious, it would've been funny.

"I'm sorry, officer, but the call was a mistake, a misunderstanding."

"I'll judge that," he said. "When a call like this comes in, I am required to check it out."

It wasn't quite true. Sheridan Police operating procedures gave him considerable latitude and discretion in such matters. They just didn't allow him to be wrong. He would be safe rather than sorry.

Mrs. Baumann didn't resist as he pushed the door open and stepped inside. Mr. Big Bully Baumann got out of a reclining chair and approached Petkowski. His face was also flushed, although there was no bruising. Petkowski assumed he'd been drinking. One whiff of his breath confirmed that.

"Like my wife says, Officer, we don't need you no more. Didn't need you in the first place," he corrected himself.

"And like I told her, sir, I'll be the judge of that." He turned to Mrs. Baumann. "Are you all right here? Do you want to come with me and press charges?"

She smiled quickly and he liked the change. "Come with you? Just how the heck would we accomplish that in this weather?" Her expression changed and she was again sad. "No, I'm not pressing charges. There's nothing to press. It was a misunderstanding."

"How'd you get the bruise?" Petkowski asked. "Did he hit you? That's a criminal offense if he did."

"She fell, if it's any of your fucking business," Fred Baumann said. He positioned himself so that he towered over the shorter Petkowski, who was beginning to really wonder why on earth he'd taken the run alone. "So why don't you go back to ticketing speeders and get out of my house?" Baumann snarled. "What me and the lady do is my business, not yours."

Petkowski shrugged and smiled broadly. "Hey, you're right, Mr. Baumann. She's yours and you can do whatever you want with her. Tell you what, I'll run along. Why not walk me to the door?"

Fred Baumann laughed and walked a pace behind Petkowski. When they reached the doorway, Petkowski stepped out into the whirling snow, and Baumann followed. Petkowski turned quickly and snarled at him. "You are an asshole, Baumann, and a fucking coward for hitting a woman."

Enraged, Baumann grabbed for Petkowski's shoulder. Petkowski wheeled, grabbed Baumann's wrist and launched the larger man headfirst into a snowdrift. When Baumann got up, sputtering and confused, Petkowski planted his right knee in Baumann's gut. Baumann doubled over and puked at least two cans of beer into the otherwise pristine white snow. A second knee to the face straightened him up and bloodied his nose.

Baumann was dazed and vulnerable. Petkowski slapped and punched him a half dozen times. "I'm not going to give you a ticket, dickhead. It wouldn't fly because you've scared your wife into silence. This time you get off with a warning. Did you like my warning? You made me come all the way out here in this miserable fucking weather for nothing. That does not make me happy."

"You're not allowed to hit me. I'll sue," Baumann said as he spat out blood and tried to keep from retching.

"See any witnesses? Hey, I don't even see Frosty the Snowman." Petkowski slapped him a couple of more times and Baumann began to whimper. Despite his size, Fred Baumann was not a fighter, and for that Petkowski was thankful.

"Besides, you started it by grabbing me and taking a swing at me. You're so much bigger than me, so who'll believe anything else? Hey, you want me to stop?"

"Yes," he whimpered.

"Then leave your wife alone. I'll check back and if I see any new bruises, I'll find you and kick your ass right up between your ears. You understand?"

"Yes."

"Yes what?"

"Yes sir. Yes sir, Officer."

At that moment, Cindy Baumann opened the door and looked at her bloody and dazed husband. She did not appear upset. "What happened?"

"He fell," Petkowski said and held his breath. He shouldn't have done what he'd done. He shouldn't have pounded on her jerk of a husband, regardless of the provocation. He'd let the built-up rage and frustration of the day get to him. People were hungry, hurting, and dying out there, and these idiots couldn't get along with each other for one night in a house full of expensive middle-class comforts. If Cindy Baumann still had feelings for the jerk, and so many abused women inexplicably did for their abusers, his career as a cop was over and he might just spend time in jail. He'd let his frustrations overwhelm him and now he might be in big trouble.

Cindy Baumann nodded solemnly and again permitted a trace of a smile. "He fell? I believe it. There's a lot of that going around, especially if you've been drinking like a fish. He's so sloshed he won't remember much of anything tomorrow."

"Would you believe the snow is actually tapering off?" Wally Wellman said.

Mort Cristman, the young anchor, smiled wanly. He was staring at a window that was covered with snow two thirds of its height. It was almost like being underwater, except that you could see better underwater. "I would no longer believe anything you told me. You are a weatherman and that makes you a congenital liar. Or is it genital liar?"

"No," Wally answered, "lawyers are genital liars because they're such pricks. Hey, I didn't say it was stopping. Like I just said on the phone to the governor—who, by the way, called me and not you—and told her the rate of snowfall has slowed down. It is now no longer a deluge, merely a rotten heavy snowfall. It's like a man who was drowning in fourteen feet of water being told that the water's only twelve feet deep."

Cristman stretched and yawned. They were seated in Wally's cubicle. "Does that mean I can go home now? My mommy gets worried when I'm out after dark and it's almost midnight."

Wally laughed. The kid was beginning to grow on him. "I'll bet you didn't even bring a change of underwear, did you? How about a toothbrush or a razor?"

"Hell no. I had no idea I'd be camping here with you and all the other Scouts. Don't tell me you bought a change?"

"I always keep fresh clothes in my file cabinet," Wally said. "Emergencies are always unexpected. That's why they call them emergencies. Tomorrow I will look fresh and bright, while you will look like road kill."

"At least there's a shower in the men's room," Cristman grumbled. "I won't stink all that badly. Of course, who'd know?"

"I would," said Wally. "By the way, there's a couple of extra toothbrushes in my closet and, if you're real nice, you can have one. A new one."

Cristman yawned again. "Gracias, amigo. So tell me, is it true that you and the governor were once an item?"

Wally sighed. "Once upon a time when the earth was young, I thought that Lauren Landsman and I would spend eternity together. Then she found someone else and the rest is history. Eternity was a lot shorter than I expected."

"And you found someone else, too, Wally. I know about your loss and you know I'm sorry. My mom died when I was eleven and I felt all alone and lost for so long. It took a lot of time to get over it."

"To the extent that you ever do," Wally added softly. "And thanks for the thought. Now I won't charge you for the tooth-brush. However, the toothpaste is extra."

Strange, though, his conversations with Lauren had begun friendly enough and quickly achieved a level of comfortable intimacy that surprised him. During the last days of her life, he and Ellen had discussed his future. She hadn't wanted him to mourn, or go into a shell and feel sorry for himself, which is exactly what he'd done. He'd known it was a betrayal of his promise to her that he would continue to live life to the fullest, but he simply couldn't shake the depression until recently.

His conversations with old flame Lauren Landsman had been a surprising tonic. Better, he knew that Ellen would not complain one bit. He smiled inwardly. Who says a blizzard doesn't have a silver lining? Now if he could only get Cristman a clean change of underwear before no one wanted to sit next to him.

CHAPTER 11

THE TEACHERS AND OTHER ADULTS MAROONED IN PATTON Elementary had started a routine of four hours on duty with the kids and four hours off. The number of children had declined only a little as the parents who were going to be able to pick up their children had done so, and it looked as if they were stuck with themselves and the remainder for the duration, whatever that meant. The teachers made jokes that some parents who could pick up their kids had decided to let the schools provide free babysitting. Even if every student somehow disappeared, and there were those who thought that would be a good idea, there was no way for the teachers to depart. No one's car would be able to navigate through the snow and they'd all heard about the roads blocked by thousands of unmoving cars.

"We're going to be here until spring," Maddy said in mock despair. "At which time someone will find our mummified corpses and we'll make the national news or a National Geographic special. Our fifteen minutes of fame. I hope we get a nice memorial service. I just don't want a school named after me."

"I just hope we get some more toilet paper," sniffed Donna

Harris. "The little assholes are using too much." She giggled at her own bad joke.

Of course, the brandy helped loosen them both up. They were in the principal's office and each had downed a couple of shots in plastic cups. Neither was close to legally drunk, but the brandy, combined with fatigue and stress, had made them a little giddy. It was the first chance they'd had to relax and they were going to seize the moment.

Many of the kids were on their cell phones and talking to family and friends. It looked like the school's prohibition on them had been a waste of time and effort. There were hundreds of the devices along with a smaller number of laptops with webcams throughout the building. Accepting the inevitable, the kids had been told to keep them all charged in case the power went out. Modern batteries had long lives, but would not last forever, especially if the owner was hell bent on talking to everyone he or she had ever known.

Donna took a sip from her cup and smiled. "So when are you going to sleep with Officer Mike?"

Maddy shrugged. "Don't know. Soon. Maybe. Maybe never. It's a big step. I'm just not certain I'm ready for it."

Donna rolled her eyes. "Please don't tell me you're a virgin? I was fifteen when I tried sex for the first time and found that I liked it, really liked it."

Maddy was mildly surprised. She'd always considered Donna to be far more sophisticated and liberated than she, but fifteen? "You make it sound like you've had sex with a lot of guys."

"Define 'a lot.' Actually the first time was the night of the prom my sophomore year and it was with the senior boy who'd taken me. We'd been dating, thought we were in love, and it seemed like the right thing, and, wow, was it. I made him do it to me a second time, which was even better, and he nearly died on the third. After that, there were some other guys, but no one-night stands except for one time my first year teaching when I went to Mexico on Christmas vacation and got drunk and laid by some kid from Los Angeles. That doesn't count, does it?"

"Of course not," Maddy said and took another slow sip. "I've never been to Mexico, but I've heard it's like Vegas—nothing that happens there counts against life."

"That's right. It's a screw free zone. It's also where I got my first tattoo."

Maddy laughed. Donna had a surprising number of tattoos and had to dress carefully to keep some of the more interesting ones covered up. As to herself, she had but two—a small Tudor Rose at the base of her spine and a butterfly just below her navel.

"Then I met my beloved husband and have been faithful to him ever since, although we started having sex on the second date. Now, how about you?"

Maddy took a deep breath. Maybe it finally was time to talk about it. She'd kept it all cooped up in her mind for too long. Not even her parents knew the story. She'd been too embarrassed and ashamed to tell them.

"I was still a virgin when I went to college," she said quietly, hesitantly. "Not a saint, in fact a long ways from one, but still a virgin. Never knew anybody in high school I wanted to do actually go all the way with. Part of the way, yes, even most of the way, but not totally. Some of it was fear of pregnancy, and the rest of it was that I had high standards regarding guys. Funny, but I wasn't all that concerned about AIDS. That stuff happened to other people. Then, towards the middle of my junior year at State, I met Dirk."

"Dirk?" Donna practically shrieked. "There is nobody named Dirk. He had to be joking, right?"

Maddy flushed. "His name was Dirk. I saw it on his passport and his driver's license. He was from Sweden and studying architecture. He was also a slightly older man—a graduate assistant in his mid-twenties—and very sophisticated. At least I thought he was since he was so European. We went out a few times and I decided I was totally in love with him. He had money and a really nice apartment he shared with two other guys, and one night he arranged for his roommates to be out and we had sex."

"How was it with Dirk? Did Dirk have a great dick?"

Despite herself, Maddy laughed. "You are just so evil, Donna. It was the most significant moment of my life and you make fun of it. Shame on you."

And shame on me, Maddy thought, for not realizing just how funny it was. "At any rate, we dated for about a year. His two roommates, Tomas and Joe, were also from Sweden, had local girlfriends, Crystal and Jackie, and we sometimes went on weekend trips. He taught me everything about sex."

"Everything?" Donna asked with a hint of incredulity. "Or just everything you know? Don't tell me that sex with Dirk-Dick meant more than the approved missionary position and possibly included oral sex?"

Maddy smiled. "What can I say? Of course it did. We did anything and everything and I liked it. Loved it. Dirk made it wonderful. My whole life was enchanted."

"Then what went wrong, Maddy?" She had seen the sudden change in Maddy's expression. One second she'd been laughing, but now she looked grim.

"He betrayed me, and in the worst possible way," she said angrily. "I thought we had a long-range relationship with maybe even marriage in the future. I was even thinking about what it would be like living in Sweden, but then it all changed."

Maddy had gone to the apartment on a Saturday night for nothing more than the usual. There would be drinks, some music, and they'd all go to their respective beds with their respective lovers. The roommates were there along with their girlfriends, and there was marijuana, which wasn't unusual, but Maddy didn't smoke any. She didn't trust the stuff, and she didn't want a random test revealing it to the athletic department. She could lose her scholarship and that would be a disaster. Neither she nor her parents had the money to keep her away at school.

Dirk and Maddy went to his bedroom and made love. Afterwards, Dirk stood up and said he had an idea. Still naked, he left the room.

A couple of minutes later, he returned and grabbed her by the wrist. "Come on out and join the party."

She protested for a moment, but the others, also naked, came in and laughingly dragged her out to the living room. She was only mildly upset. They'd all traveled together and there had been some casual intimacy. While Crystal and Jackie had sometimes wandered around nude, the farthest Maddy had gone was wearing only her panties. Athletics and solid Polish genetics had given her by far the best figure, which made Crystal and Jackie jealous. Crystal was a twig, and Jackie needed to lose a little. This moment, she quickly decided, was just another small step in her education as an adult.

Dirk said something to Crystal and she began to kiss and fondle Jackie. The two women asked her to join them and Maddy declined. She was surprised and mildly disgusted. Jackie and Crystal were soon writhing on the floor, moaning and groping at each other while the guys laughed.

"Ever do it with a woman?" Maddy asked Donna.

"No," Donna answered and thought quickly about a sleepover with another girl when she'd been thirteen. They'd touched each other with their eyes closed in order to pretend it was somebody else, but that was all and it had never happened again.

"Me neither," Maddy said and continued her story.

A few more drinks, and Dirk again stood. He was erect and aroused. But, instead of reaching for Maddy, he grabbed Crystal by the hand and pulled her off a gasping Jackie. He led her into the bedroom. Crystal was laughing and unprotesting. "Swap time," Dirk announced.

Tomas grabbed an astonished Maddy and propelled her into another bedroom.

"I started crying," she told Donna. "I said I didn't do things like that. Tomas said I was going to start and that if Dirk could fuck his girlfriend, he could fuck me, and that Joe was going to be next."

By now, even Donna was shocked. "What bastards. What did you do?"

"I wasn't going to let him screw me. I was an athlete, but so was he. I tried to wrestle him away, but he was big and strong and aroused and angry, and obviously felt he deserved me in exchange for Dirk screwing Crystal. He said if I argued, he'd get Joe and they'd force me. I didn't want to get hurt, so I did the next best thing."

"You gave him a blow job, didn't you?"

Tears started flowing down Maddy's face. "No, although I said I would. He may have been stronger and bigger but he was drunk and stoned. When I agreed he relaxed and then I kneed him really hard in the balls. Then I found Dirk and now he was screwing Jackie, and told him I never wanted to see him again. It must have been a weird scene, because we were all still naked and everybody was screaming, including Tomas who was on the floor and couldn't stand up. Dirk told me to get out and that I was a frigid American bitch and that he deserved better than a lower-class loser like me. The others pushed me out of the apartment, still naked, and then threw my clothes out. There were people in that hallway and they saw me and they laughed at me. I knew some of them and I wanted to die. I wanted to find a rock and live under it."

"God," Donna said and took another sip of her drink.

"I got dressed and went to my room. Later I saw a counselor who suggested I see a psychologist, which I did, and she helped a lot, but I still couldn't get over it. At least I wasn't suicidal or anything like that. I talked to the police, but a woman cop told me it was unlikely I could prove rape. She said five people would testify that I consented to everything and besides it would become public record, so I dropped the idea. I don't think she was really all that interested in pursuing it. Dirk and his buddies told everyone that I liked group sex, so I had a lot of interesting date offers. I just stopped going out until I was out of school."

She wiped the tears from her eyes and took a swallow of the brandy. "I ran into Crystal a few weeks later, and she told me that she and Jackie were always having sex with Dirk, and nobody seemed to mind so what the hell was my problem. I wanted to punch her lights out, but she was so thin I was afraid I'd break her. God, I wanted to, though."

"I'll bet."

Maddy sighed. It did feel better to have told Donna. "So I gave up any thoughts of a love life and concentrated on grades and volleyball. When I tore up the ligament in my right knee it killed me a second time because I really thought I had pro or Olympic potential. After all, I'd been honorable mention Big Ten. Later, my coach said I should stop feeling sorry for myself because I really wasn't all that good. Great coaching, huh? At any rate, I focused on classes and wound up with a great grade point average when I graduated. And that helped me get a job in Sheridan, which meant the whole ordeal hadn't been a total waste."

"And you've never dated since then? I'm not too sure I blame you, at least for slowing down, but not all men are pricks like Dirk and his sadistic little chums."

"I've dated some guys since I graduated, but I've never allowed anyone to get close to me. Of course, I never found anyone I wanted to get close to me. That is, not until Mike and I'm still surprised that it's happened."

"And now you want to get up close and personal with him like you've never been since Dick the Prick, I mean Dirk."

Maddy laughed. "That's right. Dirk is back in Sweden and I hope he freezes to death. Or at least his balls freeze off. Tomas is in Europe as well, and I don't know what happened to Joe. Crystal is a nurse in Chicago, and Jackie is an accountant with GM, and lives a few miles from here. Jackie called me once to tell me how sorry she was and how foolish they had all been and how she'd like to forget it. Of course, she's getting married to some older guy lawyer who's thinking of running for Congress, and she really would appreciate it if I didn't tell anybody about the weekend sex and marijuana parties. I told her my lips were sealed."

Maddy took another swallow. "Everybody always thought of me as an all-American girl. I was always so healthy, so intellectually and emotionally well rounded it was disgusting. I was wholesome, although, thank God, no one ever called me perky. I would have belted them. I showed them all, didn't I? I screwed up royally."

Donna checked her cup. It was empty. She poured them both a little more brandy. They would have to ration the bottle or they'd be out of liquor before the school ran out of toilet paper.

"So are you really over it?"

"Yes," Maddy said, finally meaning it. She was crying again, but this time it was in relief. In retrospect it had been stupid on her part to let it dominate her life for so long. She'd known that, but acting on it was a different matter. Telling Donna was the smartest thing she'd done in a long while. Now, should she tell Mike? No, she decided. Not yet, but she would. He deserved to know.

Donna kicked back another swallow and looked at Maddy intently. "What they did to you was a rotten, shitty thing. I'm glad you're not thinking of getting even with Jackie. I think Dirk and his boys used her as much as they used you."

"Agreed."

"What have you told Mike?"

"Nothing. He knows there was something that happened back in college, but I think he assumes it was date rape. Actually, in a strange sort of way, it was. He's very understanding and helpful, but I'm not ready yet to admit that I was somebody's sex toy. But for Mike I will be ready."

"Good," Donna smiled. "Now, is there any other way I can help you?"

"Yes," said Maddy, laughing while tears still streamed down her face. "Get the hell out of here and bring in Mike. I want to get my hands on his tight hard butt and I want it now."

"Stan, please tell me you didn't beat up that nice citizen?" Mike asked in a worried tone of voice. As before, they were in DiMona's office where they had some privacy. Stan was purging himself of the Baumann incident and looked distraught.

"I defended myself, Mike. He grabbed me and took a swing. I was all alone and had to protect myself."

Mike shook his head. It was so easy to sue and cry "police brutality." A few lawyers seemed to salivate at the prospect and too many cities and insurance companies were willing to roll over and pay them whether it was justified or not. Of course, it often resulted in a police officer's career being ruined, but they didn't care.

"How many times did you defend yourself?"

"Uh, I sort of lost count, Mike. I maybe hit him eight or ten times before he fell in the snowbank."

"Jesus, Stan, that goes beyond defending yourself. That's an ass-kicking. You got any bruises on you to show that he hurt you?"

Stan thought quickly. "No, but I could arrange for some if you'd like." Stan's anger flared. "Hell, where is it written that my actions aren't justified unless he hurts me first? What level of pain and injury do I have to take before I can strike back? None, Mike. He grabbed me and took a punch at me. Like it's my fault he didn't connect? If he had, he's big enough that he could have knocked me silly and worked me over and then left my Polish ass in the snowdrift. And it's not my fault that I had to make the run alone, damn it."

Petkowski had a point. Domestic violence disputes were nasty and there was always the potential for escalation to lethal violence. Petkowski should not have been sent out alone. He should not have punched out the Baumann guy. Why hadn't he used a Taser? Hell, it should not be snowing so heavily and they shouldn't have a lush for a chief.

But what else could they do? Maybe they should announce that they weren't going to make domestic dispute runs in the first place. Sure, and a woman gets beaten up, or maybe pulls out a gun or a meat cleaver and solves the problem her own way. Then, of course, there would be even more recriminations and lawsuits. They had to respond to every call as best they could, and if the Sheridan Police Department was spread so thin that only one man was available, then so be it.

"All right," Mike said, "work on a report and file it before Baumann does it first."

"His wife will back me up."

Mike shook his head in disbelief. "Aw shit, Stan, they're probably kissing and in the sack making up right now. How many times have the cops been to their house and nothing ever happens? The Baumanns are regulars. Regular idiots, that is."

Stan flushed. "This time it's different. She's going to dump him and get a divorce."

Mike now thought he understood. Stan Petkowski had feelings for the woman. Stan had a crush on her. "And then you, the cop in shining armor, or at least a shining badge, will show up and sweep her off her feet?"

"Something like that," Stan smiled weakly. "What do you think? How does Sir Stanley the Cop sound?"

"I think the snow's seeped into your brain, but I wish you luck."

Petkowski was going to make a further comment, but he was interrupted by Mayor Carter, who barged into the room. "I need you guys right away. There's some damn reporter wandering around and taking pictures. She's got a TV camera and she's interviewing everybody."

"What would you like me to do about her, sir?" Mike asked calmly. "To the best of my knowledge, city hall and the police station are public property and stopping a reporter is difficult under the best of circumstances. The snow is a definite news story as are the refugees in the buildings."

"You don't understand, Stuart, that broad has been into Chief Bench's office. She tried to interview him, but he's drunk and incoherent. I want you to stop her and get that tape from her before we're made to look like fools."

Tower and Raines dragged the numb and unresisting Traci down the stairs. Her mind was an incoherent whirl. How had they found her? How had they known she was in the house? As they hustled her past the foyer and into the living room, she saw why. Her purse was wide open and on the table where she'd left it. Her keys were beside it. She groaned slightly at the injustice of it, but neither man heard her.

Raines had Tower sit her on the couch. Raines sat across from her and Tower beside her. His powerful arm easily restrained her.

"Now this is interesting," Raines said as he pawed through her purse. "Your name is Traci Lawford and, according to your driver's license, you're thirty-four years old. You wear a ring, so you're married. Where's your husband, Traci?"

Her mind raced. "He's down the street and he'll be back in a little while. He's a cop."

Raines leaned forward and slapped her hard across the face. Lights flashed in front of her eyes and she would have fallen over, but Tower held her firmly in place.

"Don't lie. Nobody's down the street. Now, where is he?"

Traci licked blood from her lip. Her face burned from the slap. "He's in Indianapolis."

"Better," Raines said. "Now, are you afraid we're going to kill you?"

She began to whimper. "Yes."

"Well, we're not going to kill you, at least not unless it's absolutely necessary. If things got ugly, you'd have a lot more value as a hostage than as a corpse, so, if you don't fuck up, you stay alive. The cops doubtless know who we are and they are looking very hard for us because we already killed some people. However, if you don't cooperate, or if you try something stupid like escaping, we will hurt you. We will hurt you so badly you will wish we had killed you. Understand?"

She started to nod, and Raines slapped her again. This time she did fall on the floor. Raines nodded to Tower, who took out a large military-style knife he'd taken from the house with all the weapons. The short, powerful man grabbed Traci by her hair, and she screamed in pain and fear as he yanked her to a standing position. He held the knife under her chin, and then in front of her right eye, the blade almost touching it. Her eyes focused on it in stark terror. She could almost see it penetrating her eyeball.

"First test, Traci," Raines said. "You don't move. You don't move at all. A quarter of an inch and you're blind in that eye. Understand?"

She whimpered a yes as Tower slowly removed the knife, unsure as to whether the sound she made constituted moving. It didn't.

Tower used the knife with consummate skill, slicing her clothes off her body. In seconds, she was naked with pieces of cloth at her feet. She wanted to cover herself with her hands, but she willed herself to stand still, perfectly still, just as she'd been commanded. She didn't even move when her bladder emptied. Tower and Raines thought it was funny.

"Not bad," Raines said, "a little skinny, but not bad. You'd think a woman your age would have bought better boobs for yourself. I understand they sell them on Amazon. Tell me, Traci, do you love your husband?"

"Yes," she said, her voice a half cry and whimper.

"Good, 'cause if you don't cooperate, my friend here will cut small pieces out of your face and your tits and your pussy so that your husband and anyone else will puke when they see you. Then my friend'll take a cigarette lighter to you and you'll look like one big scar. You'll be alive, but you'll be blind and deaf and you won't have any lips or tongue or lots of other things. You'll be a walking freak show. But if you work with us, you won't get hurt and you might even have a good time. Again, do you understand?"

"Yes."

"Good. Now tell me, do you want to fuck me?"

Her eyes widened with shock at the question, then half closed and a tear ran down her cheek. "Yes. I want to fuck you."

"How much?"

She knew what she was supposed to say. "Very much. More than anything in the world."

Raines laughed. He was getting aroused. "Excellent, because that's exactly what's going to happen. First me, and then my friend with the knife. Then we'll start all over again. First, though, clean up that piss on the floor."

911 supervisor Thea Hamilton stuck her head in Mike's office. "You're not going to believe this, Mike."

"What kind of silly call did you get now?"

"Not a call. I've got a lady right here who wants to go home. She stopped into the call center to tell me that, since, in her opinion, she has an emergency and we're supposed to be good at that stuff."

"And let me guess," Mike grinned, "you respectfully disagreed with her."

"Respectfully my ass," she said. "I threw her out. You know what she wanted? She wanted us to take her home so she could take care of her dog. And it's a poodle, too. God, I hate poodles."

"I'll keep that in mind the next time I get a dog."

"She fed the damn thing this morning before she left for work, so it won't starve to death, and it's got a bowl full of water, but she's afraid the damn thing will pee all over her carpets. She says it has a weak bladder. Hell, my husband has a weak bladder, but I trust him to find someplace like a toilet."

"Did it ever occur to you that dogs can't use a toilet?" Mike said without even trying to stifle a grin.

"Of course, and, to tell the truth, my husband sometimes misses, too. But I'm not going to put anybody in danger by calling this an emergency. Her little FiFi, or Foo-Foo, or Fart-Fart can take his own chances. I told her she could leave if she felt that strongly and—know what? She actually started out in the snow. I had to get a policewoman to reason with her and keep her inside. Can we ticket someone for stupidity?"

Mike shook his head. "We'd have to ticket everyone, I'm afraid." Why was he getting another one of Thea's complaints? Because DiMona was out of town and the chief was out of this world, that's why.

"War is hell, Thea."

"Screw you, Mike."

"Stoner" Wilson had been amazed when one of the teachers had agreed with his request to go to the library and study. She must have been new or a sub. The older teachers knew that he hadn't studied in years and that his nickname came from the fact that he was always stoned. Even more than that, he was the main source of marijuana and other drugs for the students, and he even had a couple of teachers as part of his steadily growing clientele.

Stoner was sick and tired of watching people pretend that nothing was happening or going to the other extreme and totally freaking out because of the storm. He just wanted some privacy where he and his buddies could smoke some weed. Normally they did it in their cars during lunch and after school, but their cars had disappeared, transported up to the starship *Enterprise* in puffs of white snow. He giggled. That was really funny.

Red and Gus, his buddies and fellow seniors, didn't get the joke. They were too wasted to think, not that they ever thought much anyhow. In return for free marijuana, they ran errands, made deliveries, collected money, and had even used their muscle to collect on bad debts.

Stoner had begun to wonder if the three of them would be able to set up business after they graduated this spring. He giggled again as he realized what a joke graduation would be. The school was going to push him out the door whether he was prepared or not. He dimly recalled some advisor saying that he'd better start studying if he wanted to get into college. College? Hell, he wasn't certain he could spell the word. What he liked to do along with smoking stuff was make money and maybe have some sweet little thing trade her body or at least her lips on his toy in return for a joint. Lately, he'd begun branching out and offering other more powerful drugs, especially prescription drugs, and he thought soon he could get his hands on heroin.

Still, a community college would have to accept him, even though he could barely read. There were those who felt that he should have been held back at several points but no teachers wanted him, no administrator wanted the extra expense. Ready or not, he and his buddies were going to leave Sheridan High School this June.

Man, he thought, some parents would really be shocked at what their precious little daughters were capable of, especially the giggly ones in middle school. He understood that much of what he was doing was statutory rape, but he couldn't care less. He was the gingerbread man, and catch me if you can. But nobody was going to catch him. Someday the snow would end and he'd have to go back to the real world. For now it was as good as good gets.

Then the power went out.

CHAPTER 12

MADDY WAS AWAKENED FROM A RESTLESS SLUMBER BY THE SOUND of high-pitched, frightened voices. She sat upright and was suddenly aware that the office was dark. "What the hell?" she said and then noted that Donna Harris had left the room and that the door to the office was open. The hallway was dark as well.

The power had finally gone out. *That's just what we need*, she thought as she ran down the hallway to the gym where the children, now frightened and crying, were being comforted by the teachers. Or at least the teachers were trying to comfort them.

Then, as her eyes became accustomed to the dark, she realized it wasn't all that bad. The snow outside was doing a wonderful job of reflecting what little light there was.

After a few moments, the children calmed down. Some were still scared, but weren't going to admit it in front of all the others. Even the small ones stopped crying.

She sat by Donna and began to tease some of the children into believing that nothing was wrong. She felt a chill in the air and realized that the furnace, her best friend when she was drying off, wasn't working. Of course not. The blower was run by electricity.

Mr. Wilson, the maintenance man, sat down beside Donna, close enough for Maddy to hear. "It's not just us," he said. "Street lights and everything else is out all down the street."

"What do we have in the way of emergency stuff?" Donna asked.

"Not much. No generator or backup lights, if that's what you're thinking of. It was proposed but never put into the budget. Too expensive. There are a few lights, but not very many and none in the classrooms. Nobody ever planned for a blackout because nobody's supposed to be here at night. If the power was to go out during a PTG meeting, everybody was supposed to go home. I've got a flashlight and some spare batteries, and a box of candles, but that's it."

"And no heat," Maddy injected.

"That's right, and it's likely to be off for a long time. Technically, the furnace is on, but the blowers can't circulate hot air without electricity. Also, we've got no land line phones until I can rig up something that bypasses the computer system that now ain't working either. I've got an old piece of crap phone in my office that maybe I can plug into the jack."

"Do it," Donna said. "Of course, we can't charge up cell phones any more so we're really going to ration calls." She looked directly at Maddy and smiled when she said that.

"Don't worry, I'll ration my already inadequate love life on behalf of Patton Elementary," Maddy said with mock bitterness. "We've got to make sure the kids do so as well."

"We'll both go from room to room and tell them," Donna said. "And maybe we'll have to confiscate phones if things become tight. I've got a charger in my car that we could run off the battery, but who knows where my car is."

"Same here," said Maddy.

"What about food?" Donna asked. "We don't have that much left and not much that requires cooking, do we? Oh yeah, this means the freezer and refrigerator are off. Not a problem. If we have to, we can chill milk and stuff outside."

"Or bring snow inside," Wilson suggested and Donna agreed it made more sense to do it that way. The abundant snow also meant they wouldn't have to worry about going thirsty if the water stopped flowing. She didn't think it would, but she didn't know that much about how the utilities operated. Heck, they just worked. Lights went on when you flipped the switch and nasty stuff went away when you flushed a toilet. She'd never thought about the mechanics of public utilities and didn't want to have to start now.

"I guess we use body heat for warmth," Maddy said and the others nodded. They would gather everyone on the mats in the gym and keep them close together. Those inside the group would rotate periodically with those on the outside. Of course, a lot of kids would still want to run around and that would keep them warm until they wanted to sleep.

"It'll work," Wilson said. "Some kids'll be uncomfortable, but there's nothing else we can do. Nobody'll freeze to death. If everybody stays together, I doubt it will go below fifty degrees in here. Heck, if we have to, we can rotate them in and out of the furnace room. It'll still be warm."

Maddy became aware that half a dozen fourth and fifth graders, boys and girls, were standing in front of them in the darkened hallway.

"Yes, kids. What do you want?"

A pretty little girl with blonde hair smiled sweetly. "Can we tell ghost stories?"

Mike found the television reporter Carter was worried about talking to an older couple who were trying to sleep on the floor of the library. Their annoyance was tempered by the possibility that they might be on television. Of course, they hadn't figured out that they wouldn't be home to see themselves if they were.

The reporter was young, blonde, attractive in a too-thin sort of way, and aggressive. She had a small video camera and appeared to be working alone. He thought he recognized her as a street reporter from the local ABC affiliate.

He went to her and introduced himself. Her name was Sandy. "I've got to ask how you got here." Mike queried. He hadn't seen her in the building before, not that it meant anything.

"Snowmobile," she said, "just like everyone else who wants to move around. Got my own and drove myself in."

"Okay, why?"

She smiled coldly. "Hey, I'm the reporter and I ask the questions."

"And I'm a cop and I do it too."

"Fair enough," she admitted grudgingly. Reporters had two choices—work with cops or work around them. "With" was so much easier. "I live a little ways from here and got a call that it might be interesting to interview people who are stranded here."

"And was it?"

Sandy smiled again, still without warmth. "Yes, and there's no way I'm going to give you the tape of that drunken lout of a police chief sprawled on his desk and babbling incoherently while his city goes down the toilet."

Mike chuckled. "I never asked and never thought you'd give it to me if I did."

"Of course you didn't," she said and this time there was warmth behind the smile. Ground rules had been established. "Let me guess, though. Someone, probably the mayor, since the chief's too drunk to talk, told you to get the tape and now you can tell your boss that you tried, but your only option was to use force, and that wouldn't work since there's such a thing as freedom of the press."

"Close enough. Are you going to stick around until he sobers up so you can do a before and after?"

"Nope, I'm leaving in a few minutes so I can put this on my computer and send it to the station. The quality won't be good, but it'll work."

"You'll be ruining a good man."

Sandy laughed. "If he's so damned good, why's he drunk as a skunk during the middle of this crisis? He should be leading the troops instead of sucking on a bottle of schnapps. And guess what? I don't think you're the slightest bit sincere when you say he's a good man. A lot of people in other towns think he's a joke, only nobody's laughing. I don't think it would break your heart at all if he got canned."

With that, she turned and walked away. Mike had known she wouldn't give up the tape, and he'd been correct—he'd made the attempt to stop her and Mayor Carter would have to live with it. If Carter didn't like it, well screw him.

But why had this Sandy reporter chosen Sheridan? Just like the line in *Casablanca* regarding all the gin joints, why pick Sheridan as a place to do interviews when there were so many other towns in the area? She'd said she lived close by, but was that a good enough reason? There were a lot of communities "close by," depending on how you defined the term. According to the mayor, Sandy had made a bee-line for Chief Bench's office, just as if she'd known what she'd find. How had she known?

The riot began in ladies' clothing and quickly spilled over into housewares. At first it was nothing more than a pushing match between several middle-aged couples over who was taking up too much floor space. People were packed closely and not every inch of floor was covered by carpeting. Thin though it was, commercial carpeting was better than tile, and parents were especially concerned about their children. Power was out and that had added to the cumulative stress levels as the emergency lighting was very dim. To add to the problem, the vast store was little more than a giant, uninsulated box and it was getting cold real fast.

Fighting quickly spread as pent-up frustrations were unleashed and flailing arms took in other families, and people fought back to protect their children and spouses.

By the time an exhausted Tyler Holcomb got to the fighting with two of his four security guards, at least thirty people were involved, although most of it was nothing more than pushing and shoving punctuated with obscenities. One person lay on the floor, apparently unconscious, and blood flowed freely from a cut on his scalp. Still, Tyler thought he could bring things under control. He silently thanked the fact that Sampson's did not sell rifles or pistols.

A primal scream pierced the gloom and a man lurched from the mob with blood running from his large belly. "I've been stabbed," he screamed.

With only the emergency lights on, the effect was like a horror movie. Which, Tyler realized, it actually was, only it was real and not a movie.

One of his guards grabbed the man and headed him towards the pharmacy section. Good move, Tyler thought. A pharmacist was on duty and ought to be able to do something for the man. Someone else dragged the unconscious man out of harm's way and started trying to revive him.

The stabbing seemed to shock the brawlers, who stood frozen. All of a sudden, what had been a turf fight had turned potentially deadly, and nobody wanted to go that far.

With wry amusement, Tyler Holcomb noted that all the participants were white. No one was ever going to call it a race riot. His people weren't going to be blamed for anything this time.

Then he saw the gun and his heart skipped. A tall, rangy white man in blue jeans and a hoodie sweatshirt had a pistol in his hand. Oh Jesus, Tyler thought.

"Police," the man said and Tyler nearly fainted in relief. A badge was in the man's other hand. "Just everybody sit down and we'll sort this all out."

Holcomb went to the cop and introduced himself. The officer's name was Hardy. He was off duty and had been shopping for a birthday present for his wife when he'd gotten stuck in the mess on MacArthur. He smiled grimly and walked through and disarmed everyone in the now thoroughly cowed groups. There were a number of knives, some of which had come from the kitchen goods section, and a couple of handguns. The gun owners insisted they had the necessary permits and the right to carry them, but Officer Hardy wasn't in a mood to listen. He confiscated the weapons and told the owners they could pick them up when they left the store. He added that if they didn't like that, they could leave right now and freeze to death.

The man who'd done the stabbing was identified and hustled off to the store's offices, while his wife sobbed in disbelief that this could be happening to nice people like themselves. She held a small child tightly to her body, and the child was also crying. Sheridan police would come, but not for a while. Maybe they would take her husband in and maybe they wouldn't.

The off-duty cop said there might be other cops in the store and volunteered to find them. In a little while he came back with four men and a woman, all police officers, and all from other cities. It didn't matter. They'd be happy to help keep order in Sampson's. After all, several of them had their families with them.

Tyler sighed in relief. However, he couldn't help but wonder why he hadn't thought to check for cops in the store in the first place. Management training hadn't covered this sort of contingency. He decided to canvass the crowd for medical specialists. With luck, they might have a doctor in the building, or a nurse. Hell, he'd settle for a veterinarian.

A clerk from pharmacy came over with a note. The stab wound was more like a slash into skin and fat, and nothing vital had been touched. They were going to treat it with disinfectant and butterfly bandages that they had in stock. The victim was embarrassed that he'd gotten into the mess and relieved that he was going to live. He did not want to press charges. Also, the unconscious man was awake and alert and had no idea who'd conked him. Tyler thought he really did know and was confident that it was the guy who'd been stabbed. Paybacks are hell, he thought.

Help me make it through the night, Tyler mused, and then realized it was a line from a song. By whom and from where, he was too tired to remember. He didn't care. He just wanted to get the hell out of this place. Why hadn't he done something less dramatic and dangerous with his life, like joining the Army's Special Forces?

Her mouth hurt where her teeth had been loosened, and her nose throbbed. She felt dirty and she was alone. Cindy Thomason wanted to go home. She wanted a shower and she was afraid that her period was going to start from all the stress she was enduring. She wanted the accident to go away. She was sorry she'd ever taken her brother's Corvette. She didn't want to see her boyfriend, Boyd. He'd urged her to take the car because it would be neat to drive around after school. What an asshole. Then she wondered which of them deserved the title more.

"I'm in so much trouble," she complained softly. A woman sitting beside her and also leaning against the wall heard her and smiled. It was far too late to offer advice. The woman had said that she thought that Cindy was a spoiled brat.

Cindy was also hungry. It struck her as odd that a city hall and police station would have nothing to eat. The vending machines were long empty, but there was a rumor that food from local restaurants would soon be arriving. It wasn't helping at the moment. Her stomach growled again.

Cindy was spoiled, not totally stupid. She knew that her problems were her own doing, and that her mild pangs of hunger were nothing compared with the gaunt and starving creatures she sometimes saw on television from Somalia, or India. Still, she was a sixteen-year-old kid with a broken nose and loose teeth and she wanted to go home, even though it meant facing some really ugly music.

She took her cell phone from her purse. Crap. The battery was getting low and the charger was in the car, which was buried under a mountain of snow on MacArthur. She'd looked out a window a few minutes earlier and what used to be the highway was barely visible. Still, she felt she had to do something, anything, a lament she'd heard so many older people make.

First, she swallowed her pride and tried calling her boyfriend. There was no answer. She could only conclude that neither Boyd nor his parents had made it home. *What a surprise,* she thought as she looked around at all the people in the hallways with her. An old lady said it reminded her of the London Blitz, whatever that was. She thought she remembered a rock group by that name.

That left her family. Her mother had been home when she'd called earlier, and Dear Mom let it be known that she was totally pissed at Cindy for having wrecked the car and for being stuck in a police station. Cindy knew she was being unfair about Mom. She knew her mother was genuinely concerned and frankly relieved that she was safe. Hey, how much safer could she be than in a police station surrounded by cops, and with a face so swollen and bloated that no one would even think of trying to hit on her.

As the phone rang, she hoped her brother wouldn't answer. Of course, he should be safe and far away at Michigan State in East Lansing where he'd be drinking beer or pretending to study. A sleepy voice answered. It was her father.

"Dad, you made it home!" she said with delight.

"Kind of looks like it, princess." He yawned. It was the middle of the night.

"Why didn't you call me?"

"You didn't have your phone on. Check your messages."

"Oh. I kept it off because I'm low on battery."

"So am I, kid," her father laughed, and the familiar sound warmed her. "I had a devil of a time making it in. Had to walk the last mile or so. So, to what do I owe the honor of this call?"

"I want to come home. I'm hurt and I'm ugly."

"Aren't they caring for you?" he asked with sudden concern. Her mother had told him about her predicament and he too had come to the conclusion that she was as safe at the police station as anywhere on the earth.

Cindy saw her opening and jumped in. "My face hurts and I haven't seen a doctor, and I'm hungry. There's no food. And now some cop is talking about jailing me for endangering another cop and causing that big tie-up. It wasn't my fault, Dad. I'll be put in a cell, Daddy, with hookers and drug addicts and lesbians."

"The hell you will," he snarled. "You just hang on there and I'll figure out a way to get to you."

Cindy realized she was crying and not faking it. She desperately wanted to go home. So what if she lied just a little.

Lauren Landsman, Governor of the State of Michigan, stared at the men gathered around the table. They were Brigadier General John Soames of the Michigan National Guard, and Dennis Consiglio, Commander of the Michigan State Police. TV6 Weatherman Wally Wellman was represented through a speaker phone.

"Wally, are you there?"

"Yes, Governor, and at your disposal." Wally's voice came through tinny and nasal, but she grinned at the familiar inflections.

And how considerate and professional of him to not call her by her first name. "Do you still speak for the consortium of weather experts in the area?"

"I believe so. I've been speaking with them fairly regularly and I believe we're all on the same page for once."

This was essentially the truth. Confronted with the reality and magnitude of the natural disaster that was still developing, genuine attempts were being made to share knowledge in the hope that some sense could be made from the arrival of the huge storm. Wally had been selected as their spokesperson because he had been so right and because he knew the governor. Still, there were a couple meteorologists who wouldn't mind if he fell flat on his face.

Lauren stole a glance at a large video screen on the wall. It was a satellite view from the Weather Channel feed and showed the snow line running over southeastern Michigan as a white crescent that started in Ohio and ran northeast into Ontario. Of course, both Ohio and Indiana, along with Ontario, were experiencing their own share of extreme weather, but she was the governor of Michigan, not anywhere else.

"So what's the prognosis, Wally?"

Wally's voice came through clearly. "Believe it or not, the rate of snow does seem to be diminishing. However, it is still extremely heavy and being compounded by fifteen- to twenty-mile-an-hour winds that are whipping up what is already on the ground and causing serious drifting. We've had reports of drifts almost ten feet high, if you can believe it."

"Just for the heck of it, Wally, about how much snow has fallen?" Lauren asked, knowing that the exact depth was almost irrelevant. At a point, all that mattered was that a huge amount of snow was on the ground and still more was coming.

"Officially, thirty-eight inches, but a lot of places have received a lot more. Even though the snow front is a relatively narrow band, it still covers quite an area."

The governor looked again at the weather map on the television. The satellite photo showed the snow line as a clearly delineated white streak across her state. It looked about fifty miles wide. To the north, where she was, the skies were cloudy, but they'd get no snow. South of the snow band, there was rain and flooding, but, again, no snow. The scene switched to a closer-in radar view that overlay towns and major roads. All were covered in a blanket of brilliant white. The sophisticated radar could show particular streets and key locations, but what was the point? Everything was in the snow field.

"So, Wally, for one million dollars, when will it stop?"

"Within twenty-four to thirty-six hours would be my educated guess," Wally answered. "Like I said, the storm is weakening and will continue to weaken. Unfortunately, the cold front coming from the north has also weakened. It's like two heavyweights that have punched each other out and still achieved no advantage. As I said, the snowfall rate has diminished slightly, but not enough that it's apparent to anybody stuck in it."

"And how much more snow?" Lauren asked.

"At least another two feet."

"Jesus Christ," General Soames blurted. "Sorry, Governor."

"No problem," she said. "Wally, is two feet a maximum estimate?"

There was a pause. "Governor, do you realize you want firm estimates from people who didn't even think it was going to snow in the first place? That's almost funny. No, two feet is a minimum. My guess is at least a foot more than that."

"Mr. Wellman, this is General Soames interrupting again. I appreciate your caution after everyone got burned in the first place, but that raises a point. How come nobody saw it coming?"

"Because we deal with what we know and develop probabilities from it, General. We've watched literally scores of storms like this one come north and head east without ever a flake of snow falling up here. Therefore, in our collective wisdom it was determined that what had happened in the past was likely to happen again. There was a margin of error, just like there is in political forecasting, but nobody took it seriously. Even if we did, what would we have said? That there was a one in a hundred chance of a major storm clobbering us? Who would have paid any attention to that? I said something like that a little while back and got reamed by my manager for not being upbeat. It's like when we say there's a thirty percent chance of rain. That also means there's a seventy percent chance it won't. Hell, is the sky partly cloudy or partly sunny? Choose your poison. As much as we'd like to believe that weather forecasting is a science, it's still very much of an art."

"So what made this storm deviate from the norm?" Lauren asked.

"Who knows? Maybe the clouds were thicker than we thought, and that made them stronger. Maybe a herd of cows in a field all farted methane at the same time or maybe some butterfly got squished and all that caused a deflection in the course of the storm that multiplied as it went. Frankly, we may never know and, worse for us forecasters, it may never happen again. This may be nothing more than a mindless aberration to remind us that we're not in charge. Stop me, I'm starting to preach. Next I'll start lecturing on chaos theory. People are going to want scapegoats and I wish them good luck finding one."

Lauren grinned. "Go back to bed, Wally, or try to stop the cows from farting. We'll have dinner together after we dig you out. That is, if we can find you."

When the line disconnected, she turned to the two men. "All right, what now?"

Soames spoke first. "I've got several thousand National Guard people with tanks, armored personnel carriers, trucks, and plows trying to work their way down the major roads. It's slow and tedious and the snow keeps covering up the path behind us."

"Same here," said Consiglio. "We've contacted a number of civilian construction firms and other companies that have heavy equipment, and they're coming in, but getting them to the roads in the first place is a problem. We're all making progress, but it is so damned slow. Even when it stops, it'll take forever to clear."

"Have you found any more, uh, casualties?" Lauren said, thinking of the family dead in a car in Sheridan.

Both men nodded and Consiglio spoke, "Sadly, yes. An older couple was found frozen to death and people in at least half a dozen other cars and trucks have suffocated."

Lauren sighed. "The mayor of Detroit was on the phone a few minutes ago. He was hysterical and I don't blame him. Hundreds of fires are raging out of control in Detroit. What can we do for him?"

Soames and Consiglio looked at each other. In older cities like Detroit, many of the homes were within spitting distance of each other. A fire in one could—would—easily spread to its neighbors and continue to devour buildings until either stopped by the fire department, or by fire breaks. Fortunately, so many abandoned houses in Detroit had been torn down that there were a number of such fire breaks. This was no consolation to people whose homes were being destroyed by fire.

"Not much," Consiglio said and Soames nodded. "They're still on their own and likely to stay that way."

Lauren Landsman's stomach tightened at the response, even

though it was what she'd expected. At least a hundred and fifty people were known dead from the storm and cities were being destroyed. And there wasn't a damned thing she could do.

Like many of Sheridan's homeowners, Tim Cassidy had bought a gas-fueled generator to power essential items like the furnace and freezer if his electricity should ever fail. The utilities in his subdivision were underground, but they had to be above ground elsewhere in order to feed into the sub, and that's where the problems would occur and leave him stranded. In a previous house he'd lost electricity for a week and everything in his freezer and refrigerator had thawed and gone bad. It had cost him hundreds of dollars, and since his insurance deductible was higher than his loss, he'd had to pay for everything.

Thus, when the storm knocked out the electricity, he felt a sort of vindication. He fueled up the generator and turned it on, after prudently turning off the main circuit breakers to the house in case the electricity should unexpectedly come back. Fat chance of that, he thought, and went back inside. At least his furnace would run and his family would be warm. If he didn't open his freezer and refrigerator, his food should be safe for a while. He also kept his garage door open for ventilation.

No one ever found out what went wrong. The most likely villain was a loose connection that caused a spark that ignited some leaked fuel. For a short while, only the leaking fuel burned and easily could have been put out if somebody had been there and seen it. But Tim had been satisfied that everything was okay and had gone inside.

The generator's tank exploded with a roar, sending flaming gas over everything in the garage, and that included two cars and a couple of five-gallon cans filled with gas and kerosene. The cans went up quickly while the cars burned.

Tim Cassidy responded immediately upon hearing the roar of the explosion. He opened the door to the garage and was thrown back by the wall of flames that was feeding on his garage and which craved the new source of oxygen his opening the door provided.

"Out!" he screamed as he picked himself up and slammed the

door shut. He checked himself over. Other than some singeing and a shoulder that wasn't working right, he was okay. His wife and two kids grabbed coats and ran out the back door. The front was too close to the burning garage. Cassidy grabbed his cell phone and called 911. It was all he could do. He hoped the fire department would arrive soon. As he stood outside and watched his beautiful home burn, he realized that there were no tracks of any kind in his street, and that drifts were up to his head.

Fast food places tend to congregate together. Not only is it good marketing in that a customer has a number of choices, but all of them have similar profiles when it comes to an ideal location, high visibility and good traffic flow being among the most important.

Along MacArthur a half mile north of the City Hall campus, there was a row of such outlets. McDonald's, Wendy's, Burger King, Taco Bell, and Pizza Hut all peacefully coexisted in a brightly colored array of buildings. The parking lots were adjacent and connecting; thus facilitating those family outings where one child (or parent) wanted a beef burrito while another wanted a Big Mac. Only a little farther down Panera Bread, Starbucks, and Tim Horton lurked.

Before the snow started, the restaurants were all geared up for a typical busy Monday lunch. Students from the schools who thought that fast food was better than cafeteria barf and business people and other workers with limited lunch time would soon be lining up at the counters and the drive-ins in a rush that was a daily challenge to handle. Parents with little kids who thought that a Happy Meal was a culinary adventure would complete the scene. It was organized chaos that was repeated every day and made the owner-franchisees a ton of money.

But not today. It soon became apparent that the only people in the stores would be the employees. Fred Halavi, an immigrant who'd arrived from Lebanon ten years earlier, owned and managed the Burger King. It offended him that so much food would go to waste. Although he was now a U. S. citizen and quite prosperous, he would never forget the days of his youth when food was scarce and malnutrition common. He recalled his mother rooting through Beirut's garbage cans for leftovers that hadn't rotted too badly. Luckily, the money from other relatives already in America rescued them and delivered them to the land of plenty. Where the Halavi family had worked hard and thrived.

He glanced at the two older women who'd shown up for work. They were middle-age plus housewives with grown children who liked to make a little money on the side while their husbands were at work. They were ten times more dependable and hard-working than the high school kids who worked the afternoons and evenings, and sometimes only if they felt like it.

"Now what, ladies?" he said affably. He considered the ladies his aunts, not his employees. He could talk to the women like adults and equals, not like the kids. Sometimes kids mocked him for his accent, although, he had to admit, not all of them. Many of the kids were real nice; it was just that they didn't have much life experience. Certainly, they'd never rooted through garbage for their daily bread. If this snow was going to precipitate the crises he expected, kids would be useless.

"I think we're going to eat well," one of the women laughed. "Thank God we're in a place with all this food."

"Yeah," said the other, "think about those places without food. It's just a shame there's so much cholesterol around here and I'm trying to watch my weight. There'll be a lot of hungry people in a little while who'd like to have what we have."

Halavi did think about it. The snow was piling up rapidly and nothing was moving in the street outside. People had abandoned their cars, but no one was coming to the fast food places. The larger stores in the mall across the street had drawn them in. Halavi's Burger King might have Whoppers, but the mall had furniture, more and larger restrooms, and, yes, restaurants. The malls would be much better places to wait out a nasty snowfall.

"I feel sorry for the kids stuck in schools," one of the ladies said.

"So do I," Halavi said softly. He'd had a thought.

Halavi picked up his phone and made a conference call to the other fast food managers and then more calls to the nearby Starbucks, Tim Horton's, and Panera Bread. He knew them all and the rivalry, while intense and serious, was also good natured. They all knew their success was mutually dependent, and, together, they were all extremely successful. After getting through a layer of jokes regarding fast-food pub crawls and dog-sleds at the drive-thrus, Halavi got to the point. They had food that was going to go to waste and the schools probably didn't have enough to feed the children. How then were they to solve the dilemma?

A whirring, whining droning noise interrupted his thoughts. Two teenagers on snowmobiles raced by, serenely confident in their vehicle's ability to handle, even defeat, the growing piles of snow.

"You see what I see," he asked his fellow managers. Two of them did. "Now all we got to do is get us some of those things and find out where the food should go."

CHAPTER 13

THIS TIME IT WAS DIMONA WHO SOUNDED SLEEPY, A SMALL FACT that delighted Mike Stuart. "What's the matter, beloved Lieutenant, were you sleeping?"

"Yes, damn it. Las Vegas may never sleep, but I do. I'm losing my shirt and my wife is doing even worse. Tomorrow I'll have a hangover and I haven't even been laid lately. What do you want now? Has it stopped snowing so I can come home?"

"No, and maybe it never will and I don't understand why you went all the way to Nevada to piss away your money when we've got so many perfectly good casinos right here. Y'know, you could really save a lot of time by simply flushing your money down a toilet."

"Screw you, Mikey."

Mike grinned into the phone. "Actually, I've got a question for you."

"Shoot."

"Why did you sic that nasty blonde television reporter on Chief Bench?"

There was a moment's silence, and DiMona began to laugh. "Gee, and here I thought I was being so sneaky."

"So you admit it? Hell, I was just guessing."

"Your guess was on target, Mikey. I did it and I'm proud. I called up a guy I know at her channel, told him about Bench and that he was a danger to mankind, and he said he was going to send her over since she lived only a couple of miles away and had access to a snowmobile. Obviously she made it and stirred up some shit, and ain't that just wonderful."

"Yes, but why?"

"Because beloved Chief Bench is a drunken incompetent son of a bitch who's trying to force me to retire and now I nailed him good. Is that enough?"

"Sounds fair, but first off, I thought you wanted to retire. I never heard anything about you being forced out. That's news to me and maybe a lot of people, Joey."

"That's 'cause the people who are screwing with me are pretending to be making like being gentlemen and keeping it quiet so I don't sue them. I do want to retire someday, Mikey, I just want to do it on my terms and at my time. I still like my job and I like the people I work with, even you some days, so I'd just as soon not be out on my ass like some unwelcome party-crasher.

"Bench wants me out now because I argue with him when he makes dumb decisions, and point out his many imperfections, one of which is drinking himself into a stupor on company time. Whenever we've had a crisis, he's never been around. Why not? Because he's always stewed. He's got a lot of people fooled. He can sit in his office, or in the mayor's, and make pontifical noises and not harm anybody. But tell me, when's the last time you saw him at the scene of a crisis?"

"Joey, this is Sheridan. We haven't had that many crises."

"But we still have some, and we have a big one now, likely the biggest in Sheridan's history. Remember when you met Maddy? Some bus driver had run over a kid and the whole thing made the evening news on all channels. So where was Bench? In his office fast asleep like a little kid taking a nap, or maybe a bear hibernating would be better. You were there at the scene since that's where you met Maddy, and that's where I was too, and I looked great on television, but Bench was nowhere to be seen.

"And where's he been since the snow started falling? This is when leaders lead and give us the wisdom of their experience. Instead, the city's got you and, not to knock you since you're working so hard and generally doing the right things, but weren't there occasional moments when you would have liked to have someone to bounce thoughts off of?"

Mike had an uncomfortable thought. "Joey, are you saying that the family who died in their car might be alive if Bench had been functioning as a real chief? Or that we might have caught those two killers at the motel instead of having them get away? I find that hard to swallow."

"Nah, nothing anybody could have done was going to change a thing in those cases, but are you confident that everything that could have been done had been done? At the very least, Bench's intoxication left you one important person short, didn't it? And that meant one less person checking cars or backing you up at that motel."

Mike agreed. He and Detective Hughes had been left to fend for themselves, and the numbers of people available for support had been, and remained, limited. Now he did wonder if better leadership might have helped.

"And, Mike, it's going to get much worse before it gets better, because it's going to go beyond the snowfall."

"What do you mean?"

"Remember I said the FBI was investigating our beloved mayor? Well, chew on this. Years ago, the mayor's construction company low-bid on a number of major development projects in the city and got them. The bids were extremely low, but Carter still managed to make a ton of profit and gave some of it to charity so everybody thought he was a good guy as well as being a real canny business-man. Hell, he even got some awards for being so damned smart and civic-minded, but there's another reason, isn't there?"

Mike thought quickly. "Oh, Christ, he chintzed on construc-tion and materials, didn't he?"

"Bingo, bunky. At least that's what the Feds think. Y'know, I don't know nothing about building stuff, but let's say you just pound in six nails per foot of wood instead of nine like the plans and city code requires, or maybe you use a lower grade of lum-ber or metal struts a little cheaper and farther apart so you can have fewer of them and you can save a fortune. Or maybe you put inferior materials into the cement. Of course, the buildings aren't as strong as they should be, but that's okay since nothing's happened to them in years so they must be strong enough, right? It just proves that the legal standards were too strict. And now all those crappily made buildings are piled up with more than three feet of snow, aren't they? Bet you can hear the roofs creaking right now, can't you?"

Mike instinctively looked to the ceiling. As if he was in the room with him, DiMona laughed. "Don't worry. The police station is built like a fortress and not by Carter's boys. Same for the rest of the city hall compound. They were all built to last. But there are maybe fifty buildings in Sheridan that Carter and his cronies put up and God only knows how safe and sound they are. Oh, if you're wondering about the building inspectors, we only had one at the time and he was busy with residential work and didn't know much about commercial stuff anyhow, so the job was outsourced to a company that the Feds now think had connections to Carter."

Mike had visions of buildings collapsing onto shocked and horrified inhabitants. It wouldn't be anything like the collapse of the Twin Towers of the World Trade Center, but people could still die or be injured. With all the snow, it would be like an avalanche hit them. "Joey, I should know what buildings might be in danger. Do you have a list?"

"No, damn it. I'm on vacation, remember? Tell you what, in the morning I'll call my contact at the FBI and one of us will fax you the list."

Mike was handed a note and he stood up quickly. "Joey, you do that and I'd appreciate it. I've got to go, my friend. There's a big fire on Winston Street."

One more crisis, Mike thought after hanging up. He was thankful that his parents were safe and out of town, and that Maddy was in a place that was also safe at Patton Elementary. He gently kicked Petkowski in the ribs, let him swear a couple of times, and told him to get his outdoor gear on. They had yet another problem to solve. Too bad they didn't have a real chief of police, Mike thought.

✧   ✧   ✧

Wilson Craft enjoyed his job. After more than thirty years taking shit in a Chrysler assembly plant, even a relatively clean and modern one, the opportunity to be in an open and sunny environment filled with kids and intelligent adults was like a dream.

Forced into early retirement by a plant closure following Chrysler's bankruptcy, he'd applied for the job of maintenance man in the Sheridan schools, got it, and found that the pay, along with his Chrysler pension, more than compensated for his lost income. Better, the work wasn't at all difficult compared with what he'd been doing in the past. In a little more than a year he'd be eligible for full Social Security, which meant a hard decision on whether to continue his maintenance position or take the government money that, after all, was his in the first place. Or, he could wait a little while longer and do both. Since the work wasn't all that hard and the money was good, he was leaning towards continuing to work.

His new job had brought him a divorce and a girlfriend. His wife of twenty years had left him shortly after he'd left Chrysler, and his friends said it was in desperation at the thought of spending all day with him. Wilson knew better. She'd had a couple of affairs before and he'd caught her having sex with a neighbor. Worse, it was another woman. He never wanted to see her again. Thank God they'd never had kids, because he wouldn't know how to explain to them that mommy was a lesbian.

Wilson thought he was actually enjoying life for the first time. Some people disapproved, but screw them. It was his life, after all.

Sometimes he felt sorry for the teachers and other staff. Working in an automotive factory was far from fair, and layoffs and job loss were a regular possibility, especially if you worked for Chrysler. But for teachers and other government workers, it was a shock. Government jobs were supposed to be layoff proof but it wasn't working out that way. Michigan was supposed to be recovering economically, but few could see it. Property values were way down, which meant less money in property taxes which then meant less money for schools. The teachers hadn't had a raise in years. Wilson hadn't either, but he was used to that crap. Fortunately, Sheridan was both affluent and growing, which meant that layoffs had been few and selective. He was concerned that his job might be outsourced. Again, there was nothing he could do about it, so why worry?

But now, he was genuinely worried. The electricity was out and he had a bunch of squirrelly kids and sometimes equally squirrelly teachers to worry about. First, he had to convince them that no one was going to freeze to death. Wilson's father used to bore them with stories about how he slept in an uninsulated and unheated attic in a frame house in Detroit and never suffered anything worse than the sniffles. Bull, Wilson thought. Of course he suffered, but his old man had a point. The temperature in that attic rarely went below freezing and the temperature in Patton Elementary wasn't going to come anywhere close to it. It just wasn't that cold outside and the snow piling up was actually acting like an insulator. Eskimos lived in ice houses, didn't they? All the people had to do was stay bundled up and close together, and they'd be nice and warm. Well, sort of.

Fortunately, most of the teachers had brains, especially Donna Harris and Maddy Kovacs. He thought they both were good-looking and intelligent women who had knockout bodies, although Harris could shed a few pounds. He smiled at the thought of bagging either or both. Maddy might be younger and firmer, but Donna Harris exuded something that was positively carnal. All she'd have to do was crook a finger and he'd come crawling, drooling, in her direction.

Forget it, he thought. It wasn't going to happen. Neither woman would be interested in what to them must seem to be an old fart. And besides, he had a girlfriend who satisfied him. He laughed internally at his idiotic daydream, although he did wish that the Kovacs chick would loosen up and enjoy life a little more. Maybe the cop she was dating would make it happen for her. Wilson hoped so. Indecent thoughts or not, he genuinely liked and respected both of them.

The teachers and kids had abandoned the gym for the hallway between the classrooms. Smart move. It got a second layer of walls between them and the outside and it got them into an area smaller than the gym where body heat could be conserved. Some of the students and teachers remained in classrooms where they felt more comfortable. It was their call. If somebody really got cold, they could go into the furnace room. The furnace was still on, which made the room warm, but the blower wasn't working since it needed electricity. Mrs. Harris had told him she was thinking of doing a rotation of people in and out of the furnace room. The woman had a brain as well as a body. No wonder her husband smiled a lot. He wondered if Mr. Harris satisfied Mrs. Harris. Mrs. Harris would take a lot of satisfying. Maddy Kovacs, on the other hand, was a different story. Although very friendly and personable, she struck him as a little cold.

Wilson Craft, however, was worried by the possibility of suffocation in the school. He'd heard the radio reports of death in cars and elsewhere, and was deeply concerned that it could happen at Patton. As the snow piled up, normal ventilation sources were being covered. Opening the trap door to the roof wasn't possible because of the snow piled up there, and forcing open the outside doors would generate too much wind in the hallways where people were gathering, although he would do that as a last resort. He'd worked hard all day shoveling snow away from the doors so they could be used as emergency exits should the need arise. He was exhausted from the effort.

That left cracking open a bunch of windows in such a manner as to move the air without freezing the occupants. After working hard all day and night, he'd come to the reluctant conclusion that he was out of shape. It surprised him. What the hell—he'd given up smoking a decade ago, and he'd been watching his diet to the point that he'd lost ten pounds and his cholesterol level was dropping dramatically. Maybe he should have exercised like his doctor had bugged him to. He made a mental note to start when this emergency was over. He had a treadmill in his basement that was gathering dust.

Wilson Craft moved the ladder to the window in the now empty gym. He climbed the half dozen steps to the top where he could reach the latch and open the window. He tugged and swore. It was stuck. Nothing was going to be easy today. He pulled again and felt the muscles strain in his back.

Craft was stubborn and pulled again. As he did, his back twisted, and he lost his footing and began to fall. He kept one arm on the latch until his shoulder separated and the pain became too much. He screamed and let go. His arms flailed and he tried to grab the ladder. His efforts knocked it away. He landed on his head with a crack that went unheard in the empty room.

As his world spun in red circles, he thought it was funny that everything was so disconnected. He couldn't feel his arms and legs. And why didn't he hurt?

There was a strange similarity in the way houses were constructed in many parts of Sheridan, and with the way they were built in older sections of Detroit and other major cities. In Detroit, there frequently weren't driveways or garages, and any rear way access was through the stinking garbage-filled alleys in the back. The houses were small, often with only two bedrooms, and equally often only a couple of feet from their neighbors. The houses were generally wood frame, which meant that a fire could travel from one to the other with ease.

In Sheridan, the houses were larger and filled the lots that were as small as the builders could get away with. Smaller lots meant more lots, and more lots meant more houses sold and that meant more profit. The houses had garages, minimum two-car and usually three, and boasted brick facades. But usually only the facades were brick. They were still essentially frame homes built with an abundance of wood. As with their poorer relations in Detroit, they were still uncomfortably close to their neighbors.

The fire at the Cunningham residence on Winston Street quickly devoured its source house and moved on to others. The fire department arrived within minutes of the alarm, but only in the form of two men on a snowmobile that carried a short length of hose and a ton of frustration. By the time Mike and Petkowski arrived on the scene, the flames were roaring incongruously through the billowing snow.

A harried fireman tramped through the snow, as if looking for something. "What's the problem?" Mike asked. The fireman glared at him, then saw the badge and realized it wasn't a civilian who'd only be in the way with unwanted advice and dumb questions. Normally, he could put up with it, but not now. The fireman had been going all day and all night. For that matter, so had Mike and Stan. They were all almost drained, physically and emotionally.

"Can't find the Goddamned hydrant," the fireman snapped. "You want to be useful, help us look."

The only water going on the fire was coming from garden hoses that were manned by frightened neighbors. Mike, little trained in fire prevention, saw that their efforts were ineffective. Understandably, the neighbors were trying to put out the fire and save their homes, when their efforts should have been used to contain it. Three houses were burning furiously, and there was nothing anyone could do to save them, while billowing clouds of smoke carried burning ashes through the snow to others. Unless something was done, the fire would continue to spread until it hit either a playground or a street. Until that time, many homes could burn.

"You'd think all this snow would put it out," Petkowski said. It seemed logical to Mike, too. Snow was water, after all, but the heat from the fire was evaporating much of the snow before it hit the flames. Rain might have worked, but snow lacked the density.

"Might as well piss on it," Petkowski added.

"You might burn yourself and never be able to live it down," Mike said. "Instead, why don't we help them find the hydrant?"

The two men began to crawl around where they thought there was a curb. Hydrants were funny things, always around and always in the way when you were mowing your lawn or looking for a place to park. Nobody liked the ugly things except when you needed one. Every few houses had a hydrant in front, but few people would be able to tell you exactly where they were. Your dog could, of course, but dogs had different agendas and, besides, they couldn't talk.

As Mike crawled and duck-walked through the snow, he thought of Maddy and her excursions that had gotten her soaked. At least he had better protective gear, although he could feel rivulets of melting snow going down his neck and onto his chest and back.

Damn it, how far away could one be? And how far from the curb was it? And where on earth was the curb? He couldn't recall. He and Petkowski had split up. Maybe they should have stayed together? They could have held hands and walked their way through the snow until they found one.

Mike stumbled and fell face down in the snow. He picked

himself up and hoped no one had seen him. They hadn't. They were all either fighting the fire or also looking for a hydrant. A second fire department snowmobile showed up with more personnel and more hose and they joined in the search.

"Got it," yelled one of the newly arrived firemen. Mike swore in frustration at his own wasted effort, and aided in the effort to clear a mountain of snow off the hydrant.

"God, I hope this one works," the fireman said. "A lot of them don't, you know."

Mike winced. It had taken them forever to find this one. How many more houses would be ashes if they had to look again? Nonworking hydrants were a minor scandal that the mayor had sworn was corrected. They would soon find out.

Luck was with them. A hose was connected and a powerful stream of water began to soak the houses not yet touched by the fire. A couple of roofs were smoking from the heat, but the water quickly put an end to that nonsense. The second hose was just as effective. It would be a long while before the fires were out, but, for the time being, they were contained. A couple of homeowners were pissed that more effort wasn't being made to save their houses, but it quickly became obvious that nothing could be done.

"We're covered with snow," Stan said. "I look like Casper the Friendly Ghost and you look like Frosty the Obscene Snowman."

Mike took a deep breath and grinned. "Screw you, Polack. I'm the Grinch."

Traci Lawford lay naked and huddled on the floor of her bedroom. Her entire body hurt. She was numbed from pain that was both physical and psychological. She had promised to cooperate in return for not being mutilated and she had done her part. But she never dreamed that anything this awful could happen in her life. Until now, she never realized how fortunate her life had been.

Traci could have lain down on her bed instead of the floor, but her bed had been defiled, profaned by the repeated assaults upon her. She would stay on the floor.

They had taken her up to her bedroom and Raines had raped

her first. It wasn't as horrible as it could have been when she closed her eyes and willed her mind to be elsewhere. Then the little guy, Tower, had assaulted her with a degree of violence and built-up anger that stunned her, and she'd screamed from the pain. She quickly realized that women didn't like Tower and he was taking out his rage and frustrations on her, and that she shouldn't provoke him. He thought her screams were a rejection of him, which they were, and they made him angrier. With more emotional strength than she thought she possessed, she willed herself to silent endurance.

Then Raines wanted oral sex and she complied, hating every moment of the humiliation as she knelt before him. Tower watched them and laughed, which made it worse. She considered biting down on Raines, but rejected it. What they would do to her wouldn't be worth the momentary satisfaction.

A moment later, Tower was ready again and she complied, this time in silence. Tower was an animal with incredible sexual recuperative powers. Time and again he assaulted her, and long after Raines was satisfied. Raines thought Tower's stamina was funny.

Tower hit her once, splitting her lip. She'd begged him to stop when he was forcing himself on her for perhaps the fourth time, and it had angered him. She didn't scream again, not even when he'd sodomized her, which was far more painful.

Finally, Tower grew tired and left her in the bedroom.

For a few moments after they'd left her, she wanted to die. She rolled from the bed and lay on the floor of her bedroom and wished her world would end. But it wouldn't. Traci was not going to commit suicide, even if she knew how, considering that there was nothing resembling a weapon in her room. In their contempt for her, Tower and Raines hadn't even tied her up. Therefore, she concluded reluctantly, she was going to have to live. She thought about escape. They had taken her clothes and emptied out her closet and removed the bedding. She was on the second floor and scared to death of heights. A jump to the ground would hurt her, perhaps breaking bones and leaving her to freeze to death in a mound of snow. Even if she were to make it to the ground safely, where would she go? She would leave a trail through the snow that they could follow to where?

A neighbor's? Do that and she'd endanger others, and she could not bring herself to do that. At least not yet.

Of course, she had their word that they would not kill her. Sure. She'd seen their faces, and heard their voices, and they already were killers. Like they'd said, what would one more murder mean? If it was to their advantage to keep her alive, they would do so. But if it wasn't, she had no illusions. They would cut her throat just like the others they'd bragged about. Traci shuddered from a fear she couldn't control.

Traci had to do something. She couldn't leave the room because they'd locked it and barricaded it from the outside. She thought about barricading it from the inside with furniture, but that would only delay them for a moment. Her own bedroom had become a jail cell.

She wasn't thinking rationally and knew it. The abuse and the terror had overwhelmed her. She had to take back some control or she would die.

Muffled voices came through the heat vent. Traci crawled over to it and pressed her ear to the metal grill. The acoustics in old houses were funny. Sometimes you could hear things you didn't think you could. And sometimes you heard things you didn't want to.

Joe Gomez and Tommy Hummel had finished the six cans of Coors in a very short while, and had gotten thoroughly bored playing cards. The news from the radio and on the small portable television told them nothing they didn't already know—it was snowing. The television news said that power was out in many places but, knock on wood, not yet in their corner of the world, and even if it did, they'd hook up to a truck battery.

They'd dozed fitfully on the uncomfortable furniture in the office. Joe'd pulled rank and claimed the old, beat-up couch and wondered if he'd made the right decision. All the springs seemed to be broken and attacking his kidneys. At least they still had heat and the toilet flushed.

"This is stupid," Joe said.

Tommy yawned. "Agreed."

"We just can't sit here all night. We've got a big-ass truck with a plow and lots of power. We ought to be able to do something useful."

"It'd be easy if we could actually drive it somewhere. We could get through the snow if the roads weren't jammed with tourists."

"What if we don't use the roads?"

Tommy giggled. "Tell me you are not suggesting that we go cross-country, through parks and over people's lawns with that gigantic thing; are you? Christ, we'd break anything we rode over and get sued."

"If it's an emergency, why not?"

"If we knew something was an emergency, I suppose we could do it. But who's going to tell us what an emergency is?"

Joe smiled and reached for the phone. "First, I think I'll phone the cops and tell them we're available and see what they think. Then maybe we can go out and play."

Tommy thoughtfully examined an empty Coors can. "If we're going to be on call, I guess we should stop drinking. Too bad we ran out of this stuff several hours ago. Stopping would have meant something. Now it just means I gotta go take a tremendous piss."

They didn't find Wilson Craft for a while. He wasn't one of the kids, so no one was keeping track of him. He'd always come and gone as he wished; doing whatever job he thought needed to be done. Technically, he worked for the principal, but the staff thought of him as basically self-employed.

He wasn't discovered until one of the teachers, young Sue Stapleton, wandered into the gym to see if there was anything else in the way of padding to help make the hallway floors more comfortable. Her screams brought Maddy and Donna. Wilson lay on his back. His eyes were wide open and he seemed to be conscious, but wasn't responsive. There was a huge bruise on his head and blood seeped from an ear. The ladder was on its side in mute explanation of what had transpired.

Maddy and Donna checked for a pulse—it was steady but weak—and tried to talk to him while a distraught Sue called 911.

They were lucky. An EMS snowmobile just happened to be a couple of blocks away and arrived within minutes. The two technicians checked him briefly and radioed for more help.

"Possible fractured skull and possible broken back" was the rough and grim prognosis. Obviously, he had to be transported to a hospital for proper care and, equally obviously, that wasn't going to happen for a long while.

Instead, one of the techs took the snowmobile and returned shortly with a doctor who lived a couple of blocks away. The doctor confirmed the technician's diagnosis—it was either a broken back or a fractured skull or both.

"Doctor, can he hear us?" Maddy asked. The doctor shrugged. He didn't know. Wilson Craft would have to be transported with extreme care to a hospital and in an ambulance, not a snowmobile. In a perfect world, they would place a wooden board under him, wrap him in cushioning material so he wouldn't shift and hurt himself even more, gently place him on a stretcher, and then put him in an ambulance. He would be driven carefully to a hospital where experts would evaluate him, X-ray and scan him, and perform numerous other tests that would likely save his life. But not tonight. The doctor said he wouldn't survive a trip on a snowmobile and the techs agreed.

Everything that could be done was done. The doctor said he would remain and stand watch. Without proper medical care, Wilson Craft was going to die. The only question was how soon.

"Wally, do you know where I am?" Governor Lauren Landsman asked over the telephone.

"Hopefully, somewhere nice and warm and dry and holding a warm brandy in your delicate and sensuous hands," Wally Wellman responded. He was still in the TV6 studio and very tired, but it was good to hear her voice. "And may I guess what you're wearing?"

"No such luck to the first and no to guessing the second. I am outside and standing on what was once Interstate 96, and I'm just about at the Brighton exit. I guess I'm about fifty miles from downtown Detroit. I'm watching the National Guard try to bull their way through the snow with armor that took down Saddam Hussein in Iraq. This whole thing is incredible."

"How're they doing?" Wally asked.

"Slowly, Wally, agonizingly slowly."

After hours of effort, the Guard had managed to clear only one
lane of the interstate from Lansing to Brighton. Heavily falling
and swirling snow, however, threatened to overwhelm their poor
efforts. Thousands of men and women of the Guard were attacking
the mountains of snow by moving down the various interstates
that met in the metropolitan Detroit area, the approximate center
of the area's population, if not the storm.

Even though she'd seen television and satellite images, Lauren
was still stunned by the storm and the suddenness with which it
took over everything in its path. For the first several miles out
of Lansing, there was nothing, not even a hint of the disaster.
Then there was a wet drizzle and, suddenly, a wall of white. It
was as if there was an ordained dividing line between the lands
of snow and no-snow.

As everywhere, the Guard found its problems compounded
by the thousands of abandoned vehicles that clogged the roads.
They had to be moved aside far enough for plows to clear the
road and for there to be an area to dump the thousands of tons
of displaced snow.

Lauren had pulled rank as governor and commandeered a tracked
armored personnel carrier as her command post. She was aware
that others might think it grandstanding on her part, but she could
not abide the thought of sitting in her comfortable office and either
reading about the problems the citizens of her state were having or
watching them on television. No, she had to try and experience at
least some of the difficulties as she tried to resolve the problems.

All over, people were losing their homes, and those who only
lost property were the lucky ones. Fires had killed a number of
people as had a multitude of other causes. She'd been on the
phone with several of the local mayors who'd tried to convey a
sense of their tragedies.

And what she'd seen looked like a snowbound planet from a
science-fiction movie. In front of her, scores of men and women
operated tanks, personnel carriers, and heavy machinery to push
vehicles out of the way, while others used plows and front-end
loaders to remove the snow. She knew she was useless from a
practical point of view, but she hoped she was providing some
moral support. This was becoming one of the worst natural

disasters in the history of Michigan. Other than tornados and the occasional forest fire, her state had been remarkably free of much of the devastation nature routinely handed out to other areas, like Florida and California.

It's our turn, she reminded herself. There is no free lunch in life and paybacks are hell. Cripes, she thought, she was beginning to sound like Wally. The thought made her smile. Maybe next time she'd let him guess what she was wearing. Maybe she'd make it real interesting for him.

"Over here," yelled out a soldier who was standing by a car and waving frantically. All thoughts of Wally were wiped from her mind as she ran to the soldier.

Bile raised in Lauren's throat as the soldiers smashed the window of the car, opened the door, and dragged a stiff form out and laid it on the road.

"What is it?" she heard Wally ask on her phone. "What's the problem?" She had momentarily forgotten that she'd been talking to him and that the line was still open.

"A dead man," she told him, while walking over to the corpse. There would be no attempt to revive him. The man looked to be in his late forties or early fifties. He was frozen blue and his limbs were stiff. She wondered if he'd been on his way home to a family that now was worried sick about his not calling, or out selling widgets or something and wouldn't be missed for days. Why had he stayed in the car? Had he suffocated? Not likely— the ignition was off. Had he frozen to death? Possibly, but why hadn't he left the car and tried to find better shelter?

She knew the answer. They were in a rural area and the man probably couldn't see a better place to go. Hell, he probably couldn't see anything. Nor was he dressed for bad weather. The dead man wore a suit and an overcoat. He wore expensive shoes, not boots, and looked ready for a staff meeting, not a blizzard. She'd always heard that you should stay in a stranded vehicle and wait for rescue, and it looked like he'd done so until it was too late. At least they'd found the body, which might not have happened for a long while if he'd tried to cross a cornfield. She shuddered at the thought of what the thaw and animals would have done before his corpse was found.

Maybe he'd had a heart attack on top of everything else? Hell, she thought, they'd probably never really know what happened to the poor guy. It really didn't matter what the precise cause was. Death by storm should be written on the death certificate.

"He won't be the last," Wally said softly. As the storm continued, the death toll rose.

Soldiers put the corpse in a truck. It would be driven north, out of the storm.

"Wally, I think I've seen enough," Lauren said sadly. "I really wish you were here. I really don't like being alone anymore."

"I don't either," Wally answered. "It's been too long, Lauren."

Maddy Kovacs was standing in the hallway when she heard what sounded like cheers. What now, she wondered. She had just left the small group around Wilson Craft's comatose body. The doctor remained by his side, but was waiting for the end and not counting on any improvement. It was just too depressing for words, and she wanted to get away.

"The cavalry's arrived," announced Frieda Houle, "and about damned time."

Frieda always found things to complain about, and her complaints ran from pay, working conditions, the union, the school board, her co-workers, and her sex life. Donna said Frieda was only happy when she was complaining. Maddy joined her and they went into the cafeteria. Several people wearing snow gear were carrying packages into the kitchen. Maddy found Donna Harris opening a box. A wispy cloud of steam escaped from it.

"What the heck is this?"

Donna grinned. "A gift horse. The PTG got a few snowmobiles and picked up food from Burger King, Wendy's, McDonald's, and Taco Bell. They're still open because the staff's stuck there, and were going to throw all this food out until somebody in the restaurants got the bright idea to get it to us. We also got coffee from Starbucks and Tim Horton's. If you want tea, you're out of luck. Want a burrito?"

Maddy took a bite. It was still sort of warm and absolutely delicious. There was a noise behind her and she saw other teachers lining up kids to get the food. The kids looked groggy, tired, and very, very hungry. She saw some smiles as the odor of good, greasy fast food permeated the room. Maddy poured some coffee into a disposable foam cup. It was still very close to being hot. And, damn, it tasted good.

Mrs. Santana, one of the parents on the snowmobiles, grinned at the sight of the hungry kids and the equally hungry teachers. "Mine are home safe, but I couldn't help but wonder about these munchkins, stuck here and all that."

"You're a godsend," Maddy said, ignoring the fact that Mrs. Santana was concerned only about the kids and not the adults, which was about par for the course. Mrs. Santana wasn't being cruel, only typical. Maddy wondered if anyone would have thought to bring them food if there hadn't been children. Not a chance. Sunrise was only a little ways off and maybe the day would be better than the night. It couldn't get worse, could it?

"Sergeant Stuart, may I have a word with you?"

Mike looked up from the desk. A tall, thin man in his forties stood before him dressed in expensive cold-weather gear. Although Mike hadn't memorized all the faces of the refugee population, he didn't look familiar. Most likely he was a new arrival in the police station. But why? If he'd been anywhere else, it was likely better than being stuck at City Hall.

"Sure," Mike said, wiping grogginess from his eyes. "What can I do for you, sir?"

"I'd like to know if I can take my daughter home."

Mike was puzzled. "Is she under arrest?"

"I don't know. My name is Dr. Peter Thomason and my daughter is Cindy Thomason. I understand she's being held here because she was in an accident earlier yesterday morning. I also understand she's injured and I'd like to get her some proper medical care."

Now Mike remembered, as the cloud lifted from his tired brain. "Your daughter caused a major accident that resulted in the early blockage of northbound MacArthur. Thanks to her and her inability to control a Corvette, at least one police car is seriously damaged, one officer bruised, and maybe hundreds of people didn't make it home. In fact, I'd say a lot of them are right here and lying on our floors trying to get to sleep thanks to her. It is also possible that the accident she caused resulted in a number of deaths due to asphyxiation."

Thomason paled and Mike felt a twinge of sympathy. His daughter had done something stupid, not malicious.

"No, Doctor, your daughter is not under arrest, although there will doubtless be some very serious charges filed against her at a later time. If you have a means of taking her home feel free to do so, and I assume you do, otherwise you wouldn't be standing here. And when you do get her home, I strongly suggest you contact a very good lawyer."

Thomason nodded stiffly. "I would greatly appreciate it if you had the charges dropped. After all, she was injured. I checked her out. She definitely has a broken nose and she'll need major dental work on her front teeth. Also, some of the people here have been picking on her for allegedly causing the tieup, although I'm rather certain the weather caused it and not my daughter. Under the circumstances, I'm confident family discipline would be sufficient."

Mike didn't think the family had much discipline at all, based on Cindy Thomason's actions. Nor had Doctor Thomason said a word about his daughter being contrite, or that she even accepted responsibility for her actions. If Doctor Thomason felt the girl could drive her brother's car without permission, create a major accident, cause injuries and tie up traffic without anything more than being grounded for a few days, Doctor Thomason was nuts. He knew that blaming the girl for the suffocation deaths of the family whose name he was too tired to remember was more than a stretch. He'd let the prosecutors figure that one out.

"Sir, she nearly killed one of my officers, so no, I do not feel benevolent. In fact, I think she was very lucky. I can't drop charges because none have been filed. Let the district attorney and a judge sort out what should happen to her. At the very least, I hope she loses her license for a very long time along and pays a healthy fine."

"If she loses her license, officer," Thomason said with a glare, "just how is she supposed to get around? We don't have a chauffeur, or did you think we did because I happen to be a doctor?"

Mike wondered if Doctor Thomason was a proctologist and

returned the glare. "I don't know how she'll get from here to there and I don't much care. She can get rides from friends, or even take the big yellow school bus that older kids hate so much. In my opinion and based on what happened, she's too immature to be driving a car. Maybe this'll shape her up. Perhaps she should have thought of the consequences before she tried to drive a car she couldn't handle and in weather conditions that were extremely bad."

Mike knew that he had let his anger and exhaustion cause him to talk too much. Cops were supposed to keep their composure and he had almost lost his. Fatigue was no excuse. Doctor Thomason was perfectly capable of complaining about his behavior. Mike then wondered who Thomason might find around the place to complain to. Bench was disgraced and drunk, and the mayor was being investigated by the Feds. DiMona, he thought. Thomason could complain to DiMona, but the close-to-retirement cop was just as likely to tell the good doctor to go screw himself. Perhaps it wasn't such a bad world after all.

Moments later Mike watched as Thomason departed with his daughter in tow. She looked concerned, but not particularly so. Mike got up and looked out the window. Big surprise—it was still snowing. Damn, would it ever stop? The clock on the wall said it was very early morning, but the snowfall seemed to have cancelled out any distinction between night and day.

Petkowski came into the office and plopped onto a chair. "What was that all about?"

Mike sighed and then grinned. "You don't want to know, but it was all your fault."

Petkowski yawned. "What the hell else is new?"

CHAPTER 14

NOT ALL THE PEOPLE DRIVING SNOWMOBILES WERE PERFORMING works of charity, such as carrying food to shut-ins and school-children or taking medicine to sick people.

There were a number of people of all ages and backgrounds who thought the weather was a wonderful opportunity to cut loose and party. Who cared if you had a world-class hangover tomorrow? Tomorrow had been cancelled and so had the foreseeable future. Nobody was going to work or school until the snow ended and was carted away. Disaster parties were common, although most of them broke up in the early wee hours, casualties to exhaustion. Some, however, had simply run out of booze.

It was just before a dawn that no one would quite see because of the snow when a dozen snowmobiles descended on Sampson's Super Store. Tyler Holcomb heard the roar of the machines and went to the main front door. A score of people dismounted from their machines and entered the building with a chant of "Beer, beer, and more beer!"

At first, Tyler thought it was kind of like a scene from *Animal House*, one of his all-time favorite movies and one that his wife hated. But then he saw that the crowd, mostly men, was stagger-ingly drunk. Aw shit, he thought, just when he had everything settled down.

"No beer," he told them. "And no alcohol sales of any kind per the order of the police."

"Fuck the cops," said a skinny young man in his early twen-ties. Tyler thought of carding him, but there wasn't any point if there wasn't anything to sell him.

"Shelves are empty, people," Holcomb said. "I've got nothing to sell you."

"It's behind, in the back room," the skinny guy added. "I used to work here, so I know where they hide it."

Tyler fumed. He wished the skinny guy still did work there so he could fire his skinny white ass. "Doesn't matter. It's now against the law to sell alcohol."

A bigger white man stood in front of the skinny one. His face was flushed and his eyes were glassy. "I know the law. We got a constitutional right to drink ourselves silly when there's more than eight inches of snow as determined by the National Weather Service."

That was almost funny, Tyler thought. Maybe the big guy wasn't as drunk as he looked. "Can't do it and I'm not going to argue with you."

"You don't have to," said the bigger man, "we're just going to take it."

"Send the bill to my parents," said the skinny guy, who then broke up laughing. "They'll fucking crap."

Holcomb placed himself in the aisle way leading to the back. "I'm asking you to leave."

"Fuck you," said the big guy and the others cheered him. Big Guy then pushed Tyler away. He landed against a stack of canned goods that fell with a clatter.

Tyler got up and Big Guy took a wild swing. He missed and Tyler kicked him in the knee, dropping him. Tyler then wheeled and backhanded the little guy across the face, sending him skid-ding on his backside down the aisle.

"Enough," said one of Tyler's cops who'd finally decided to step in. Badges were shown and all belligerence quickly went out of the drunks. "I guess they meant it when they said no booze," lamented one of them.

"Against the walls," the cops growled to the remaining crowd and patted them down. To Tyler's astonishment they found several handguns and a number of knives. It occurred to him that he'd been very lucky.

Holcomb was congratulating himself on his good fortune, when there was a sudden, loud crack, and the building seemed to vibrate.

"What the hell was that?" someone said.

Tyler forced a smile. He'd seen the movie *Titanic* a half dozen times with his wife who loved it and even bought the 3-D version DVD. He sometimes wondered what Captain Smith was really thinking when the ship went down. Aw shit, he and his wife decided. Tyler just liked to see the white chick naked again.

"Nothing important," Tyler said, knowing it was a lie.

Traci jammed her ear against the heat vent. Raines had gone outside to investigate something and had returned. If she was careful, she could hear pretty much all that they said.

"It was a fire down the street," Raines said. "A bunch of houses were really lit up."

"Wish I coulda watched it," said Tower.

Raines thought the scene had been unusual. They'd spotted the glow through the snow and he'd managed to huff his way the couple of blocks to it. He'd been at enough fires, hell, he'd even set a few, but this was really strange. No fire trucks, no flashers and no sirens. A couple of real firemen had connected hoses to hydrants and were trying to contain the blaze.

But he'd seen badges on a couple of men and realized that the cops were not totally immobilized. They too had snowmobiles, which meant they could go inspecting abandoned houses at any time. He'd gotten close enough to hear people saying that the snow would break in a few hours, which was just what the fools on the television were saying. When that occurred, he and Tower would be better off moving. Even if the amateur weather forecasters were wrong, this wasn't the beginning of a new Ice Age. The snow would still stop sooner or later. No, it would be much better to be prepared to move quickly the instant it did.

Tower listened to the explanation in silence. "Too bad," he finally said. "This is a nice house."

"All the more reason the cops are going to check it out. They always check out the rich people's places first when something happens."

"What about the girl? We told her we wouldn't kill her, didn't we?"

Raines had been mulling that one over. He didn't give a shit about promises, but wondered if she was still useful to them.

"If we need her as a hostage, she goes with us. If we don't, she could tell them what time we left, what we were wearing, and maybe even what direction we went. No, if we don't need her as a hostage, we'll kill her. We'll wait 'til the last minute of course—she's cooperating real nice and that's kind of fun."

Tower laughed. "Yeah."

"So we'll just keep her around, keep fucking the shit out of her, and then you can slice and dice her if we don't need her, and that looks pretty likely."

In the bedroom above, Traci shook with fear as she listened through the vent. All illusions were gone. She was as good as dead if she didn't do something fast. What had seemed impractical or dangerous a few moments before looked now to be her only choice.

But if she could only tell somebody, she might stand a chance.

Tyler Holcomb was in a sweat. The loud crack had not repeated itself, but the one sound had been enough to scare the pants off him. The building had vibrated and he knew what had caused it—the extraordinary buildup of snow on the roof.

Like much new construction, Sampson's was not built to last for ages. It was a cement-walled shell built on a slab. There were steel pillars and trusses supporting a roof that was only slightly pitched. It was designed to permit rainfall to drain quickly and was, theoretically at least, sturdy enough to hold significant amounts of snow.

But had the designers anticipated anything like this monstrous snowfall? He had no idea what the building codes were, but he doubted they anticipated anything like this storm. He was the manager, not the builder or an engineer. So what did that loud noise mean? Nothing good, he determined.

Holcomb gathered his managers and security people and asked for advice. It was obvious that they had only two choices: They could stay where they were or they could leave the building and take their chances on the weather. Holcomb looked outside and saw the snow still coming down heavily and still being whipped by winds into drifts that were taller than many men. He realized that too many people either couldn't leave or wouldn't leave, and he had no real way of forcing them out into the snow and with no place else to go if they did. They would stay regardless of what was decided.

They found a couple of people who were in the construction business, and they said that a roof failure would likely come in the middle. But then an engineer said the heaviest snow buildup was along the edges and that's where a failure would occur. Tyler threw up his hands. He didn't know what to do. All his options were wrong.

With another and even louder crack, the decision was taken away from him. The west center portion of the roof, the part directly over men's clothing, opened up and, with a roar, dumped an avalanche of snow into the building while people screamed and tried to run through the crowd to safety. As the snow cascaded into the aisles, people were buried by it while others trampled anyone in their way.

There was a brief period of stunned silence and then the screams began from the injured and the terrified. Quickly, Holcomb's managers and security, along with scores of volunteers, started to dig their way through the piles of snow that now reached well above everyone's head. The roof was open to the sky and fresh snow swirled inside the shell of the store, accumulating on the injured and the rescuers.

Shovels were brought from the hardware and home sections, and scores of willing hands pulled snow and debris off of victims. At first there were only broken bones and cuts that stained the white snow red and looked worse than they were. A makeshift first aid center was set up along a wall where the injured were treated. A couple of dead were recovered. Nearly a third of the interior of the store was covered by snow, just like a Swiss town in an avalanche. Holcomb remembered watching video of that domed stadium in Minneapolis collapsing. This was worse because people were involved. Dismayed, he thought that dozens could still be buried. *Damn it,* he thought, *this sort of thing happens in Iran or some backward country like that. Buildings don't fall down and go boom in the United States.*

Finally, the first police and fire personnel arrived. Holcomb caught the name of a grim-faced officer who seemed to be in charge—Stuart.

Mike saw that the store manager had organized things fairly well and decided not to make any changes. Instead, he went to an aisle and joined in the digging. In moments, he'd pulled out a woman with a bad cut on her head and a man who needed CPR to resume breathing. They were followed by a screaming child with a broken leg. Then he found another woman, unhurt but pinned under a counter. With some help, he freed her. She crawled away, sobbing her thanks.

Next, he found a man whose skull had been smashed flat by a falling beam. There was no attempt to revive him. Mike and another man pulled the corpse to a wall with the others. They lay in an awkward row, and someone had managed to cover their faces. The latest victim made it four dead with a lot of the store yet to dig out.

A thought struck Mike and he ran over to the manager. "Mr. Holcomb, when was this store built?"

"Who cares?" Holcomb said in exasperation.

"I do," Mike snapped, and then more gently, "Humor me, it might just be important."

Holcomb thought for a second. "It was about five years ago, give or take. I wasn't here."

Mike felt his spirits sink. "Who was the contractor?"

"How the hell would I know? I just said I wasn't here then. Officer, I've got dead and injured to care for and there's no time to play like this is a quiz show."

Mike persisted. "Look, you had to have seen the records. Tell me one thing—was it Carter-Sheridan Construction or something like that?"

Holcomb looked surprised. "Yeah, I think it was something like that. Why?"

Mike felt sick to his stomach. He saw that the store was crawling with people digging for victims and that others were trying to shore up the rest of the roof. The situation was terrible, but as under control as it was going to get. He had to get back to the station and make a call to DiMona. He needed that list yesterday.

Traci crawled towards the bedroom closet. Raines and Tower had raped her again and had gone downstairs. They'd seemed distracted while they assaulted her, treating her as if she almost wasn't there. Before, they'd talked to her and tried to get a rise out of her while they assaulted and humiliated her. This time she was little more than a piece of meat. She realized that their callous behavior indicated that they'd written her off.

But it was still snowing and that was good. Unless they decided to change their plans, she thought. She crawled to the walk-in closet and looked around. There was no clothing, just as there were no sheets or blankets on the bed. The two animals had taken everything she might find useful.

Traci reached under a shelf and groped. Her hand found something solid and she sighed. Thank God that her husband was an electronics gizmo freak who always bought fresh toys and relegated the old ones to the closet.

What she had in her hand was a laptop computer that he'd replaced only a few months ago with a newer version. She'd scolded him for wasting money when the old one was still perfectly good. Now, she thought that he'd made a wonderful investment. If she recalled correctly, this one had a wireless modem that connected directly to the internet. She had no idea how this occurred, she only hoped it still worked.

However, there was no cord, so she didn't have a way to plug it into the wall. She prayed that the battery still had some life. Judging from the dust on it, the computer had been in the closet since it had been replaced. She turned it on and was relieved and startled when it beeped. Had they heard it? She adjusted the sound so no chirpy voices might tell all that she had mail or whatever.

She dialed and went online. Fast, she thought, she had to be fast. She had no idea how much life was left in the batteries, and her captors could come back to torment her some more at any time.

Traci composed a short e-mail message: "Help me. 2 killers in house. Send cops. Phone line cut. Will kill me." She ended it with her name and street address, 561 Beckett, and then sent it to everyone in her e-mail address book. Then she sent it a second time. And a third. Finally, she sensed the laptop's battery weakening. She exited and turned it off.

Please God, she thought, *please*. She crawled over to the vent.

Mike quickly realized he'd been nuts to think he could get the list of questionable buildings from DiMona at six in the morning. First off, the lieutenant hadn't answered his phone. Maybe he was taking a shit or maybe he was playing blackjack. Maybe he was through with Mike calling him.

Nor would he have been able to get DiMona's FBI contact to send the list because his contact wasn't even in his office yet. Hell, if the agent was local, he might not be able to make it in to work in the first place. He might be as snowbound as everyone else.

That left Plan B, Mike thought and smiled grimly. Plan B might cost him his career, but he had to know which buildings were in jeopardy. He opened Mayor Carter's office door and closed it behind him. The mayor looked exhausted. Mike felt no sympathy for him.

"What can I do for you, Sergeant?"

Mike stood over Carter. "I want to know what buildings Carter-Sheridan constructed."

Carter looked startled. "What?"

"Mayor Carter, don't fuck with me," Mike said with a cold fury. "You're being investigated by the FBI for putting up shitty buildings, and one of them just fell down. People are dead and a lot more hurt and I need to know about the others so we can evacuate them."

Carter paled, then recovered his poise. He rose and glared back at Mike. "First, Sergeant Stuart, I am your boss, not the other way around. Second, my attorney told me to say nothing about Carter-Sheridan Construction. However, for your benefit I will say I don't know anything about poorly constructed buildings. It's a damn shame a roof collapsed, but I think a lot of other roofs covered with heavy snow are going to fail with or without any assistance from Carter-Sheridan Construction. Now, get the hell out of here and start writing your resignation."

Mike snorted, then punched Carter in the middle of the chest, sitting him back down in the chair and gasping for breath. "I didn't think this would be easy," Mike said, "but I don't care. Now, give me that list, and if you don't have one, make one. And don't tell me you don't remember at least most of them. You know about the Feds, so you know what buildings they're looking at."

Carter tried to rise again, but Mike again hit him in the chest. The mayor gasped and sat down again. "How many more times do you want me to hit you?" Mike snarled. He reached over and grabbed Carter by the tie and dragged him across the desk. As he fell across it and onto the floor, Mike punched him in the kidney, then pushed his face into the side of his desk.

"Notice how I haven't hit you in the face? That's so there'll be no evidence of this. I'm a cop and we can do things like that real well. We can go on all day if you'd like."

Someone was knocking on the mayor's door. "Stay out," Mike commanded, then turned on the mayor who was writhing on the floor. Blood was pouring freely from his nose.

"The list," Mike snarled and made like he was going to hit him again.

They mayor said he'd had enough and said so in a voice that was little more than a squeal. Mike handed him a pad and paper. In moments he was done. "That's all I can remember," Carter said weakly and now in total subservience. "If I think of others, I'll let you know."

Mike took the list and made a copy on Carter's Xerox machine. He glanced at it before putting it in his pocket. He returned the original to Carter. It didn't seem logical that the mayor would have them all committed to memory. However, he now had phone calls to make and people to send out into the windy cold and the still falling snow. He opened the door and saw Chief Bench standing in the hallway. He was nowhere near as drunk as he had been, although his eyes were far from clear.

"Wha's wrong with him?" Bench asked, looking beyond Mike and into the room at a disheveled and bleeding Carter.

Mike recalled Petkowski and the abusive husband. "He's got the flu and then he fell."

"Bullshit," glared Bench.

Mike was about to respond when the 911 supervisor, Thea Hamilton, pushed her sizeable body between them. "Cut the crap. Chief, either be useful or go back to your office, we've got a real problem on our hands."

Wally Wellman looked at the latest satellite picture. It actually showed features of the earth to the south of them that had earlier been obscured by the storm. He waved the picture in triumph and grinned wearily. "It's going to end, folks."

"Can't be," said his young anchorman, Mort Cristman. "We've got thirty-nine days more to go and we've got to build a boat. Or maybe a really large snowmobile that can hold all the animals two by two. Preferably one with a hot tub in it."

"And you'd really put two of everything in it?" Wally asked.

Mort grinned. "Nah, I'd stuff it with chicks and beer. Seriously, are you serious? Is this thing really going to stop sometime this century?"

Wally looked at the weather map. Now the end of the storm was as sharply defined as the front that had been hanging around for an almost twenty-four-hour period that seemed like a decade. Could it have been that little time? It felt as if he'd been in the studio for an eternity. The front itself was finally moving east and into warmer air where it would become the heavy rain that had been predicted.

"It won't turn itself off like a switch, but it will begin to slow down and stop completely in a couple of hours. Sorry, but it won't turn off as quickly and dramatically as it turned on, so we're still in it for a while."

"Then what?"

"Well, for starters, young guys like you can go out and shovel. I'd really like my car cleaned off." He laughed when Mort and a couple of staffers gave him the finger.

✦   ✦   ✦

Wilson Craft was dead. One minute he was trying to breathe, and the next he wasn't. His eyes were suddenly wide open in shock as he couldn't get air into his lungs, but they quickly closed and seemed to glaze over. The doctor tried CPR even though he feared it might further complicate Wilson's injuries, but nothing worked. Maddy wept softly and wondered if it had been a blessing. The hell it was, she decided. Everyone wanted to live and Wilson had fought hard to stave off death. Damn. A simple fall off a ladder should not have been fatal, but it was.

"I'm sorry," the doctor said as he covered Craft's body with his own jacket. "We'll get him out of sight so the kids don't panic."

It seemed like the logical, sensible thing to do; only she didn't want to be logical and sensible. Maddy wanted to cry, but held it back. Once she started it would be a long time before she stopped. There'd be time for that later. She still had scores of kids to take care of.

Maddy and a couple of others helped the doctor drag Wilson's body into a walk-in storage closet where they laid him on the floor. "Hope we remember he's there," said Frieda. "It'd be a helluva note if we didn't find him before fall."

The inanity of it sent them into nervous, exhausted laughter. It felt good. The world would not end. The radio was saying that the storm would end in a few hours, so all they had to do was hang on.

CHAPTER 15

MIKE AND PATTI HUGHES LISTENED INTENTLY TO THE RECORDED call to 911. It had come in long distance, from Boston.

"Jesus," muttered Patti as she listened again. "An e-mailed distress call." She looked at Mike, uncertain. "A hoax?"

"Maybe, but we can't take a chance." He checked the city map. 561 Beckett was about a mile away. The records said it was occupied and owned by Thomas and Traci Lawford. The Lawfords had made no contacts with the police since moving in, so they knew nothing more about them other than that they paid their taxes. They were just ordinary invisible people and now they were hurting.

"If the two she's talking about are Tower and Raines, and that seems obvious, we're going to need a lot of outside firepower and help," Patti said.

"Which we're not going to get," Mike added. "We're on our own. Again."

A more detailed map was pulled out, along with some overhead photos taken as part of an aerial survey a couple of years ago. Google Earth was used as well. The Lawford residence sat

194 Robert Conroy

in the middle of a large lot. There were houses on all sides, but nothing close.

Mike tried to recall if he'd ever driven through the neighborhood and thought he had, although nothing rang a bell. The relative isolation of the house created a problem, but the falling snow would help screen their movements. With luck, they could get cops inside a couple of the neighboring houses and set up for whatever might occur. The bad news was that, like the move on the motel, they would only have a handful of officers available. There'd be no help from other departments, the county sheriff, state police, or the FBI. Once again they'd have to do it with the tools and weapons at hand.

Perhaps that's better, Mike thought. If they showed up at the Lawfords' front door with a ton of firepower, Tower and Raines might open up with the automatic weapons they'd stolen. No, maybe it'd be better to do it on a small scale.

I'm kidding myself, he thought. *Tower and Raines know we're after them and will be ready. We're screwed.* But maybe they didn't know about the e-mail? Knowing that the police were looking for them and knowing the police had found them were two different things.

"I've gotten a couple of more phone calls about the e-mail," Thea Hamilton said. "She must've sent it out to everyone she knew. I've also checked with the phone company and the phone line is out. Or cut."

Mike thought furiously. "How much time before the snow breaks?"

"A couple of hours," said Patti. "And that's when Tower and Raines will kill her and make their break. So that means we really do have no choice but to make do with the resources at hand." She grinned wanly. "What we lack in manpower, we may be able to make up for in technology. Thanks to all that Federal money, the department's got some nice bells and whistles for us to play with."

"You really think it'll make up the difference?" Petkowski asked.

"No," she said. "But what are our choices? We just can't leave her there, can we? Not that I care, but where's the chief?"

Thea laughed harshly. "Back in his office with the door closed.

Same thing with the mayor. Will somebody tell me just what the hell's going on around here?"

Mort Cristman yawned hugely. "Hey, Wally, is this really the worst disaster ever to hit this area?"

"Might be," Wally said as he rubbed the sleep from his eyes. "At least it's one of the worst natural disasters. Some man-made tragedies have been real beauts. I vaguely recall reading about a cruise ship burning and sinking on one of the Great Lakes, and, of course, there've been tornados. About a century and a half ago, there was a truly hellacious forest fire in Michigan that killed a bunch, but that's about it for so-called natural disasters. It'll all depend on the final body count."

"Jeez, how morbid. I hope there isn't some ghoul out there hoping the body count will make this disaster number one."

"I hope not too. Tell me, do you remember where you were when Kennedy was killed?"

"Sorry, Wally, but I'm too young."

"I keep forgetting you're such a child. How about when the first Gulf War started, or the September 11 attacks on the World Trade Center?"

"Sure. Of course. I was a kid for the Gulf War, but the World Trade Center will stay with me forever." He shuddered as he recalled the televised horrors. "Some things you never forget, and maybe that's all to the good. Why?"

"Nothing, really. I just wonder if we're all going to remember this blizzard a couple of decades from now. Hell, I wonder if we'll even remember it a week or two from now? I'll bet you that, in just a short while, we'll all be wondering about the NCAA playoffs and the opening of the baseball season. This'll be nothing more than a bad dream when the snow finally melts. Unless we've lost a loved one or our home has been destroyed, it'll soon be a nuisance and then, after a while, we'll barely remember this at all."

Mort grinned. "If we don't, I'll have wasted a whole night with you, sailor boy."

Eight cops on four snowmobiles moved out from the Sheridan Police Station. Two of the snowmobiles trailed toboggans stacked with equipment. One of the overhead photos of the area they'd found in the City Planning Department's files had shown them how best to lay out their small manpower resources. Mike, Petkowski, and two other cops would enter a house directly in front of the Lawford residence, while the other four cops, led by Detective Sergeant Patti Hughes, would take over a house to the left.

They did not have enough manpower to surround the house; instead, they tried to set up an L-shaped ambush that would hopefully cover any directions Raines and Tower might try to use as an escape route. That such an arrangement would reduce the possibility of officers being hit by friendly fire had also entered their minds. The strategy was very similar to what they'd used at the motel.

Only one of the two houses they took over had been occupied, and the family hadn't wanted to leave. Who would blame them? There were three adults and two children. They had a fire in the fireplace and were warm, dry, and comfortable, and here were the cops sending them out into a blizzard. Finally, reason prevailed when they realized they were in danger and the cops promised to put them up at the Sheridan Motor Inn for the duration. The motel's management said they'd cover any costs. The family swore they would not contact any of the media. They understood it was imperative that the operation be kept secret.

Mike and Hughes could only hope they would keep their word. He visualized the aggressive blonde reporter who'd been wandering the police station and city hall showing up with a camera and demanding to interview Tower and Raines, and then asking Traci Lawford how she felt about being savaged by two murderers.

Two other houses flanking the Lawfords' were quickly checked and found empty. It was highly unlikely anyone would be returning home, although someone's arrival by snowmobile or cross-country skis was a possibility they could do without. If they had any chance of rescuing Traci Lawford, they had to have a large amount of luck and secrecy.

Petkowski set out his weapons and electronic toys. Along with sniper rifles and shotguns, the police also had fully automatic M16s. It occurred to them that they had brought more weapons than they had police officers to use them.

Petkowski and Mike set up portable infra-red and thermal

imaging sensors and directed them at the Lawford house. Detective Hughes, in the other side of the L, was doing the same.

"You gonna be able to see through the snow?" Mike asked her. Their night and thermal equipment was state of the art, but still not perfect. They also both hoped their radios, which were encrypted, could not be picked up by the media or cop wannabes.

"Not as well as if it wasn't snowing, but we can't have everything, now can we?"

The world is not perfect and life is not fair, Mike thought. *And there's no such thing as a free lunch,* he added. The clichés were old and worn, but terribly correct. He squinted through the night-vision scope at the Lawford house. At first he could see nothing—the snow was distorting the view, but then he thought he saw slivers of light and heat coming through otherwise covered windows. But were they unusual? Certainly there was some heat in the house.

There was one room on the first floor and one on the second that seemed to have more than their share of heat. Mike continued to stare until he was reasonably confident in his assessment.

Mike showed the scene to Petkowski who concurred. Mike then called Hughes on the radio. "My bet is that the bad guys are on the first floor and the hostage in the room on the second."

"Sounds as good as anything," Hughes said. "I'd just love to be able to verify that scenario before we go charging in."

Mike swallowed. Going charging in was something he was not looking forward to. Somehow they had to get closer to the house without being detected. Hopefully, they could use the foul weather to their advantage. There was no reason to fear that Tower and Raines had anything like the technology the cops had.

"Oh, fuck," snarled one of the other cops.

"What?" asked both Mike and Petkowski.

"You heard the radio?"

They had not. They'd kept the homeowner's radio on as background and told the officer nearest it to monitor the local news for any developments regarding the weather.

The cop shook his head in disbelief. "Some asshole newscaster just announced to the world that the police have two serial killers trapped in a house on Beckett Street in Sheridan."

Mike groaned. Maybe, just maybe, the two killers weren't

listening to the radio. It wasn't likely they'd be that lucky. They now had to assume that Tower and Raines knew they were out there and would use every means at their disposal to keep the cops away. Charging the house against the murderers' considerable firepower was no longer an option. They had to come up with a better, sneakier way.

I will never, ever, complain about anything, Maddy Kovacs thought. Her back ached from either sitting on the floor or on strange furniture, and her stomach was in a turmoil from the cold Mexican food combined with a Whopper. She hoped she wouldn't have diarrhea. She thought that if she did, she'd use up all the additional toilet paper that had just been delivered.

She stood and tried to stretch. She belched and that relieved some of the stress on her stomach. No, she would never complain again. Just like major disasters help put values and problems in a true perspective, so too had the events of the preceding day and night helped her sort out her personal values.

First, she now had a firm grip on what she wanted her future to be. Any doubts about teaching as a career were gone. Despite all her complaints and groans, she was glad she was in Patton Elementary and able to help when trouble found them. The kids needed her and she needed them. It sounded schmaltzy, but it was the truth. She would teach until she retired, or they carried her out.

Gone too were any doubts she'd had about Mike Stuart. More than anything, she wanted them to be together and, if right now wasn't an option, then real soon would have to do. Mike had said he loved her and now she realized that she loved him as well. Hell, she wasn't some dewy-eyed kid going around proudly but idiotically proclaiming her latest boyfriend as her soul-mate or her life's companion. No, she was a mature and educated woman who now had a very clear outlook on life.

Sure, she and Mike had differences, but who didn't? Maddy wore her Catholicism sincerely, but lightly, and she thought Mike was Episcopalian, if anything. She thought hardly anybody was Episcopalian anymore, and, like many American Catholics, she wasn't all that concerned about announcements from the Vatican. She would decide how many children they would have and when, along with Mike, she added hastily. Maddy hated the thought of abortion, but would not hesitate to have one if her life was in danger, or if the child was going to be terribly handicapped. She didn't see any problems with Mike on either issue.

As to money, heck, they both had good jobs and didn't piss away what they earned.

Maddy worked on stretching some more, and reluctant muscles creaked and began to function. She belched again and grinned at her crudeness. She walked quietly into the kitchen, trying not to disturb those who were sleeping. There was a pot of hot coffee on the stove. Electricity might be out, but the old range in the kitchen cooked with gas. Thank you, God!

She poured herself a cup and took a sip of the black stuff. She shuddered as the caffeine attacked her dormant system and slapped around some nerve endings. Maybe, just maybe, she and the others would be out of Patton Elementary and back to their real homes by tonight. The weather said the storm was going to break up and maybe they could soon send home the kids still in their care. That would be real nice for all concerned.

Maddy sensed that she had an unwashed odor about her and was glad that the cold kept it down. Of course, they were all a little ripe, especially some of the kids who weren't all that up on personal hygiene in the first place. God, she would kill for a warm shower. She'd already changed into the clothing she'd brought in her backpack. Maybe Mike would be her white knight on a charging snowmobile and take both of them home. Fat chance.

"Hi."

Maddy turned and saw two high school girls standing in the doorway and smiling shyly. "Can I help you?" she asked.

"Actually, we thought we could help you. I'm Tessa and this is Lori and we heard that your boyfriend is that real nice cop who helped us yesterday morning."

Maddy laughed. "If his name is Mike Stuart, you're right. So what can we do for each other?"

"Seriously," Tessa said. "We are bored out of our minds. We've been to the library and we were weeks ahead in our homework when the power went and, besides, it's full of kids making out and smoking pot. We just thought we could be useful."

"Our parents know we're safe," said Lori.

Maddy made a mental note to have the library checked. What was that overweight cop doing besides sitting in the office? "Either of you ever babysat?" They both had. "Well, you are hired."

"Chief Bench, where are you when I need you?" Mayor Carter snapped into his phone. A few moments later, his chief of police was in his office. Bench's eyes were red, and his face was pale, almost gray. He looked nauseous, which went well with the likelihood that he had a hangover. Otherwise, he seemed fairly lucid, although he stank of booze and old sweat. Carter shook his head. The man was a pig. He would have to go before the spectacle he'd made of himself rubbed off on the office of the mayor.

"Chief, I want you to fire Sergeant Stuart."

"What?"

"Damn it, Bench, you heard me."

Bench snickered, then tried to flick some dirt off his shirt. He stopped when he realized it was a stain. "Well, do you have a reason for wanting to can him, or is it because he pisses you off? Y'know, we do have a few little rules around here involving the termination of public employees. The last time I checked, he got an outstanding personnel evaluation from DiMona, which was signed off by both you and me, which also means it's gonna be difficult to make a case to throw him out. He's not a part of the union, but we do have written procedures regarding stuff like canning his ass without just cause, so you've got to give me a good reason before I can even start."

"Well, didn't he let that reporter in?"

"No, the doors were open and she walked in."

"Damn it, you know what I mean. Someone told her to come here and spy on us. Was that Stuart?"

"Uh-uh. I really think that someone else did it. Maybe DiMona called her. He hates my guts, and he's not that fond of you, either."

"But Stuart is DiMona's boy."

"Still can't just fire him."

"Then suspend him." Carter was getting frustrated and suspected that Bench was enjoying his discomfiture.

"Can't do that either, and even if we could, we shouldn't because we don't have any extra cops around here. But why are you so gung ho on getting rid of him? Don't bullshit me. The reporter thing doesn't cut it."

"He punched me and made me give him the list of defective buildings I'd put up."

Bench laughed. "That's priceless, although it does explain why you look like shit."

Carter was desperate. "I just want all this to go away. You know the FBI's after me, don't you?"

Bench laughed again and stood up. Then he glared at Carter with a semblance of dignity he hadn't shown in years. "Of course. I'm one of the guys who tipped them off, you dumb arrogant fucker. I've been telling them all about the way you've screwed the city, and I'm getting immunity in return. Now that all my shortcomings are going to be on the eleven o'clock news, I'm going to retire and save the city the aggravation of sacking me. Have a nice day, Mayor." He turned and walked out of the office. He slammed the door behind him.

Bench grinned as he walked down the hall to his office. It wouldn't be his for much longer, but that was okay. He heard a sharp thudding sound and turned back to the mayor's office.

Traci Lawford lived by the heat vent in her second-floor bedroom that had become a prison. It was both a source of warmth and knowledge. Sometimes Tower and Raines moved off and she couldn't hear them very well, but, more often than not, they came through loud and clear.

They were arguing again and she didn't know whether that was good or bad. The snow hadn't let up, which should have meant she was safe. The snow was her friend. She needed a friend.

The argument between her two tormentors directly concerned her. They'd picked up something on the radio about her, and they were considering leaving now and not waiting for the weather to break. However, they didn't know where the cops were. Logic said they were in the closest houses, but no one was visible. Traci had gone to a window and tried to signal, but got no response. She could scarcely see the nearest houses. They were little more than shapes in the snow, which meant no one could see her either. She wanted to scream. If the police were out there, why didn't they come?

Media exposure had been one of her fears and it had come true. Someone, someone on her list of so-called friends, had contacted the media without a thought to her safety. She gritted her teeth. If she ever got out of this, she'd kill whoever it was.

The absurdity of the situation struck her and she almost smiled. If she ever got out of this, she'd thank God, not go looking for revenge. Her survival was paramount. What happened in the next few minutes, up to a couple of hours, would determine whether she ever saw her husband again, or celebrated her thirty-fifth birthday.

Now they were talking about using her as a hostage when they left and killing her when they got clear because then she would be just so much additional weight on the snowmobile. They wouldn't even just throw her off because she knew too much. No, they'd decided that they would shoot her in the back of the head. She was terrified and wanted to break down, but willed herself not to. She had to stay focused.

Traci accepted as fact that they were planning to kill her. She did not accept as fact that she had to go quietly or easily. They had shamed her, hurt her, and humiliated her, but they had not destroyed her. For some reason she recalled a line from the movie *Independence Day*. She would not go easily into the night if she could possibly help it.

Traci stood up and walked nervously to the window. It was time.

Mike squinted through the night vision scope. He thought he had seen motion at the second-floor window, and had mentioned it to the other cops.

"Thank God you said that," said Officer Charley Donlan. "I thought I was going nuts. For an instant I thought I saw a naked woman up there, but then the snow got in the way."

Mike wondered why Donlan hadn't mentioned it in the first place. Was he afraid the others would laugh at him? If it was a woman, naked or not, it had to be Traci Lawford. At least they knew where she was. His hunch that she was on the second floor was correct. Now all they had to do was take advantage of that small fact.

"How do I look?" asked Petkowski from behind him. Mike was startled by the apparition in white, then grinned.

"You look like a Russian soldier at Stalingrad."

"Nah, I thought I looked like a management trainee for the KKK."

Petkowski was wearing a couple of white sheets that had been pinned and roughly sewn together. A pillowcase hid his head. He carried an M4, the carbine variant of the military's M16 that was also covered by white bedding. Out in the snow, he would be damn near invisible to the unaided eye.

"You sure you want to do this, buddy?" Mike asked.

"Hell yes," Petkowski answered with a trace of indignation. "Now give me a kiss goodbye, sailor."

Instead Mike patted him on the head and wished him good luck. All the kidding in the world couldn't hide the fact that Petkowski was going to crawl through the deep snow to the Lawford house. Fortunately, they didn't think that Tower and Raines had anything in the way of night vision or thermal imaging gear. If they did, Petkowski was screwed.

After he got to the house, they didn't have a real plan. It would depend on where the bad guys actually were and what they might do. One of Hughes' cops was going to attempt the same thing, but from the other side of the house.

It was nuts, Mike thought, but did they really have any other choices?

Petkowski opened a door that was out of view from the Lawford house and dropped down into the snow. Within seconds it was as if he no longer existed. Night vision didn't help. Infrared, however, picked up the traces of his body heat and registered him as moving with exquisite slowness towards the foreboding dwelling.

Maddy Kovacs was confident that the worst of their ordeal was over. Now all they had to do was wait to be rescued and taken home. Well, maybe rescued was too strong a term. It was not as if their lives were in danger. They were dry and safe in a school, not bobbing around in the ocean on a lifeboat. Nor were they endangered by fire. In fact, a little warm fire might be a welcome diversion.

Wilson Craft's death had been a tragic accident, nothing more. Perhaps all they'd been was terribly inconvenienced, although the late Wilson Craft might feel otherwise.

Maddy wondered if she had a home to go to. Her condo was well built, she thought, and it did have a steeply pitched roof that should have shed a lot of the snow, but you never knew. Neither of her roommates had made it home yet, and calls to neighbors about her property had gone unanswered.

"Just where the hell is everybody," she muttered to herself and drew surprised stares from a couple of sleepy children and grins from Tessa and Lori. The two girls had been surprisingly helpful. They were able to communicate with the children at a different level than she could. No matter how friendly a teacher might be, she was still a teacher, an authority figure.

At least she had no pets to worry about. Not even a goldfish. Several teachers were concerned about cats and dogs, although they all admitted that the animals would be more uncomfortable than in any real danger. They'd all been left with water and food as on any other day, so the real worry was where a dog might go to poop and pee, and if it got bored, what would it chew on. Cats used litter boxes, of course, and were above getting bored. If cleaning up dog shit from the family room carpet was the worst that happened, they would have fared well.

She left the classroom and walked down an empty hallway. It was good to be alone, if only for a few moments. Life in Patton Elementary in many ways did resemble being on a crowded lifeboat. She opened the door to the gym and stepped in. Wilson Craft, the maintenance man, had fallen and died on that floor and there was no longer any trace of either him or the frantic efforts to save him. It was as if he'd never existed. *There must be a lesson in that,* she thought, *and maybe someday I'll figure out what it is.*

Maddy shivered. It was colder than expected in the gym. Of course, with no heat there was no reason for it to be warm. But she didn't expect it to be quite as cold as it was.

She felt a drop of moisture on her cheek. Snow. She looked up and saw a patch of light through the roof and wisps of snow filtering down. There was a hole in the roof, and, as she stared in disbelief, it seemed to widen.

"Oh God," she said and walked carefully from the gym as if the sounds of her steps would disturb anything. When she got to the hallway she called out for Donna Harris, who came up quickly, recognizing the urgency in Maddy's voice.

"What's up?"

Maddy swallowed hard. "The roof. I think it's beginning to collapse."

CHAPTER 16

STAN PETKOWSKI CRAWLED SLOWLY THROUGH THE SNOW. EACH motion was choreographed by him to make as little of his body as possible visible to anyone in the house. In effect, he was swimming, leaning forward and dragging himself with his arms while his feet tried to find the ground beneath him. When he stopped, which he did only when he needed to catch his breath, the snow came up to the middle of his chest. He thought about going into the snow and burrowing like a rabbit in a cartoon, but this was real, not a damned cartoon.

Still, he was not a fool. He did not believe for an instant that he would be totally undetected. For one thing, his crawling left a trail. When the snow finally stopped, anyone in the house would be able to follow that trail and see where it ended and his priceless body began. He would be an unmissable target. Stan hoped the snow kept up for at least a little while after he reached the house and blurred evidence of his passing. Also, as he crawled, he got wet, and the sheets that covered him were becoming translucent as they dampened, reducing their effect as camouflage.

Oh well, he thought, *who ever said this would be easy?* He paused behind a massive lump on the Lawfords' front lawn. It was a large ornamental shrub that had been turned into a snow mountain. It hid him from anyone in the house and gave him a chance to rest. He burrowed into it and tried to warm up. At least he was out of the wind and the snow no longer fell directly on him. It was almost an igloo and igloos kept Eskimos warm, didn't they? So why was he still cold?

He radioed to Mike that he was about fifty feet from the house and there was no sign of life or any indication that he'd been spotted. It reinforced his own opinion that the two bad guys, Tower and Raines, were a long ways from being rocket scientists. But Stan had not made corporal and survived a decade on the force by underestimating an adversary, especially heavily armed murderers. The thought of what the two men had done to the couple in the motel made him shudder. He had no idea who Traci Lawford was, but he could only guess that she was being subjected to an ordeal that no human deserved.

He looked up at the looming building. He had to get closer. He had to see just what the hell was going on inside that big house.

Stan radioed Mike that he was going to move closer and again began his slow, laborious crawl. After what seemed an eternity, he was up against the brick wall of the Lawford house. The building was solid brick and not a façade like new houses. It would make a helluva good fortress if it came down to a gunfight. Shit, why did the bad guys draw all the high cards?

He was beneath a window. He asked Mike if there was any indication of undue light or heat from behind it and was assured that there wasn't. As far as technology and the human eyeball could determine, the room was empty, although there was probable occupancy of the room farther to Stan's right as he faced the building.

Stan raised himself to where he could see in over the snow piled against the window and confirmed that the room was indeed empty. However, he did see a snowmobile in another room and just visible down a hallway. He radioed that info to the others. If the killers tried to escape by that route, they would have to exit the rear of the house. Petkowski was grateful he was in the front. He checked and the window was locked. Just as well. He had no urge to crawl in and confront Tower and Raines all by his Polish lonesome.

Stan checked with Mike and was told to sit tight. "Easy for you to say," he whispered in mock anger. "You're in a nice dry house while I'm freezing my ass off in a snowbank."

Stan was about to add something else when he heard the sound of a window opening above him. He looked up through the falling snow and saw a naked woman leaning out.

Officer Clyde Detmer wondered if he was making the right decision. He'd been offered a decent pension and was considering taking it. He would miss being a cop. But he already missed riding a motorcycle and giving tickets to people who thought they were either above the law or who professed blindness when it came to the speed limit and stop signs.

Still, he had nothing to complain about. He had a bad habit of being sarcastic, about work and his weight, and he knew that annoyed some people. His job this day wasn't difficult and it did enable him to work with kids, which he enjoyed. He also liked working with their teachers. With only a few exceptions, he respected them. He had an associate's degree in criminal justice and had toyed with the idea of getting his bachelor's, but his wife talked him out of it. He was fifty-five, she reminded him. Just what would he do with the degree? Teach? There were more teachers than there were jobs in Michigan; ergo, he would not go back to school.

When the severity of the storm became obvious, he volunteered to get out of the offices and help control hundreds of antsy kids. The little kids responded well. The bigger ones were different. With them, he decided, it was like trying to herd cats. Raging hormones and pent-up energy barely accounted for it. It more than kept him busy, but he did feel he was doing something useful. Along with having a cop's command presence, Detmer was a large man.

He was deeply grieved on hearing of the death of Wilson Craft. He had known the man, and while he and Wilson had never been close, his death was a tragedy nonetheless.

Even after the power went out, he still convinced himself that things were pretty much under control. However, when the fire alarms started screaming and the sprinklers went off, he wondered just what the hell else could go wrong. He told those teachers who were too surprised to think that they should get the kids under tables and desks while he went to find the source of the fire. Normally, everyone would have filed out of the building and gathered on the lawns and in parking lots. Only thing was, that was clearly impossible unless it was an act of utter desperation, and his gut said it was a damned false alarm.

"There's smoke reported down by the library," a very harassed Nancy Hamlin announced. It was her second year as principal and Wally wondered if she wasn't in way over her head.

"Then why did all the sprinklers in the building go off?" Clyde asked. Nancy said she had no idea.

A few seconds later, they and the sirens stopped. "I'm going down to the library," Detmer said. "I'll bet you a dollar that some jackass kids set it off."

Nancy smiled wanly. "I will not bet against you."

Chief Bench turned and walked toward the mayor's office again. He was more sober than he'd been in days as he opened the door and walked in. The mayor was nowhere to be seen, but there was the sound of moaning and the smell of cordite and blood.

Thea Hamilton followed the chief and walked behind the desk. "Oh, Christ," she said and began to vomit. Carter lay face down on the floor in a widening pool of blood and what looked like pieces of skull and brain matter. A handgun lay beside him. Behind them, voices yelled for help.

EMS techs and other cops arrived quickly and began to work on the mayor's limp form. Bench stepped aside to allow them through. A sheet of paper on the mayor's desk caught his eye and he picked it up. The heading was Carter-Sheridan Construction Company and it was a list of addresses. As quickly as he could without his glasses, Chief Bench read the list and the brief accompanying text. It said that these were the properties the FBI was investigating for shoddy construction, and there were nearly fifty of them. Sampson's Super Store was on it, which provided an answer to why the mayor shot himself. At least five people were now dead at the store and many injured. The mayor was looking at major jail time for his involvement in the deaths and the fraud. Bench had done dumb things in his life, but he'd never endangered anyone. He found little pity for his fallen boss.

"I didn't know the mayor could shoot a gun," Thea said.

"He can't," Bench responded. "He's still alive. Once again, he's fucked up."

Bench allowed his eyes to wander down the list. One additional building caught his eyes—Patton Elementary School. *Jesus,* he thought, *now the stupid bastards have put little kids in danger.*

"Damn you, Wally. You said this was going to end soon."

"Hold on to your delicious little gubernatorial panties, Lauren, it is ending, just not as fast as we'd all like. Besides, the word 'soon' is very subjective. How soon is soon to God, for instance? A billion years? Think about it. This could be it for the rest of our lives. Maybe a new ice age just began and we're privileged to see it."

"Shut up, Wally, and get serious. Make it stop."

Wally Wellman glanced at the computer monitor that showed the latest satellite update. Another look at the radar and satellite report confirmed what he'd said. The line of demarcation now cut through the metropolitan area like a knife. To the south and west of Detroit, around Romulus and the Detroit Metropolitan Airport, there were reports of clearing skies. The plows trying to clear the airport runways were beginning to make some progress. It would be a long time before planes moved, but there were places where the runway was actually visible.

Not so to the north of the city. "Wally, we've got more than a foot of new snow in the roadway behind where the Guard has cleared it. The plows are having to replow what they've already cleared. It's like a tar baby. We just keep getting in deeper."

"Not my fault, Governor. I only make the announcements. As they say, I'm in marketing, not production."

"Wally, don't be a smartass. I'm beginning to like you again, so don't screw it up. Oh, that's right, I always did like you—just some days more than others."

Wally grinned. He liked the idea of her liking him. "Seriously,

Lauren, it is beginning to clear, but that's the key word—beginning. When the front passes, it seems to turn off rather quickly, but it's still not going to be instantaneous and it's got a long ways to go before it reaches you. You're on the northern fringe of it, so it's going to be a while before any change comes through to where you are."

"Yeah, yeah, I know that. I just need somebody to complain to and you're the lucky one."

Lucky me, indeed, thought Wally with a smile. *And don't ever stop calling me.*

Traci Lawford leaned out the window and looked down at the deep, white snow. It looked so inviting, even fluffy like a pillow. The cold, wet wind on her bare skin told her that it was treacherous, not gentle. And it might cover something very harmful should she jump and land on it.

Even though it was her own yard, she was disoriented both by the abuse she'd endured and the snow that had wiped out any semblance of familiarity. The yard that she'd taken for granted now looked alien and threatening. Worse, she hated and feared heights. She'd gotten physically ill watching scenes of people jumping to their deaths from the World Trade Center. What terrors could motivate a person to do something like that? Now she was beginning to realize the answer—total desperation. Here, Tower and Raines were the all-consuming flames.

Put it in perspective, she ordered herself. She was not on the top of the World Trade Center. No, she was only a dozen or so feet above a snow-covered lawn. Those people in the house were going to kill her if she didn't free herself. She couldn't depend on the possibility of cops coming to help her. She had to get out of the house.

Traci leaned farther out the gabled window and eased herself onto the roof. The snow was deep and the footing slippery, especially since her bare feet got cold quickly and lost any sense of touch. She managed to get herself out onto the roof and sat there, shivering and naked in snow that was over her waist, and contemplated her next move. She was two stories above the snow-covered ground. Did she really have the courage to jump?

From inside the house, she heard the door to her room open, followed by angry shouts. She climbed up to the top of the gable. Now she was almost three floors up. Her feet dislodged some snow and a small avalanche fell.

Below her and unseen, Petkowski spoke softly and carefully into his radio. "Did anyone see that? Where did she go? I lost her."

"She's on the roof," Mike answered, "and just out of your view. Oh, shit. Someone's at the window and it's got to be one of the bad guys looking for her."

Mike gave the radio to Officer Donlan and picked up a rifle. The range wasn't all that great, but he only had sight of part of the target's body and the blowing snow distorted the view. He only assumed the person in the window was either Tower or Raines, but he wasn't certain. He didn't want to kill an innocent person. What if Traci Lawford wasn't the only hostage in that house? They'd assumed she was alone, but what if she wasn't? What if there was a girlfriend, or a lover, in that house? Hell, what if it was a small kid?

The man in the window disappeared. Had he realized that their prisoner had flown? It occurred to Mike that the man might have assumed that Traci Lawford had jumped instead of being just above him on the roof. Good—let him think that.

But she couldn't stay up there forever. Minutes would be more like it. Mike didn't know how long it would be before hypothermia set in. Considering her total nakedness, the snow depth, and a wind chill well below freezing, it wouldn't take long before she was incapable of functioning and not much longer after that before she was dead.

Across the yard, Traci Lawford's cold hands lost their grip on the roof and she slid off the gable. As Mike watched in horror, she slid down the roof and, arms flailing, fell soundlessly into the snow by the house, only a few feet from where Petkowski waited. A second later, Traci Lawford began to scream in agony and flop around in the snow that trapped her.

The roof at Patton Elementary fell in sections that seemed like waves. Still, it happened fast enough that there was no real way to escape the torrent of white snow and roofing debris that buried many in the school.

One moment Maddy and Donna were looking up at the shuddering ceiling and wondering what their next step might be, and then they heard a roar and the roof came down on top of them. They tried to run, but were quickly engulfed and buried.

Maddy was covered by the white stuff. She tried to move and couldn't. She was pinned. With great effort, she twisted her body, while at the same time, more snow and debris poured down on them. She heard something snap, and then she screamed from the searing pain in her left arm before she passed out. Before losing consciousness, she realized that being able to scream told her that she was buried in an air pocket.

Maddy awoke to more pain and cold. Something hard was sticking her in the side. She could breathe, but not see. Gritting her teeth, Maddy started to use her good arm and hand as a scoop to try to dig her way up and out.

Officer Stan Petkowski stood in stunned disbelief in snow that came to the middle of his chest. One second he'd been contemplating a way of getting into the Lawford house, the next Traci Lawford was writhing in agony a few feet from him. Her leg was twisted and a piece of bone had burst through her skin—a compound fracture. Worse, it looked like she might slip under the snow and drown. Or freeze to death. Christ.

Petkowski yanked off his now filthy white sheets and pushed the few steps to the screaming woman. He threw them over her in a pathetic attempt to cover her and keep her warm. She stared at him with horror-filled eyes and continued to scream.

The door to the house opened and a man with a rifle stood only a few feet in front of him. Petkowski recognized Raines from the photo he'd seen. Petkowski scrambled for his rifle, but a confused, hurt, and panicked Traci Lawford chose that moment to grab for his leg, throwing him off balance.

Raines fired a burst from his M16. The bullets stitched across Petkowski's chest and hurled him into the snow that rapidly began to turn red. Raines looked down at the fallen woman and realized she was no use to him as a hostage.

"Useless bitch," he muttered and aimed his weapon at her.

Across the street, Mike Stuart watched through the telescopic sight. Thermal imaging showed one man down and he knew it was Stan. Inadvertently, the other cop had been in Mike's line of fire. Now the only one left standing was the shooter, framed in the doorway. From where he was, Mike had no idea which of the two killers he had in his sights. He didn't care. He saw the target raise his weapon and aim it down.

Mike fired a short burst of three. At a little more than a hundred yards, it was an easy hit. The man silhouetted in the doorway lurched back, crumpled, and lay still. He heard Patti Hughes yelling "Go, go, go," to the other officers. Mike headed towards the door and joined the charge. There was still one man to go and a couple of people to try to save.

Maddy Kovacs's head and shoulders were finally free of the snow and she gasped in relief. The pain in her arm had receded to simple agony. It was endurable. Other teachers, along with Tessa and Lori, pulled her the rest of the way out. She had to tell them that she was hurt and to leave her arm alone. They got the message when she howled as someone touched her. A sobbing Tessa took off her coat and wrapped it around Maddy's shoulders.

Finally, she stood on the snow-covered floor, clutching her bad arm with her good one. Donna Harris lay unconscious and bleeding from a head wound. Frieda Houle finished checking Donna over. "She's alive. Other than a probable concussion, I don't know what else is wrong with her." Frieda caught a look at Maddy's arm. "Oh shit, come here."

While Frieda tied on a rough splint, Maddy tried to figure out what remained to be done. Snow mountains were everywhere and more snow was falling through the opened roof. Kids were crying and several adults looked like they were in shock.

Maggie Tomasi grabbed her by her good arm. "Four kids are missing."

Maddy looked down at Donna. Her eyes were blinking open, but she was only barely conscious, if that much. "Everybody digs," Maddy ordered. She felt wet and realized the sprinkler system had just activated. Along with the snow, it was raining.

✧   ✧   ✧

Jimmy Tower was panicked. He'd run down from the second floor, and been behind and to the left of Raines when Raines had shot the ghostly white apparition standing over Traci Lawford. He'd started to lunge forward when Raines suddenly fell backward a second before he heard the sound of more distant gunfire.

One look at Raines was enough. Two bullets had entered his chest and exited through giant holes in Raines' back. Raines' insides were splattered all over the floor and walls. He'd gurgled for a couple of seconds and then lay still.

Tower knew he wasn't considered very smart, but even a dumb animal knows when to flee instead of fighting overwhelming odds. Surrendering was out of the question. He'd been in prison and been badly treated by both inmates and guards. Other inmates had thought he'd make a great boy toy, and he'd been raped on a number of occasions. No, he'd rather die than go back to jail, and endure the pain and the shame again.

"Gotta get out of here," he said to himself. Through the snow, he thought he could see shapes converging on the house. He ran to the back of the house where the snowmobile was and opened the family room doorwall. He didn't have his winter gear on—there simply wasn't enough time. He might freeze his ass off, but he'd be okay if he could get far enough away from this house.

Tower hopped on and turned on the ignition. It started with a roar and he gunned the machine out into the snow-covered backyard.

Mike arrived at the fallen Petkowski just seconds after the other officers. Wading through the chest-deep snow had taken what seemed to be an eternity of supreme effort, and Mike was breathing heavily from the exertion. EMS personnel had been waiting behind the houses where the police were stationed and were slowly converging on the two fallen people. There was still a shooter in the house and they were supposed to wait for the all clear before tending to any injured. Still, they found it impossible to wait while people might be dying.

Of the two people down, Petkowski was obviously in worse condition. There was blood all over his chest and head. His eyes blinked feebly and his breath was raspy. His Kevlar vest had stopped most of the bullets but at least one had penetrated near his shoulder. Traci Lawford had stopped screaming and looked about in wide-eyed shock.

The roar of an engine brought Mike back to his senses. He was in the way of the medical personnel and there was still a killer on the loose. The sound was a snowmobile. Mike ran around the house in time to see Sergeant Patti Hughes plant herself in front of a monster that was bearing down on her. She never got off a shot before the snowmobile struck her and flung her against the side of the house like a limp toy.

Mike screamed in anger and frustration as the vehicle turned in front of him. Still, he couldn't shoot indiscriminately. It wouldn't be like shooting Raines where there was a brick house directly behind the target. Now there were houses behind him and there were people in them. An M16 round could travel more than a mile and could pierce walls. He fired a short burst down, towards the ground. If he hit anything it would be the driver's legs. If he missed, maybe the shots would go into the snow.

There was no response from Tower. The bullets had all missed him. But one had hit the snowmobile, piercing the gas tank, which erupted in a ball of flame that wrapped itself around Tower and threw him onto the snow-blanketed ground only a few feet from Mike. He flailed and tried to stand up. He had a pistol in his hand and howled in pain. He seemed to point the gun at Mike. "Thank you," said Mike and he fired three more rounds into the stocky little man's chest.

Mike lowered the rifle. He walked back to the house through the trail he'd made. EMS personnel were rushing to aid the fallen. Traci Lawford's leg was clearly broken and they began to move her into the house. Setting it there would provide little more than first aid. She needed a hospital.

Petkowski was in far worse shape. He had to go to a hospital right now for him to stand any chance at all. The EMS tech shook his head and said they'd do their best, but it didn't look good at all.

Patti Hughes was trying to sit up. "My leg's broken too, damn it."

Mike started to shake with relief. He'd never before even drawn his weapon, much less shot anyone, and now he'd killed two men in a matter of minutes. That they'd deserved all they'd gotten and more was scant consolation. He'd killed. He didn't like it.

Another EMS tech began to examine Hughes. She was yet another person who needed a ride to the hospital. Out of the corner of his eye, Mike sensed a large, even monstrous shape, coming across the lawns. At its front a huge plow bulled the snow out and away. It pulled up in front of Mike. The logo on the door of the truck said Gomez Snow Removal.

A Hispanic-looking man leaned out the driver's side. "I heard you got people who got to go to the hospital? Put them in the back. I know a way to get there if I stay off the roads."

EMS and other cops put all three people in the back of the dump truck. Mike turned to Gomez. "Who told you to come?"

"Thea Hamilton," Gomez said. "I called her a while ago offering help, and she called me when you guys left for here."

With a roar, the big truck took off through the snow. It wasn't going fast, but at least it was moving. The hospital they were headed to was more of an industrial clinic than a real hospital, but it was a lot better than trying to do a bunch of medical procedures in a living room. Maybe, finally, things were going to settle down and turn out right.

"Hey, Sarge!" yelled one of his cops. "We got problems at one of the schools. Roof's down and people are trapped and, oh yeah, there may be a fire."

"Which one?" Mike asked with a feeling of dread.

"Patton."

CHAPTER 17

WHEN THE POWER WENT OUT, STONER THOUGHT IT WAS AN inconvenience. Now he realized he was getting cold. Red and Gus were looking at him for leadership.

"Okay," he said. "Do we want to go back to the classrooms?"

"Hell no," said Red, and Gus nodded.

"Then we'd better do something to get warm. This is a library and it's empty because it's cold but it's full of books and stuff that will burn and keep us warm. The power won't be out for too long so let's just get some old encyclopedias and burn them." He giggled. "Nobody uses them anymore. Maybe they'll even thank us."

The others agreed and they quickly accumulated a pile of old books. Gus had once been a Boy Scout, which they thought was hilarious, and knew how to start a fire. They would keep it small and on the floor, which they didn't think would burn. The floor felt like it was slate.

In a few minutes, a decent fire was burning and keeping them warm. Stoner thought they'd be able to stay there forever if the power didn't come back. There were plenty of books that nobody read anymore thanks to Nook and Kindle and other things. Food would be a problem, though, and Stoner's stomach was beginning to grumble. They'd already eaten everything in their backpacks.

They were smoking pot and discussing their fate when a gust of wind from somewhere took their fire and blew the burning pages around the library. To their horror, some of them settled in wastebaskets and other places that contained something to burn. They ran around and tried to stamp out the embers, which only sent more swirling into the air.

The fire began to spread as embers flew down hallways. This activated the smoke detectors, which, being battery operated, were still functioning. As they commenced their ungodly screeching, the sprinkler system turned itself on. The fires were quickly extinguished, but the damage had been done. Everyone in the three connecting buildings was now wet as well as cold. Surrounded by smoke, and dripping, the three young men stood in the library, too stunned to move. They were still standing by the remains of their original campfire when several teachers and Officer Detmer found them. A horde of students followed them. Almost all of them were recording the event on their phones and cameras. Detmer was out of breath, but smiled when he saw the soggy joint that was still in Stoner's hand.

Detmer took the joint, smelled it, smiled again, and put it in a plastic bag. "Damned if this doesn't look like probable cause to search everything you've got, including body cavities. I have been waiting to bust your worthless ass for a very long time and now it's happened. Hallelujah."

Detmer kicked their backpacks, which were soaked and on the floor. They came open and more bags of marijuana spilled out along with vials of prescription drugs. "The mother lode," Detmer crowed. Some of the kids watching applauded, but he felt that a number had groaned. He secured the three dealers with plastic ties and then rifled through their possessions. Still more marijuana was discovered, along with an assortment of pills that Detmer said looked like ecstasy. Stoner moaned when Detmer got to his pack and a flash drive fell out. The officer plugged it into a laptop—luckily a teacher had found a dry one—and turned the screen so nobody else could see what was on it. Not only did the flash drive contain records of all Stoner's business transactions, but there were a number of pictures of female students either undressed or giving the three of them sex. Stoner was eighteen and an adult, but Detmer recognized some of the girls. A few were as young as twelve.

"I think I want a lawyer," Stoner muttered as he considered the consequences of statutory rape on top of drug possession.

Mike steered his snowmobile through the hidden streets of Sheridan as quickly as possible, but it still seemed like an eternity before he arrived at the school.

Scores of people were digging in and around the collapsed building. Parents and neighbors had arrived to help, along with police, fire, and EMS. As he watched, a snowmobile with a child strapped to a sled departed. An adult was also on the sled helping to comfort the child.

With his badge clearly visible, people moved aside and let him into what remained of Patton Elementary. A woman with a bandage on her head stood against the hallway wall. Dried blood caked her face. If the wall hadn't been there, Mike was certain she'd have fallen over. With a jolt, he recognized Donna Harris. Had it been only two days ago that she'd had them over for dinner? He touched her shoulder and she reacted suddenly.

"What?"

"Donna, it's me, Mike Stuart."

Her eyes focused a little. She was concussed and having difficulty identifying people. "Oh yeah, Mike. How are you? Maddy's okay, by the way. I'm fine. Thanks for asking. I look like shit, but I'm fine. The fire's out and the sprinklers have stopped."

I'm better off than you are, Mike thought, although the news about Maddy lifted a weight from him. But what the hell was she talking about fires and sprinklers? "You really okay, or should you go to the hospital?"

"I can think a little. This isn't my first concussion and there are people who are lots worse off than I am. The doctor's checked me out and told me to stay right here, so that's what I'm doing. People think I'm a hero because I got hurt. Can you imagine that?"

Mike grinned despite himself. "Wonderful. Where's Maddy?"

"In the classroom at the end of the hall. The one with all the snow in it."

Mike pushed his way through a crowd of people passing snow and trash through and out like a bucket brigade, only they were using their hands and wastebaskets and not buckets. Finally, he made it into a classroom that was the focus of their efforts. Maddy, her arm in a sling, was directing traffic. There was a cheer and a small form was lifted from the snow. It was a little girl, maybe eight years old, and the sight of the child choked him up. Then the girl started crying and everyone cheered again, because that meant she was alive, and that made the girl wail even louder. She was placed on a piece of plywood that was doubling as a stretcher and moved to another room.

"That's it," Maddy said triumphantly. "All present and accounted for." She saw Mike and grinned. "Bumps and bruises, and maybe one broken arm, not counting mine," she said to everyone around, but to him in particular, "but no one's in really bad trouble from the collapse."

She felt the caveat was necessary since Wilson Craft had died before the roof's collapse. His body was still in the storeroom and buried in snow. Cold storage, she thought.

The crowd cleared out of the classroom, leaving Mike and Maddy alone, if only for a moment. She kissed him quickly and put her head on his shoulder, again thinking that he wasn't that much taller than she.

"Where've you been keeping yourself, policeman?"

Mike laughed. "I've been busy."

"The two guys? Did you get them?"

"Yeah, we got them," he said and gave a summary of the events. As he reached the conclusion, he began to shake all over and she looked at him in alarm.

"Maddy, I shot them. I killed both of them."

She wrapped her one good arm around him while he tried to regain control of himself. "It's all right, Mike, you did what you had to. You saved the woman and you probably saved a lot of other people if either one of them had gotten away."

"I know," he managed to say. The shaking was subsiding. He had to have someone to talk to and he was very glad it was Maddy.

"God, Maddy, I'm being very greedy with my problems. You must have been going through hell. Look at this place. It looks like a bomb hit it."

She too started to shake and it was his turn to hold her. "Hey, school's out, isn't it? I was strong for as long as I had to be and now I don't have to anymore."

"You needed here?"

"No," she said. "The last of the parents are here for their kids. I am finally superfluous."

Mike realized he'd been on duty for a very long time with little more than catnaps to sustain him. He was both hungry and sleepy. He kissed her gently on the forehead.

"Y'know, I think the world can get along fine without us for a few hours. I still have a snowmobile and your place is the closest. After getting you to the hospital, that is."

"Sounds good to me." Then she looked up at the bright blue sky. "Well, I'll be damned. It's stopped snowing."

"Hallelujah! It's over," exclaimed Mort Cristman. "Maybe we can go home."

Wally stretched and yawned. "Tell me how, buddy. The sun may be shining, but there's still more than five feet of the ugly white stuff on the ground. I still cannot fathom why people would voluntarily go out and play in it. Mankind was meant to stay indoors. That's why God took away all our fur."

The last official measurement of the snow's depth had pegged it at sixty-three inches, and that didn't take into account the considerable drifting that had doubled the depth in some places.

Cristman sobered. "And the death toll is so high. What're we at now, nearly a thousand?"

"That's what they say, and it's going to get worse. More bodies are going to be found and now idiots who are out of shape are going to get heart attacks from trying to shovel their way out of this mess. The body count may be well over fifteen hundred before this is finished. Oh, did you give any thought as to where the snow's going to go? My forecast says the temperature's going over forty tomorrow and will be in the fifties by the weekend. That means major melting and there's too much snow for the sewer system to absorb, so there'll be deep water all over the place. We prayed for the snow to stop and now it has. Always be careful of what you wish for—it may come true."

Cristman shook his head. "You are such a bundle of happiness. Why don't you call your governor friend and ask her what she's going to do about it. Maybe I can get a low-interest loan to dig my car out."

There was a picture of Wally's late wife on his desk. He looked at it and smiled, and he could have sworn she smiled back. Nah, he was just too tired to think. But calling Lauren seemed like a great idea. He picked up the phone and punched in the numbers.

EPILOGUE

MIKE WATCHED FOR ONCOMING TRAFFIC AND TURNED LEFT, AWAY from the imposing bulk of the hospital located a few miles south of Sheridan. He was in his own car, not a squad car, which meant that a degree of caution was required. He was also wearing civilian clothes, not that any driver could tell. Maddy said he'd look like a cop regardless what he wore. Still, he didn't want the embarrassment of being pulled over by another cop.

He'd left the hospital buoyed by a degree of good news. Petkowski was continuing to improve, however slowly. The stocky cop would never regain full use of his left arm and, thus, would never again patrol the streets of Sheridan on his beloved motorcycle. For that matter, it was unlikely that he would ever drive a patrol car. The city would find a place for him—somehow, someplace—while he collected a pension for partial disability. Petkowski was appreciative of this as well as the simple fact that he was still alive and able to use his arm at all. He'd nearly bled to death and his shoulder had been turned to mush and crushed bone by Raines' bullets.

He'd told Mike that he would take some of his convalescent

time to go to college and get more education in computer science. Mike hadn't known about his friend's interest in computers, and thought there would be a place for someone knowledgeable about cyberspace and computer crime. They'd joked about Stan pretending to be a fourteen-year-old girl in a porn sting. Mike then told Stan that he was going to start law school in the fall, and Stan feigned disappointment that Mike had chosen a life of white-collar crime.

As to Stan's love life, well, for the short term that had gone from bad to worse. Cindy Baumann had inexplicably made up with her abusive and obnoxious shit of a husband and they'd moved away, thus dashing any hopes that he would be her knight in Kevlar armor. Petkowski had been disconsolate for about ten minutes until he realized that one of the nurses was a) paying a lot of attention to him, and b) very attractive and single. *Stay tuned,* Mike thought with a smile. Stan might finally get truly lucky. God knew he deserved it.

Detective Patti Hughes was back at work, although with a cane and a lousy disposition because she was essentially desk-bound, and that really frustrated her. Her husband and kids were just happy to get her out of the house.

Chief Bench had retired and left town, and some jokers suggested that he'd bought a brewery in Milwaukee and retired to live inside a vat. Whatever, he wasn't around and had been replaced by Joey DiMona, who held the rank of acting chief, just as Mike now held the rank of acting lieutenant in charge of the Traffic Division. If they succeeded in dragging the job researches out long enough, the city council might just give the jobs to them on a permanent basis. Mike would like that.

Mike, Patti, and Stan had all been decorated and commended for their actions. Mike had gotten two paragraphs in *Newsweek* as the magazine summarized the ravages of the storm and its unexpectedly high human cost. After several postponements, an appearance on the *Today Show* was cancelled when the public lost interest in the story.

So what was the cost? Mike gave it some thought. In total for the area, the estimate was about five hundred dead, not the thousand or more some had forecast. Sheridan alone had suffered disproportionately and people wondered why. Of course, just how many had died depended on who was counting and what they were counting.

Obviously, the five people asphyxiated in the car needed to be counted, as did the old guy who froze in the snow and the five who were killed when Sampson's roof caved in. But what about Tower and Raines and the two people they killed? If it hadn't been for the snow, they'd all be alive. So too with the UPS driver who'd been shot by a homeowner who was now facing manslaughter charges, and there was the woman who'd bled to death from the deer slashing her.

Then add Mayor Carter, whose suicide took days to become official. He'd lingered on for nearly a week before they finally pulled the plug on his brain-dead body. And don't forget Wilson Craft, who wouldn't have been on a ladder if it hadn't snowed. Add other people who'd suffered fatal heart attacks and you had a current total of twenty-one fatalities. Quite a lot for a smallish city like Sheridan.

Mayor Carter's death seemed to have halted, or at least slowed, the FBI's investigation into the construction scandal. Bench had offered to turn state's evidence, but it then turned out he didn't know enough about it to make it worthwhile.

The death toll continued to rise as the snow melted. All over the snow-covered portion of the state, bodies were still emerging and after a couple of people were found in drifts, great care was taken while removing snow. Some of the workers had been caught referring to the bodies as "popsicles" and had been chastised by the media.

Some of the bodies were those of senior citizens with dementia who'd managed to wander away from the facilities that were supposed to be caring for them. Criminal negligence charges were being considered against those responsible.

Many others were injured by the storm. While broken bones like Maddy's could heal fairly quickly, psychological problems did not. Traci Lawford, for instance, had left the hospital on crutches after a few weeks, but was under psychiatric care. She and her husband had moved and vowed never to return. Their house was now on the market at a bargain price. After what she'd endured, who could blame her? Mike thought the Lawfords would likely leave the Sheridan area altogether. In a follow-up interview, a haunted-looking and gaunt Traci had confided to him that she thought people were staring at her. Sadly, Mike thought she was right. Everyone in town seemed to know what horrors had gone on in the old house.

Damaged buildings were still common sights as local contractors had been overwhelmed by the number of collapsed or damaged roofs. Nothing was quite as dramatic or tragic as the collapse of Patton Elementary or Sampson's Super Store, but hundreds of roofs needed repair in Sheridan alone. A change in the building code was contemplated. Likewise, there was dismay that the storm sewers had been overwhelmed by the melting runoff. If a building had a basement, it had gotten a lot of water in it. Insurance companies were taking a beating, and that meant rates would rise next year. One car insurance company was contemplating suing the State of Michigan for damaging so many cars that were insured by them when the tow trucks and dozers had to move them. Life just wasn't fair, some people complained, but no one was listening. At least the media had finally stopped referring to the damaged buildings as looking like a "war zone." Mike hated that phrase.

Residents of Sheridan and elsewhere had given up on having green lawns this year. As the snow was finally removed or melted, what lay beneath was brown and dead. Landscapers would get rich. The federal government had declared Michigan a disaster area, which meant low-interest financing for all the repairs would be available.

Sampson's Super Store was not being rebuilt. The company was filing for Chapter 11. Wal-Mart had won. Tyler Holcomb, Sampson's heroic and hard-pressed manager, would not be around to see it. He'd been hired away by Wal-Mart to be a regional manager at just about twice his pay at Sampson's. He deserved it, Mike thought. There was a hell of a lot of stress at Wal-Mart, but the consensus was that Holcomb could handle it.

In the midst of the tragedies, it seemed almost trivial that the governor was going to marry some local weatherman from TV6. At least someone gets to get married, Mike thought.

Maddy had told him that she looked forward to life being normal, whatever that was. She said she would never complain about parent-teacher conferences or lesson plans. Mike thought that vow would last about two weeks.

Mike turned down the street that led to Maddy's condo. It still seemed strange to see parts of brown lawns. Despite steadily rising temperatures, the snow had been a long time disappearing. The schools and stores hadn't fully opened for more than two weeks after the storm stopped as mountains of snow were removed to make new mountains of snow out in fields and parks. A couple of radio stations had run contests regarding when the last snow would disappear from such and such a place. One station offered an Antarctic cruise for two as first prize and tens of thousands had entered. Another station had a "Mow the Snow" contest when the piles hung around too long. Contestants painted their snow green and decorated the piles with deck chairs and other paraphernalia and pretended it wasn't there. Some environmentalists put pressure on the station to stop the contest because the paint would damage the soil when the snow finally melted.

The roads were eventually brought back to normal and the flooded basements were ultimately drying out.

A quarter of a million cars had been abandoned in the metropolitan area, and many still hadn't been picked up by owners who probably hoped insurance would pay more than they were worth.

Good luck, Mike thought.

Mike pulled into the driveway. There were no other cars to share it with. Maddy's roommates had moved out and Mike wasn't sure why. He did know that Maddy couldn't afford the place too much longer on her own. Maybe she would move in with him? Maybe he could move in with her? Either way struck him as a winner.

Although he had a key, he knocked to announce his presence before using it. Everybody needed their privacy. He opened the door when he heard Maddy's voice telling him to come in.

She was seated on an overstuffed chair and wore a long white robe. Mike idly wondered what she was wearing underneath it. Automatically, he removed his gun and holster from his ankle and put them in a drawer.

Maddy had pulled up the sleeve of her robe and was staring at her left forearm. It was pale and withered where the cast had been and there was a raw scar where she'd been stitched. It turned out that the break was more serious than originally thought. An infection had set in and she'd required surgery.

"This is horrible," she said, staring at the prune-like white flesh. She'd had it removed earlier that day. Mike had offered to go to the doctor with her, but Donna Harris had taken her instead.

Mike silently agreed that her arm looked like hell, but said nothing of the sort. "It'll be all right in a short while. You'll never know it happened."

"No, Mike, I don't think I'll ever forget."

"That's not quite what I meant," he said, getting them each a drink, Chardonnay for her, and Heineken for him.

She stared at the offending arm. "I'll never be able to play the piano again."

Mike laughed. "You never did play the piano."

She took the wine and smiled. "I was hoping for some sympathy. Tell me," she said looking around the room, "do you miss my roomies?"

"Not at all," he answered truthfully. Even though they'd been alone on several occasions, there had been nothing like the sexual close encounter-near miss they'd had the night before the great storm. Even the few stolen hours after getting her arm fixed resulted in exhausted sleep. It was as if Maddy was holding back and still trying to sort things out.

"I've been a bitch, haven't I?" Maddy asked.

"You've had a lot on your mind," he answered with an attempt at tact.

"I know and I appreciate your trying to be polite. It's taken a while to think things out and figure out what I really want. Watching people get hurt and die helps put a whole new focus on what is and isn't important."

"Tell me about it," Mike said. He'd been bothered by nightmares and cold sweats after shooting Tower and Raines and later seeing Maddy hurt. Sometimes a strange noise would startle him and cause him to jump. It was tapering off, but he knew it would be a long time before the reaction totally went away, if ever. He'd talked to a much older cousin who'd been in combat in Vietnam, and some other guys who'd been in Desert Storm along with Afghanistan and Iraq, and they all felt the same way. It would never totally go away.

A conversation with DiMona had helped put it in perspective. "Get your head out of your ass, Mikey. You saved Petkowski's life and probably that Lawford woman's as well. And don't forget the people those dirtbags were going to kill in the future. Sometimes you have to kill, Mikey. That's why you carry a gun, or did you think it was for show and tell? Did you know I killed a little kid in Iraq?"

Mike hadn't. He hadn't even known DiMona was in that war.

"Yeah," DiMona had continued. "I was a young private and scared shitless and this kid runs up with what looked like a gun in his hand. I yelled at him to stop, but he didn't, so I killed him, almost blew him in half. Know what? He didn't have a gun."

"That's awful," Mike said.

"Yeah," DiMona continued. "It was a grenade instead. Dumb fuck hadn't pulled the pin, though. I guess they hadn't read the instruction manual. Anyhow, he's dead and I'm not. Just like Tower and Raines are dead and you're not. If you hadn't killed them, they might have killed you. Quit feeling sorry for yourself and deal with it."

Time would help, but what had happened would forever be a part of Mike's life. And Maddy's. He'd shared his thoughts with her and she'd reciprocated. It was good knowing that they could confide in each other.

Maddy stood and faced him. For a while she'd lost a lot of weight and he'd been worried. She'd seen both death and people hurt in a school, a place that was supposed to be a sanctuary, and that was traumatic. But lately she'd managed to work her way through her own demons and had regained both her appetite and her normal looks. He liked normal.

"Like I said, I had a lot of decisions to reach, and I've made most of them."

"Do they involve me?" Mike asked tentatively.

"Follow me," she ordered. When he hesitated, she took him by the hand and led him to the bathroom. The overlarge tub was half full and steaming.

"I'll bet you've had a few fantasies involving this," Maddy said with a smile.

"Just a few," Mike replied in an understatement. Actually, there'd been scores.

"Well, so have I."

Maddy undid her robe and stepped out of it. She was naked and Mike breathlessly thought that she was the most beautiful woman he'd ever seen.

"Michael, I will marry you if you promise to never call me your 'soul mate.' I hate that term. It's so banal. Not even teenagers use it anymore. Just keep telling me that you love me."

"Promised," Mike said huskily. "Is it warm in here, or is it just me?"

Maddy slid into the tub and stretched herself out. "If you're going to be my husband and claim privileges, you have to earn them. Get me my wine, please." He did as requested and somehow managed not to spill any, although his hands shook. He was fascinated by the way her breasts seemed to float in the churning water, and he let his eyes wander to the pale thatch of hair between her thighs.

She smiled invitingly, lovingly. "Now take off your clothes and get in here."

"It'll be a tight fit."

"I'm counting on it."

Wally could just see the headlines. "Weatherman and the Gov caught canoodling in the Caribbean." He wouldn't care. In fact, he'd be proud to be caught canoodling with the lovely Lauren Landsman. But Lauren would. So that was why they were at her sister's house a few miles away from Lansing. Their relationship had renewed and rekindled with astonishing speed. Soon it was like they'd never shut it down for several decades. Wally thanked the late Ellen for keeping them in touch. He sometimes thought she'd planned it this way all along. Maybe she was watching them now and was smiling. Wally wasn't particularly religious, but he liked the thought.

The first time they made love, Lauren insisted on keeping the lights off, saying that she wasn't ready for him to see her older body and compare it with the younger version. He told her he felt the same way. Fortunately, they both quickly got over that silly hang-up.

He reached across the bed and took her hand. "Will it be the Senate then?"

"Yep, and I'm going to kick everyone's ass. I'm not going to let a silly law about term limits derail my political career just when it's heating up. A couple of total nobodies are going to be running against me in the primary and the Senate incumbent is in his eighties and on the verge of being declared mentally incompetent. He even tried to block emergency federal aid to his own state. He's going down. The Savior of Michigan is going to trample him."

Wally laughed. The title had been pinned on her by one of the major newspapers and had stuck. She had gotten a reputation, well deserved, for working tirelessly to clear the storm area and to bring relief to the inhabitants. She would be unbeatable. As for himself, he'd gotten an Emmy for his wall-to-wall reporting. Now he was brought in by the major networks as a guest expert.

"Then I will have to go with you as your official Weather Wizard."

She laughed and rolled next to him, resting her head on his shoulder. "Sounds like a plan, O Wizard. Do you think you could wave your magic wand one more time?"